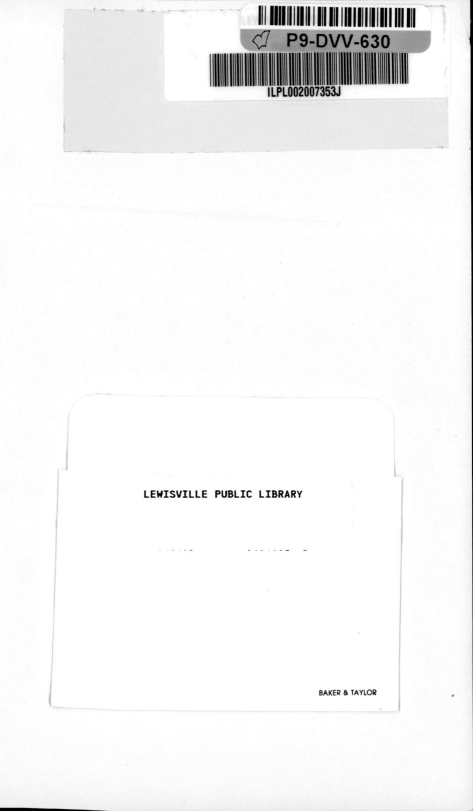

I've travelled the world twice over,
Met the famous: saints and sinners,
Poets and artists, kings and queens,
Old stars and hopeful beginners,
I've been where no-one's been before,
Learned secrets from writers and cooks
All with one library ticket
To the wonderful world of books.

© Janice James.

The wisdom of the ages
Is there for you and me,
The wisdom of the ages,
In your local library.

There's large print books
And talking books,
For those who cannot see,
The wisdom of the ages,
It's fantastic, and it's free.

Written by Sam Wood, aged 92

MATLOCK'S SYSTEM

In Matthew Matlock's England, the population explosion has been controlled; on Budget Day, the national Expectation of Life is regulated according to what the economy can bear. Matlock introduced the system. Now, forty years later, he is fighting desperately against it, with little support. But suddenly, inexplicably, he finds he has become important — to the Prime Minister, to the Scottish Ambassador, and to the head of a sect called The Meek. He discovers nothing is constant, not even the most basic of principles and relationships. Sometimes it's even difficult to tell the living from the dead . . .

Books by Reginald Hill
Published by The House of Ulverscroft:

REGINALD HILL

◆

MATLOCK'S SYSTEM

Complete and Unabridged

ULVERSCROFT
Leicester

First published in Great Britain in 1996 by
Severn House Publishers Limited, Surrey

First Large Print Edition
published 1997
by arrangement with
Severn House Publishers Limited, Surrey

Originally published in 1973 in Great Britain
under the title *Heart Clock*
and pseudonym *Dick Morland*

British Library CIP Data

Hill, Reginald, *1936* –
 Matlock's system.—Large print ed.—
 Ulverscroft large print series: mystery
 1. Detective and mystery stories
 2. Large type books
 I. Title II. Morland, Dick, *1936* – Heart clock
 823.9′14 [F]

ISBN 0–7089–3792–6

Published by
F. A. Thorpe (Publishing) Ltd.
Anstey, Leicestershire

Set by Words & Graphics Ltd.
Anstey, Leicestershire
Printed and bound in Great Britain by
T. J. International Ltd., Padstow, Cornwall

This book is printed on acid-free paper

FOR BRIAN AND MARGARET

Matlock's System

An introduction by
Reginald Hill

Nowadays hardly a news broadcast passes with a lead item about the Economy. A quarter of a century ago, to the non-political and non-politically correct economy was something practised by Scotsmen in jokes and inflation had something to do with Germans taking home their worthless pay in wheelbarrows back in the twenties.

But things they were a'changing. The buoyant sixties had sunk, the punk seventies were rolling in, and people were beginning to be dimly aware that what the Chancellor did on Budget Day had consequences a little wider than the price of fags and beer. And I found myself fantasising, what if instead of balancing national income to cover proposed expenditure a government decided to regulate population to fit within national income?

MATLOCK'S SYSTEM (first published as HEART CLOCK) was the result. It enjoyed a modest success. Naturally I wished it might have been a best-seller. Until the eighties, that is. Then, realising we now had a government to whom anything was possible, I spent a whole decade fearful that someone in one of the Think-Tanks might come across my book and think, *Hey, I wonder if they've thought of this at No 10 . . .*

Perhaps they did.

Reginald Hill
Summer 1996

1

MATLOCK looked carefully round the hall as the Chairman's voice droned on. He had heard the introduction, or ones like it, too many times to listen any more. There had been a time when they flattered him, but that was long ago. Now he used these moments to take in the meeting, look for trouble spots, recognize old supporters, old enemies.

The hall itself was as familiar as his own living-room. There were cobwebs in corners and a smell of damp stained the air. The cream-coloured walls (white originally, he seemed to remember, but now darkened by a patina of cigarette smoke and grime which invited brave fingers to trace slogans and abuse in it) were cracked and rutted. The whiteness of the powdery plaster shone against the dark background.

There will be more cracks tonight, thought Matlock.

1

The only advantages of this hall were not his. It was in the middle of the oldest, most decaying district of Manchester. It was several narrow, ill-lit streets away from the nearest transport-stop. It was in a curfew area.

There were halls like this available to Matlock in every major population centre. Dingy. Unattractively situated. Scarred. More scarred after every meeting.

Matlock had protested. He always protested. It was good policy to form patterns of behaviour. Sometimes the unexpected could work if the conditioning had been good.

"You're not suggesting that your freedom of speech is being interfered with, are you?" the Chief Constable had asked. "You've never been refused permission for a meeting in my area. This just happens to be the only hall available."

"Like last time. And the time before."

"You've been unlucky, Mr. Matlock. Still, you couldn't hope to fill a larger place, could you?"

Matlock had smiled.

"With your own contribution, we might

2

manage it, Chief Constable."

"I'm sorry you're not satisfied. We like to co-operate. I'll tell you what I'll do. I'll call an early meeting of the Watch Committee and put you on the agenda."

"That would be kind of you."

Matlock had halted as he left.

"Do you remember a time, Chief Constable, when Watch Committees gave instructions to the police?"

"Good day, Mr. Matlock. And please remember, no trouble. You're getting a bad reputation. The Committee will have to take that into consideration as well. For your own sake, keep things quiet. You're sixty-nine now, aren't you? You might as well end your days peacefully."

At the back of the hall, which smoke and the place's own miasma made an area of almost impenetrable shade, Matlock could dimly make out a row of figures on whose breasts glinted the silver circle of the police. He let his eyes drift slowly forward. It wasn't a bad audience even when you removed the 25 per cent he knew to be provocateurs, plain-clothes men and layabouts looking for fun. There must be well over a hundred people present. Then he laughed inwardly and humourlessly at his estimate of a hundred as a 'good' audience.

There were five million living within a radius of thirty miles.

He let his drifting gaze halt when he reached the front row. There were only four people sitting there. Three of them he knew. More than knew. They were his, and he belonged to them. Colin Peters, his agent. Ernst Colquitt his chief assistant and heir-apparent. And Lizzie Armstrong, his secretary. She smiled broadly at him as his eyes paused on her. He drooped an eyelid in reply, then moved on to the fourth.

He had never seen him before, but him he knew also. At least he knew him in general terms. Sitting two or three seats away from the others; dressed in a charcoal-grey suit, brilliantly white shirt, dark-blue tie split down the middle by a thin silver line; holding an elegant leather document case on his lap; he was present at all the meetings and sat as impassively as his fellows had under Matlock's close scrutiny.

4

The Chairman's voice changed gear and Matlock brought his attention back to the figure beside him. Percy Collins was a few years younger than Matlock, but looked considerably older. In this day and age it was strange to see a man looking so old. Matlock's own hair was still mainly brown, his face relatively unlined, his cheeks full, his teeth sound. Percy on the other hand looked like an octogenarian in the old days. His crown rose in wrinkled baldness out of a few wisps of white hair which clung round his ears and nape. His face skin hung in leathery pouches and his jaw-bone protruded like a loop of wire through muslin. But his eyes were clear and alight with enthusiasm, and as always they reassured Matlock when he felt doubts about the kind of image people like Percy gave to the movement.

"Ladies and gentlemen. Matthew Matlock!"

He had allowed his thoughts to drift again and was not quite ready, but years of experience in public speaking took him smoothly to his feet as applause, enthusiastic from the front rows, rippled

5

back and lapped itself out in the shadows at the back. Matlock's practised ear told him that things were worse than he had expected. He readjusted his estimate of the sympathetic audience to nearer seventy five than a hundred.

"Thank you, Mr. Chairman, for those kind words," he began, smiling down at Percy. They were the only occupants of the platform. If I am to be a target, he had said at an early stage, let us at least put a premium on accuracy and award marks only for bullseyes, not for inners, outers and magpies.

"Tonight I want to concentrate your attention on one thing and one thing only. Budget Day. In a few weeks' time the Government will be bringing in yet another Budget, its thirty-fourth since it first came to power. Since then there have been nine years in which the Government did not feel it necessary to introduce a formal Budget and merely contented itself with using its majority to bulldose through one or two more economically restrictive measures in the normal course of Parliamentary business."

"We elected them to make laws,

Matlock. What's wrong with that?"

Matlock nodded genially at the interrupter.

"I shall answer you in a minute, friend. But let me continue. This means that this Government has had forty-two years of uninterrupted power. It is forty-two years since the Unirads first won office. And it is thirty-eight years since the introduction of the measure which has been central to all Budgets since. I mean the Age Bill."

"That's history, Matlock!" a derisive voice jeered.

"How did you vote then, Matlock? You were keen enough then!"

"Getting on a bit now, aren't you?"

"Anarchist bastard!"

Something swung through the air and dropped at his feet. It was an egg. Matlock was unmoved. He didn't mind eggs.

"My friends," he shouted. "Listen to me. In a few weeks we'll get a new Age. And you know and I know which way it's going. It can't go up. It MUST come down. In a few weeks, Jack Browning, our beloved and ageless Prime Minister, will be covering up *his* mistakes with years of *our* lives. OUR LIVES!"

There was a lull in the tumult building up below. For a brief and rare optimistic moment, Matlock thought he might get a hearing.

The neat man in the front row, still impassive, straightened up and half-looked round.

"My friends," said Matlock in a quieter tone, then gave a gasp of pain and clapped his hand to his face. A marble hurled from the back of the hall had struck him just below the eye. A cheer went up mixed with mocking laughter and suddenly there was a tremendous rattling as a shower of marbles and ball-bearings bounced on the bare boards of the stage. Matlock and Percy turned their backs on the audience and bent forward to protect their heads. This also had the effect, they had learnt from experience, of inviting the missile throwers to aim at their behinds. A politician's arse can absorb anything, Percy was fond of saying, and besides it puts the audience in a good mood. The English have always found the backside comic.

There was some more laughter now,

but things were obviously planned to go further. A couple of dozen men were moving purposefully towards the platform, pushing chairs and their occupants to one side with equal violence. Others were tearing down pro-Matlock posters from the walls. Matlock's own supporters protested vociferously. The neat man settled in his seat and relaxed.

The hail of marbles eased off as the hecklers found other work to do, and Matlock turned round. Below him in the hall a small riot was developing. Much of it was still verbal and the noise itself was bent and twisted by the warped acoustics of the old room. Here and there pushes were changing into punches and already there was the splintering noise caused by the breaking of legs off chairs.

Matlock took his handkerchief from his breast pocket and blew his nose.

"MY FRIENDS!"

The harsh, ear-shattering, metallic tones cut almost contemptuously into the hubbub and stilled action and noise alike.

"MY FRIENDS, WHILE YOU ARE FIGHTING EACH OTHER, JACK BROWNING

9

IS TRIMMING YOUR LIVES. IT IS NO SECRET THAT IF HE DARED HE WOULD GO BELOW THE SO-CALLED BIBLE BARRIER. EVEN THOSE OF YOU WHO BELIEVE IN THE AGE LAWS MUST BE DISTURBED THAT ALREADY WE HAVE THE LOWEST EXPECTATION OF LIFE IN EUROPE!"

The neat man rose to his feet and looked round at the audience. The hecklers were puzzled, uncertain what to do. One tried a shout but the metallic voice, now clearly recognizable as Matlock's, swallowed up the sound without trace.

"BUT MORE DISTURBING STILL IS THE CRIMINAL INCOMPETENCE WHICH HAS PERPETUATED THE VERY CIRCUM-STANCES WHICH MADE AGE CONTROL ACCEPTABLE IN THE FIRST PLACE."

Some of the audience began to sit down again. The neat man nodded to someone in the shadows.

"FORTY YEARS AGO THIS COUNTRY ALONG WITH MANY OTHERS WAS BANKRUPT. THE CAUSE, WE WERE TOLD, WAS OVER POPULATION. THE REAL CAUSE, THEN AS NOW, WAS UNDER

PRODUCTION; THAT IS, BAD MANAGE-
MENT, AT THE HIGHEST LEVELS."

From the shadows at the very rear of the hall a line of policemen moved forward on a word of command. They wore crash-helmets and carried truncheons.

"Come on now. Break it up, will you. Come on."

They picked their way methodically through the overturned chairs.

"IT WAS THEN THAT THE PARTY WHICH HAS SINCE SPAWNED BROWNING PUT FORWARD ITS SOLUTION. I KNOW. FOR IT WAS MY SOLUTION."

Only the hecklers and the police were still standing. Even some of the former were taking their seats. Then Matlock saw one of their number, a swarthy, burly man he had already recognized as some kind of leader, turn to the nearest policeman and knee him viciously in the crutch. His agonized scream rose above even the recording and within seconds the police were full into the seated audience swinging their truncheons indiscriminately.

Matlock rushed to the front of the platform.

"Colin! Ernst! Get Lizzie out of here!"

Even in speaking he saw he was too late. Already the fighting had reached the front of the hall. He reached forward to pull Lizzie up on to the platform but his own arm was seized by a fresh-faced youth who dragged him down to the floor. He lay stunned, his arms instinctively raised to protect himself from the blows the youth was raining into his face.

"You old bastard — you old bastard — you want to live for ever — I'll show you what you'll get — what you deserve — you old bastard! bastard! bastard!"

The youth was weak with hysteria, his rosy cheeks stained with angry tears, and his blows were losing force. For a moment Matlock saw Ernst trying to drag his attacker off him, but he in turn was seized from behind and disappeared backwards into the mêlée. Matlock carefully thrust his index fingers up the youth's nostrils and rose with him, then gently deposited the screaming boy on the edge of the platform. He could hear his own recorded voice still booming out in the background — but very much in the background now.

"Lizzie!" he called, "Lizzie!"

There was no sign of her in the mass of struggling, wrestling, punching bodies. He tried to force his way forward to where he had last seen her, but found it impossible to make any progress. Women were screaming all over the hall and he was certain he recognized her voice in one of the screams. Leaping forward again, he began dragging men out of the solid heaving wall in front of him and casting them to one side. He seized a uniformed figure by the shoulders and pulled him back. The man turned round with great agility and swung his truncheon. Matlock's arms were trapped against his sides by sheer pressure of bodies and he watched the truncheon's back swing with helpless horror.

But before it could descend, a delicate white hand touched momentarily on the policeman's wrist.

"Not this one, thank you, Sergeant. Come along, please, Mr. Matlock."

It was the neat man, unruffled by the violence. He guided Matlock through the crowd with no more difficulty than he would have found moving through a

13

well-attended cocktail party.

"In here, please, Mr. Matlock," he said opening a door. They stepped out into the corridor and he closed the door behind them which cut out most of the noise except Matlock's voice booming out of the hidden loudspeakers.

"WHAT HAVE WE LEFT TO FEAR? WHAT HAVE WE LEFT TO PREVENT EVERY ONE OF US LEADING A USEFUL, ACTIVE, COMPLETE LIFE TILL NINETY? TILL A HUNDRED? WE NEED HARDLY FEAR DISEASE. MEDICAL SCIENCE CAN CURE THEM ALL. WE NEED FEAR ACCIDENTS, I SUPPOSE. BUT CARE CAN PREVENT THEM.

NO. ALL WE REALLY NEED TO FEAR IS . . ."

The sound ceased without preamble. The silence fell strangely on Matlock's ears.

"The recorder must have been well hidden. It has taken us rather too long to find it," said the neat man with a pleasant smile.

He moved forward along the corridor and stopped outside a room marked 'Private'.

"After you, please."

Matlock went in. Seated beside an electric fire, smoking a cigarette, was Lizzie.

"Thank God you're safe!"

She rose and flung her arms around him.

"How are you?" asked Matlock. "How did you get out?"

"The Inspector kindly removed me."

Matlock turned to the neat man.

"Thank you for that."

The Inspector smiled and nodded.

"It is our job. Now, Mr. Matlock let us get down to business. I have here . . . "

The door burst open and Colin rushed in. His face was bloody and his tunic torn so that it flapped down behind him like a tailcoat.

"Matt," he said, and staggered against the wall.

Matlock stepped forward and took his arm.

"OK Colin. Come and sit down."

"No, Matt. It's not me. It's Percy. He's been hurt — badly I think."

Matlock left the room without a pause and ran down the corridor.

15

The hall was almost empty now except for the police and one or two casualties. But lying near the edge of the platform, his head cradled in Ernst's lap, was Percy. His bald crown was a ruin of congealed blood but his face was relaxed and almost content.

Ernst looked up at Matlock and did not seem to see him for a moment.

Then, "He's dead, Matt," he said. "He's dead."

Matlock looked down at the face which had always seemed strangely old but now seemed strangely young.

"Leave him be, Ernst," he said, then spun round to confront the Inspector.

The neat man had been handed a chair leg, brown with blood and a few white hairs sticking to it. He examined it unemotionally then returned it to the sergeant.

"I am sorry we could not prevent this, Mr. Matlock."

"Prevent it?" said Matlock. "I believe you have caused it. Chair-legs, truncheons, they're all the same, except that one used to go with an honourable profession."

The neat man reddened, but his voice

was still pitched on the same even key as he replied.

"As you will realize, however, this unfortunate death is merely the most serious of a succession of serious incidents, Mr. Matlock, most of which can be traced back directly to the deliberately provocative tone of your own meeting."

He opened his document case and extracted a typewritten sheet.

"I have here an order, signed by the Chief Constable and approved by the Watch Committee, for your removal from the area of his jurisdiction forthwith. Any subsequent visits must be notified within twelve hours to the Central Police Station and any request for permission to hold a further meeting within the area must be preceded by a written request at least three months before the date of the proposed meeting. It's all in this." He handed the paper to Matlock who received it wordlessly.

"Now if you please. Seats have been reserved for your party on the nine-thirty Autotrain for London. We must hurry."

Matlock folded the paper carefully and put it into his pocket.

"Thank you, Inspector," he said looking at him with emotionless eyes. In the doorway beyond he saw Lizzie's pale face with Colin's, still paler, beside.

"Come on, Ernst," he said abruptly. "Let's go."

"Percy?" said Lizzie. "Is he . . . ? Oh, Christ."

Matlock led her gently away and Ernst, with Colin leaning heavily on his arm, came behind. Matlock took one look back before he left the hall. Policemen were quietly picking up the overturned chairs and putting to one side those which were broken. On the walls, as he had forecast to himself, fresh scars had appeared in the plaster. The result of missiles. Chairs. Truncheons. Heads. Scrawled along the entire length of one wall were the words *Matlock is getting old*.

He went out into the night.

There was a hovercar waiting for them outside, as always, and a still corridor of police led them to the open door. Matlock looked up and down the street. Not a spectator in sight, not a face at a window.

They climbed into the hovercar, the door slid silently to behind them, the magnetic-lock clicked.

"Reporters, Colin?" said Matlock.

Tonight he had no interest in reporters but needed the normal political reactions to still his confusion of thought.

"I'll let them know, Matt, of course."

The strain in Colin's voice told the same story.

The opaque glass sheet which separated them from the front compartment of the car filled with a pale blue light then slowly cleared. Sitting beside the driver, but facing them was an ornately uniformed figure.

"I'm afraid we had to declare this an early curfew area this evening. Part of the Watch Committee's new Social Drive. So it wasn't worth while letting any reporters in, was it?"

Matlock looked at the Chief Constable with a surprise he did not show.

"You honour us tonight. Why let the meeting start if an early curfew was in force?"

The Chief Constable laughed.

"You had been given permission,

19

Mr. Matlock, and the Committee does not give its word lightly. But I'm afraid that even without the unfortunate interruption, we would have had to bring you to an early halt. About now, I should think."

As if on a word of command they heard the slow bell of the Curfew Patrol quite close and a moment later the solid bulk of the Curfew Wagon moved majestically by. Matlock had never been in one but he felt his usual tremor of revulsion as he watched the great shape slide past them. He remembered the description given him by a friend who had been inside. A dungeon on wheels.

"Chief Constable," he said, "we will soon be at the station. What do you have to say to me? You are not here just to keep us company."

"Nor from choice, Mr. Matlock. Despite what you may think, I am non-political. Merely the instrument of law and order, the organization of which is the politician's business. I have been particularly instructed to have you removed from my patch this evening. I am merely ensuring that this is done."

"Your instructions must have been very particular to bring you out in person."

There was a pause while the Chief Constable lit a cigarette. The hovercar turned onto the brightly lit ramp which coiled its way over the centre of Manchester to the A-Train station.

"Very particular, Mr. Matlock. I will say good-bye now. I am sorry about your friend's death. That may be a weakness, but I do not anticipate seeing you again."

"Hardly a weakness in a *law*-officer," began Matlock, but the panel was already tinged with blue and in seconds had resumed its former dull opacity.

The hovercar drew to a halt so close to an open door of the A-Train that they stepped from one to another without touching the platform. The train door slid shut behind them and they moved forward into their comfortably appointed compartment. Their luggage was already there, neatly stacked in a corner. The train began to move as they sat down.

For a long time nothing was said. Matlock sat by Lizzie who had not spoken a word since they left the hall.

21

He put his hand over hers and pressed it gently, but there was no response. Finally, Colin, obviously determined to break the silence, said, "I'm sorry they managed to keep the papers away, Matt. Shall I get in touch with the nationals in town?"

Matlock shook his head.

"It's not worth it. They won't be interested. Or if any of them are, the news will be stale by the time they get licence from the Committee. Or at best it'll get a para. It's not worth it."

Ernst leaned forward and put his hand on Matlock's knee.

"Couldn't that be the point of tonight? That it's not worth it, I mean?"

They digested this for a while.

"This would mean," said Colin, "that Percy's death was planned. A warning. Not just an accident (if that's the word) in the general fighting."

"Yes."

"Why not one of us?"

"Because," said Matlock, "this way they can shovel us out of the area as a complete, unsullied unit and sweep poor Percy and the rest of the meeting under the carpet. Maximum warning, minimum fuss. I think you're right, Ernst. It's a new part in the jigsaw. It's a different picture."

Lizzie, who had been staring dully out of the window apparently not attending to a word, suddenly turned and dragged her hand from under Matlock's. They saw that her face was wet with tears, but it was anger that twisted it now.

"So that's good-bye to Percy, is it?" she snarled. "A piece in a jigsaw now. He was alive an hour ago. Our friend. Telling everyone how bloody great you were, Matlock. Then someone cracks his skull wide open and suddenly he's a piece in a jigsaw, part of a game, more significant dead than he ever was alive. Then he was just an old friend we could rely on. Now he's important. Now he's dead."

The tears had started again. Matlock reached out his hand, but she slapped it aside, stood up and flung out of the compartment.

The three men sat in silence for a moment.

They're waiting for me to say something,

do something, thought Matlock. They're all waiting. Friends and foes alike. All waiting. And I'm no longer ready.

His right hand had involuntarily moved inside his loose jacket till it rested lightly over his heart. He increased the pressure till he could feel the rhythmic beat.

A machine. A machine running down. Ticking off years, days, hours. It is not many years since that was just a metaphor, he thought. It changed in my lifetime. I helped to change it.

The thought made him clench his hand into a sharp-cornered fist. Abruptly he stood up and followed Lizzie out of the door. She was standing staring through one of the observation ports and did not turn as he joined her. He put his arm over her shoulder but she shook it off impatiently.

"Go away, Matt."

He looked through the port with her. Their own faces, shadowy, transparent, stared palely back at them. He forced his eyes to pass beyond and looked down at the blur of lights which was all that was visible of the Multicities over which the great elevated track of the Autotrains ran.

He did not try to touch her again and she showed no sign of awareness of his presence.

Finally he began to talk softly, monotonously.

"Lizzie Armstrong. Age forty-seven. Height five feet five inches. Weight eight stone two ounces. Blue eyes; brown hair; good teeth; mole on left hip; appendix scar; left breast slightly larger than right. Born Perth, Scotland. Resident in England twenty-three years, eighteen of them spent in the employment of Matthew Matlock. Took English citizenship seventeen years ago. A competent secretary, consistent in her errors. Two 'm's in amount. Two 'c's in necessary. Has been known to correct an audio-type machine."

Lizzie's eyes had come up to meet his from the shadow world in the port. He went on, expressionlessly.

"Loyal to a fault. Has served her master with unquestioning devotion. Intellectually. Spiritually. Sexually. Tends to boast that she knows him inside out."

Lizzie turned to him.

"I know, Matt. Yet she seems incapable of understanding what he truly feels on the death of a friend. I know what you're thinking. But it wasn't that. It wasn't just Percy. It is this whole business. It seems so aimless somehow. Why not make a run for it, Matt? Go for Op. We can afford it. Or at least, duck out. Retire. Marry me. You've got six years at the present rate. Let's make them easy, carefree years. Six contented years."

Matlock grimaced.

"Less after the Budget."

"Five then. Or four. Browning won't dare go nearer the Bible Barrier than that. I'll settle for four. And who knows? Things may take a turn for the better of their own accord. A boom perhaps. It could be ten."

"In a free economy it could be twenty. It could be fifty."

Lizzie stamped angrily.

"It could be none. I'll settle for five. I think Ernst was right, you know. Percy was a warning. That could be you next time with blood on your head and your head in someone's lap."

Matlock shook his head.

26

"They wouldn't dare. That at least I'm sure of. Not like that anyway. But you're right in part, Lizzie. I'll take part of your advice at least. I'll give the meetings up. They can win that round."

Lizzie had watched her employer's expression closely as he spoke. Now she put her hands lightly on his lips.

"Matt, you're talking about politics again. You're retreating from yourself, from us."

"It's my life."

"Not any longer. I've been watching you change for two or three years now. It was your life once; all your life. But now these plots and plans and policies are at least fifty per cent a refuge. You can hide in them. You didn't really want to go to Manchester tonight, did you? It was pointless long before some thug split Percy's skull."

"No," said Matlock defensively, "we achieved something. At least I got some of my words heard."

Lizzie laughed derisively.

"You mean the tape and the loud-speaker? A prank. A joke. Oh I know, it took them by surprise. It broke the

27

pattern. Percy broke the pattern too. Have you thought, perhaps *they* fixed Percy because *you* broke your precious pattern. In any case Matt, this wasn't your idea was it? Not much lately has borne your mark. This stinks of Ernst."

Matlock drew away now.

"Let's not start on that tack again, Lizzie. Ernst is my chief assistant, my successor. And my friend."

Lizzie shrugged indifferently and lit a cigarette as Matlock turned and re-entered the compartment. The two men in it were talking earnestly, but stopped as the door opened.

Ernst's boyish face broke into a smile. He was by far the youngest there and looked another five years younger than his forty. Matlock smiled affectionately at him. There had been no doubt at all in his mind who to publicly declare as his successor when he had reached the statutory age four years earlier. The Age Law declared that every man in a position of public responsibility must at age sixty-five appoint a successor (or 'understudy' as he was generally and frivolously known) at least ten years younger. 'In a position of public responsibility' had needed a great deal of qualification and modification, and Matlock was still not wholly certain whether he as the 'leader' of a non-representational 'party' came under this section of the Bill. Dentists, youth leaders and newspaper reporters didn't; doctors, civil servants of the top grade, broadcasting administrators did. These were only a few of the categories where doubt had arisen. Matlock had decided to be on the safe side.

To attack a law, he always declared, one must first make sure that one does not break it.

I must have been young and certain when I said that, he thought.

Now Lizzie had openly suggested (among other things admittedly) what had begun to stir in his own mind recently — what must begin to stir in the minds of many men of his age.

Go for Op.

It sounded flippant, casual, put like that. He forced himself to think what it really meant. It was a favourite theory of his that verbal abbreviations were often euphemistic to start with and morally blinding to finish with. To 'go for Op' meant, he formulated carefully, to use one's wealth illegally and selfishly to pay for a criminal operation which would extend one's life above and beyond the maximum permitted by the laws passed by a democratically elected government. So stringently applied were these laws, moreover, that it involved illegal exit from one's country with (if it were to be worth while) sufficient funds to maintain one during the illegal extension of one's life-span.

That just about covers it, he thought. Put like that, it is obviously out of the question.

Obviously?

Not obviously or I would not be thinking about it. This is the natural panic of age. These are last, and worst, growing pains.

Yet who would I harm? I have no one touchable by the law. I'm lucky in that respect.

Lucky?

Why had he not married Lizzie when Edna, his wife, died eighteen years ago?

Because I had not the right to involve her so closely with me in a dangerous struggle, he cried inwardly.

Suddenly he realized that he was twisting round in his seat and the others were looking at him with concern. Matlock had always set the tone of gatherings of his intimates, they respected his silence and had not spoken since he relapsed into his brown study. Lizzie had re-entered the compartment unnoticed and was regarding him with such loving concern that he forced himself to relax and smile at her.

It was still not too late, he thought. Perhaps that was the answer, a few final years of domestic contentment. At sixty-nine he was in the prime of life. Well, just a very little out of it. But sexually he was as active and as potent as ever he had been. He had hardly a grey hair; his body was tanned and fit. Lungs, liver and lights all in order, he thought, recalling this odd list from God knows where.

And heart?

Oh no trouble there. No one ever had any trouble there any more. Since the first transplant attempts in the nineteen-sixties, things had come a long way. Hearts could be popped in and out with vast speed and almost 100 per cent certainty of success.

And everyone had at least one heart operation in a lifetime. His hand strayed again to his chest. There running down his breast bone was the only large scar on his body. He had been the first, but since then the tidying-up had become so good that nowadays there was rarely a mark to be seen.

He had been the first.

He looked across again at Lizzie and thought of her soft round breasts which he knew so well. They had done a good job there. Scarcely a mark. Of course, with Lizzie's generation they were already doing them much younger.

He had been the first.

He suddenly saw in his mind a vision of a young girl, naked on the operating table while white-coated men with rapid efficiency carved a hole in her chest and inserted a large clockwork device, all cogs and springs. This was always how he thought of it, though he knew well the actual electronic device was a mere millimetre in circumference.

He had been the first.

He was among those responsible that every man, woman and child in England had embedded in the heart a clock which after seventy years plus was going to sound an alarm, then stop. And the heart with it.

He stirred again and the others moved too. But this time it was because the smooth deceleration of the A-Train told them they were near their destination. He glanced at the wall-clock. It was ten-fifteen.

Colin followed his gaze.

"These bloody things are always late nowadays," he said.

Ten minutes later they were standing silently in the lift which bore them down to street level.

"Come back to my place for a drink. We can talk things out," said Ernst.

They all looked enquiringly at Matlock. He shook his head.

"No, thank you. We must talk, but not tonight. Nine-thirty tomorrow morning."

He watched them move away, felt the

urge to call Lizzie back. Instead he turned west and began his own slow walk home.

After a while he quickened his pace and paid more attention to the night and his surroundings. As always he admired the ingenuity of the store-artists. Nearly all the big shops were constructed of the new poro-glass which was window or wall at the turn of a switch, with the area and shape of transparency as easily controlled. He stopped outside Selfridges and watched as scene after scene revealed itself in depth as successive walls were cleared. It was like the transformation scene in the old pantomimes, he thought. It was also a very effective anti-burglar device. Though nowadays the new penalties had caused a considerable drop in the crime-rate. This was inevitably used as an argument in support of Age Laws, of course.

Matlock shivered and started walking again. Fifteen minutes later he was approaching the main door of the block of flats he lived in. When he was about thirty yards away, he noticed two things. The first was a large grey hovercar parked opposite the entrance. The second was a man coming towards him and about the same distance on the other side of his door. It was still early and even in this highly mechanized age walkers, especially in London, were fairly common. But the man's strange, loose flapping, one-piece garment — a cross between a cloak and a dressing gown — caught Matlock's attention. There was something about it which touched a chord in his mind, but odder still was the certainty growing in him that this man was going to speak to him, was there for the specific purpose of meeting him.

He increased his pace. So did the other, and they arrived at the door almost simultaneously. Matlock halted and the two men looked into each other's face. Matlock saw a pair of deep-set, grey eyes, a flattened, pugilist's nose and a fiercely unkempt brown beard. He had the feeling that the other was looking deeper into his own face and he resisted the strong temptation to speak first which this uncomfortable sensation produced.

But before he could learn whether his effort was to be rewarded, the silent contest was interrupted. The door of the hovercar slid smoothly open and a young man as extreme in his elegance as the bearded man in his disarray, stepped out.

"Mr. Matlock, Sir?" he said with the near insolent deference of office. "I have a message for you. Will you sign please?"

He handed over a small plain envelope and Matlock stabbed his forefinger automatically in the proffered receipt-wax. The bearded man had resumed his walk immediately the door opened and was now almost out of sight. Matlock could hardly believe that he had stopped at all.

The young man followed his gaze.

"Strange fellows about these days, Sir," he said. "Goodnight to you, Mr. Matlock."

He stepped back into the hovercar which pulled away instantly and noiselessly.

Matlock waited a few moments to see if the bearded man would return, but the street remained silent. Finally he operated his sonic key and entered the building. Immediately he was in his own flat he opened the envelope. Inside was a single sheet of paper. On it in an almost indecipherably ornate hand was written, 'I would be awfully glad if you could call in to see me first thing tomorrow morning. Yours, Browning.'

He had been summoned to see the Prime Minister. Instead of his usual coffee and brandy, he took three sleeping tablets and went immediately to bed, knowing that if he sat up in thought for any time at all, he would in the end telephone Colin and Ernst. Or Lizzie. It might be interesting to see which 'phoned first.

But best of all was sleep.

2

"**M**Y dear Matt! Do step in." Jack Browning came forward with his hand outstretched and a smile of apparently real pleasure on his face.

"Thank you, Clive," he said to the smooth young man who had ushered Matlock into the room, then to Matlock, "I hope you didn't mind my sending the hovercar for you."

"Not in the least," said Matlock, and he was speaking the truth. "I enjoyed its company."

Browning looked at him quizzically. The smooth young man who seemed reluctant to accept his dismissal said acidly, "Mr. Matlock did not care to be driven here, Prime Minister. He walked with the car behind him."

"Did he now? How very odd of you, Matt," said Browning his smile re-appearing, even broader.

Matlock began to wonder how clever

he had been. It had seemed a good publicity stunt to approach the House with the large official car crawling at his heels like a monstrous but obedient dog.

Several photographs had been taken and a large number of questions asked by the horde of journalists whose prowling ground this was. It had seemed a useful and entertaining manoeuvre.

Now faced by Browning's enjoyment of the jest, it all seemed rather silly. Worse, he felt that something like this might have been exactly what Browning had planned. Then he reminded himself that Browning's strength as a politician had always been his capacity for being unsurprised. It was said of him (by friends and foes alike) that he could turn a disaster into a forecast within a day, and into a plan by the end of the week.

The reluctant Clive having removed himself, Matlock was ushered to a chair, upright but comfortable — a compromise between the official and the domestic which he felt rather suited the situation. The Prime Minister himself looked very relaxed and unofficial. He was casually but immaculately dressed, and wore no tie. His crinkly brown hair had just that touch of untidiness which gave an effect of vigour and energy and which it was said took two hairdressers three hours a week to maintain. His square farmer's face was aglow with health and he carried his fifteen stone lightly on his six foot plus frame. As always, Matlock felt physically diminished by the man, by his bulk, his lightness of foot, his vigour, the very richness of his voice.

"Now what about a drink, Matt? Whisky?"

"It's too early in the morning to be patriotic, Prime Minister," he answered.

Browning boomed with laughter, then came over to Matlock with two brimming glasses and sat beside him.

"We don't see enough of you, Matt. This bunch of sycophantic moles I'm surrounded with make me take myself too seriously."

"Only those in danger from delusion of grandeur need deflation," said Matlock.

He took a sip of his drink and recognized without surprise his favourite

40

Scotch. It was a long time since he had tasted it.

"They wouldn't like this in Yorkshire," he said, indicating his glass, referring to the main source of English whisky since the secession of Scotland.

"They're not bloody well going to get it in Yorkshire," laughed Browning. "Anyway, we've got to support our neighbours. It's like liar dice. You look after the man on your right."

"I would hardly have thought the Scots, or anyone for that matter, were on *your* right, Prime Minister."

Browning stood up and leaned against the mantelshelf. It was a perfectly casual move and one which fitted perfectly with the appearance of the man — a gentleman farmer elegantly at home in his own parlour. Not that such a creature had existed for half a century or more, but Matlock recognized it. He also recognized the picture behind Browning's head.

"Careful, Matt. You're talking about the party you helped to make great."

It was a photograph of seven men and three women talking casually against a background of fruit trees in blossom.

Browning followed Matlock's gaze and nodded twice.

"That was it, Matt. That first Cabinet. I was only a toddler then, but that picture means something to me."

Matlock rose and moved towards the mantelshelf. Browning stepped aside.

"Have a good look, Matt. Those must have been great days."

He watched with approval as Matlock reached up and unhooked the photo from the wall, and the approval remained as Matlock placed the picture face downwards on the mantelshelf and looked quizzically at the small oval-shaped discoloration on the wallpaper.

"It can only have started meaning something to you quite recently, Prime Minister. I would be interested in purchasing the miniature that used to hang here if you have grown tired of it."

Browning downed his drink with gusto and went to pour himself another.

"It's like a game, Matt; a great game. It's marvellous to meet someone who's almost as good as me at it. Or at least to meet someone who dares show he's almost as good as me. I don't surround myself by fools. Never did. That's a fool's policy. But they only let me see so much cleverness, no more. That's what being clever is."

"I take it you're practising what you preach, Prime Minister?"

Browning slapped his thigh. Matlock had never seen anyone slap his own thigh, and he mentally applauded the naturalness of the innately ludicrous gesture.

"So you see me as a kind of subtle Iago? Dishonest even in his protestations of dishonesty? Why do you think I brought you here, Matt?"

"Invited. You *invited* me. I accepted your invitation."

"And damn decent of you it was. Why?"

"Why what? Or rather, which why?"

"Answer what you will, Matt. It's been all counter-punching so far. Let's have some aggression."

"How curious your terminology is. Boxing has been outlawed in this country for thirty years."

"I travel a lot, Matt. It goes with the

job. Go on talking."

"All right. If you will. You're obviously fishing for a cue. I'll endeavour to pander to your theatrical whims and supply you with it. I think you would like to do a deal. I have some small nuisance value — perhaps more than I am aware. Your government is approaching Budget Day with greater trepidation than ever before. It's worth an hour of your time trying to buy me off. But no more. Am I right?"

Browning looked full at Matlock, his body tense and now with no trace of merriment on his face.

"No, Matt. Wrong. I brought you here to have you killed."

Matlock's stomach twisted violently and he felt the blood drain from his cheeks, leaving his head light and giddy.

Then Browning's great jovial laugh filled the room, echoing and re-echoing as the Prime Minister doubled up with mirth.

"I had you there, Matt. For a moment, you believed me. Admit it, eh?"

Matlock could say nothing. He took a long pull at his drink and sat stiffly, filled with self-loathing.

44

It's true then. I fear death that much. It's true. I am terrified. I am paralysed with fear at the awareness of death. It is true. This is the reality in the midst of all my moral abstractions. It is true. I am afraid, selfishly, egotistically, isolatedly afraid.

Browning was speaking again, with a serious note in his voice now.

"But all the same and joking apart, Matt, it's a bit sad that it's come to this between us. That you could really believe that, even for a moment, that I had the inclination *or* the power to have you killed. This is a democracy we live in, not a police state. I'm a civilized man, a politician. You're an opponent, but I hope I can still keep you as a friend. And even politically we were once on the same side of the fence."

Matlock still did not trust himself to speak. Browning went on.

"You were right of course. I've brought you here to offer you a deal. But before I do, there's something I'd like you to see. You're always ready to tell me what I am, Matt, to use my own words against me, to show the world how you feel I am being dishonest, deceptive, immoral. Sometimes what you say hits home, rings a bell. You may not think so, but it does. Well, I'm going to offer you a chance to take instead of give for a change. I'm not going to accuse, to point, to decry. Just show. We should all face our origins some time. Are you ready to do that here and now?"

Matlock pulled himself together. This was no time for introspection. He wondered how much of his reactions had shown and was thankful that he too was not unskilled in the use of political masks.

"I never forget my origins, personal or public, by day or by night, Prime Minister." He decided to test how much Browning wanted him to stay. "It seems a shame to waste your time in reminiscence. I think I should be off."

Browning leaned forward and stabbed a button on his desk, then stood up and made for the door.

"That's very good of you, Matt. But there's no need to worry about me. I'll leave you to your own devices for a while and catch up on a bit a work. See you soon."

He slipped through the door which clicked with ominous finality behind him. The poro-glass windows blackened and the room was engulfed in total darkness. Matlock started to his feet, the terror back, then subsided again as a white square glowed in the wall opposite him and he realized what was happening. He was being shown a film.

Back projection was being used of course, so there was no stream of light pouring over his head. Also it was obviously a poro-glass screen, the advantage of which was that its shape and size were easily altered.

An impersonal voice began to speak. There was still no image on the screen.

"Matlock Matthew. Born Carlisle, Cumberland, Committee Region 62. Parents . . . "

And now the picture appeared. His mother, long haired, bright eyed, her lovely face animated as she mouthed silent badinage at the camera-man; his father, tall, thin, a trifle ascetic, but touched as always by the fullness of

47

life which overflowed from his wife. These were home movies. Matlock dimly recollected having seen them before. If asked where they were he would have guessed in one of the trunks that contained all he had wanted to keep of his childhood home and which had lain in storage untouched for forty-five years. Untouched by himself, at least.

Matlock saw himself on the screen now. A mere child. An only child.

His education and adolescent life were dealt with briefly, but with a remarkable attention to essential detail. It didn't surprise him. No one grew up without leaving traces of his passage. Everyone left a trail of pictures and tapes and documents marking a clear path from birth to the grave. Since the passing of the Age Act, the necessity for close documentation had become still more acute.

But soon he felt a growing unease as it became apparent that ever since his earliest successes in politics, his every move had been carefully supervised.

The voice went on: "The accidental death of his parents in May 1982 came at an opportune moment. He had been moving further and further towards the Uniradical Party and only his emotional loyalty to his father and mother had prevented him from openly joining at an earlier date. Now he accepted the Party discipline, was soon adopted as a candidate and was elected at his second attempt."

The film now was all professionally shot. Some of it was newscast material; much wasn't. In an effort to be fair, he reminded himself that much of it must have been shot at the instigation of the Lib-Lab coalition then in office, and only later inherited by the Unirads.

The years in Opposition were soon disposed of, but not without a clear picture being sketched of Matlock's attitudes to the big questions of the day. The drive, the force, the sense of mission, the ruthlessness of this ghost from his own past were always apparent.

The events which led to the expansion of the Unirads from one of the smallest Parties in the House (five or six new Parties had gained representation in the seventies and eighties of the twentieth century) to the first Party in nearly ten years capable of governing without coalition, were clearly and honestly indicated. The world was in economic chaos, due mainly to the population explosion. America and Russia had turned their backs on their former allies and retreated into self-sufficient isolation in which the only things that mattered were employment and food. Their moonbases were abandoned by both nations and the planets handed back to the science fiction writers. The European common market was creaking along in an atmosphere of mutual distrust at Governmental level and hatred at national level. The Lib-Labs had put all their eggs in the European basket and when the Great Consult of Brussels in 1987 broke up in confusion and recrimination, the British Government fell. The Unirads, who had been advocating a return to insularity for years, were returned to Parliament with a slender overall majority.

It was a great year for Matlock. He was elected with the largest personal majority ever known in modern Parliamentary history, he married Edna Carswell, only daughter of the party leader, and he was made at the age of twenty-seven Secretary of State at the Ministry of National Re-organization.

The photograph above the mantelshelf appeared now for a moment. Matlock looked at his fresh young face, brown against the apple-blossom of Carswell's orchard, and found he was clenching his fist till it seemed that these savagely sharp knuckles would cut through his skin.

Now the voice was stressing, gently but insistently, that the main policy-making responsibility of this first Unirad government was Matlock's. His own post was a new creation. He made it the most important in the Cabinet.

"The decision to quit Europe was the Party's. The speed and completeness with which it was put into effect were Matlock's," said the voice. "He rescued more for Britain than had ever seemed possible and left the other European nations bewildered at the fate which had overtaken them. Within weeks every other British overseas commitment had been cancelled. The national enthusiasm which had brought the Unirads to power reached incredible proportions and Matlock's personal popularity was so vast that many felt he would have taken over the leadership of the Party had it not been in his father-in-law's hands."

Matlock smiled for the first time since the film had started.

It amused him for once to be wrongly assigned a virtuous motive instead of the other way round. The reason he had not taken over the leadership of the Party was practical, not sentimental. Indeed, old Carswell had offered to stand down.

But his smile faded as the voice continued.

"The truth is that Matlock was not yet absolutely certain of his authority, whereas Carswell could only be challenged by Matlock. And he still had the biggest step of all to take.

"In January 1991 Matlock introduced the Age Bill."

Matlock who had felt uncomfortably hot for some time began to sweat profusely. On an impulse he rose, knelt in a corner and put his hand over the airconditioning duct.

The gentle stream of air was burning hot. He almost heard Browning's appreciative chuckle and the air began to grow cooler even as he took his hand away.

Back on the screen, the effects of the introduction of the Age Bill were being described. Comfortable again — in body, but not in mind — Matlock watched as the strikes, the demonstrations, the protest-meetings unfolded on the wall.

Then he saw himself, young, confident, poker-faced, being escorted by the police through booing crowds from the House to the Westminster Bridge Hover-launch. He had seen this sequence a hundred times. Until comparatively recently it had appeared at least a couple of times a year on the popular Tele-recall programmes. It was still, so he was told, a leading request item on these shows.

As he stepped on to the pier, over the heads of the demonstrators in full view of the cameras soared a small round object. The sun glinted on it as it spun in the air. The young Matlock stepped forward casually, cupped his hands close to his chest like a seasoned cricketer, caught it;

then, changing sport, turned, dropped it on to his foot and booted it far out into the clear blue waters of the Thames.

It exploded just below the surface. A fountain of water arched into the air and its outermost fringe rained down on the pier where the police were plunging into the bewildered crowd in pursuit of the thrower.

Matlock, with a cool wave to the onlookers, stepped into the launch which swept away up river.

"It is not impossible that this incident as much as anything else turned the tide for Matlock," said the voice. "It has been suggested that Matlock himself arranged it. Whatever the truth, it created a breathing space. Matlock's next step was a mammoth statistical attack upon his opponents. The main burden of his arguments was that . . . "

The voice droned on, the pictures flickered by. Matlock neither saw nor heard. A voice in his head and a picture behind his eyes were much clearer, much closer.

Population had outstripped production. The causes were partly inefficient management, partly a steadily increasing birthrate, but principally the rapidly decreasing mortality rate. The country was top-heavy. He was not rationing children, he was not denying the right to procreate. He was giving the old a term to their years; an equal term for rich and poor, great and small; he was offering what could be a great boon to mankind — the chance to know the moment of one's end and the chance to meet it with dignity and serenity.

He was proposing that every man, woman and child in the country should be fitted with a heart clock; a minute device, fixed in the main valve of the heart, which at the end of a determined number of years, would stop.

Euthanasia had been legalized eight years earlier. It was now an accepted part of the nation's life.

The heart clock involved a kind of economic euthanasia.

What a phrase! gibed Matlock bitterly to himself. How they had all liked it. Or nearly all.

"Let us, as we have so often done in past centuries, let us lead the world to a new kind of freedom and prosperity. And let us show that we are aware that true freedom is only possible through voluntary restriction; and true prosperity is the fruit of democratic sacrifice."

His thought bitter and self-mocking, had joined in perfect timing with the voice, youthful and vibrant, from his face on the screen. He covered his ears and closed his eyes, careless of the eyes he knew were watching him.

When he looked at the screen again, he was lying naked on a table and a knife was cutting into his chest.

The film was well edited, the whole sequence here took only five minutes.

This had been his final card, of course. This had been his greatest gamble.

The Age Bill had not yet been voted on. Opposition throughout the country, though slackening off, was still considerable. And within the ranks of the Unirads themselves there was not enough certainty of support to guarantee the vote.

So Matlock presented the most bizarre Party Political Broadcast ever. It consisted of live coverage of himself undergoing the first heart-clock operation. Recorded television surgery was a commonplace; open-heart surgery, heart transplants, these were as familiar as visits to the dentist had been in mid-century. But this was something new and had hitherto uncontemplated audience appeal. Ninety-eight per cent of the television sets in the country were tuned in to the operation that February night.

The operation went smoothly, smartly. The programme ended with Matlock opening his eyes in the recovery room. Blinking in bewilderment at the camera for a second. Then with a faint smile saying into the microphone, "That's all it is, ladies and gentlemen. I will bid you good-night now. I must get some sleep. I have a hard day in the House tomorrow."

His car had driven to Westminster the following morning between cheering crowds such as had not been seen since the crowning of the King.

His reception in the Commons was not so unanimously applaudatory. The Leader of the Opposition congratulated him on his recovery, then enquired what part of Matlock's anatomy they could hope to see dissected in the next episode.

When the laughter had died away, it was Carswell, not Matlock, who stood up to reply. His speech was short, but it stunned the Opposition, and a great many members of the Government too. This was too important a matter for a Government with such a small majority to push through, Carswell said. (Cries of "hear, hear," from the Opposition.) Therefore he thought it best that the people should themselves give the answer, and consequently he had formally requested the King to dissolve Parliament.

There had been uproar, Matlock recalled. For a man who had been calling on the Government to resign since it came into being, the Leader of the Opposition looked remarkably displeased.

The rest was history. This became the biggest single-issue election campaign ever. Matlock's teams were superbly drilled. No one not wholly and publicly committed to the Age Bill was put forward as a Unirad candidate. The country, in love with the hero-figure of Matlock and readily reacting to the appeal to self-interest implicit in the Bill (for all those under sixty anyway), returned the Unirads to power with a majority so large that the Government's side of Chamber could not seat all its members.

On the screen appeared the film of that first re-assembling of Parliament. Matlock saw himself entering the House, heard the great roar of applause which greeted him, saw himself advancing to his place on the front bench with a slight deprecatory smile on his face. Then the film stopped and held his face there quite still, until suddenly it began to expand and spread out till it covered the whole wall. Till the pores of his skin pitted his face like the craters of the moon. Till only his mouth was visible, vast, canyon-like, but still holding that vilely modest smile.

Then it stopped. And the lights went on.

"Hello Matt," said Browning from behind him. "Hope you're enjoying the show?"

He must have slipped in in the dark. He

had certainly gone out earlier. Matlock wondered how long he had been back.

"It has some historical interest," he said in reply.

"Yes, hasn't it? Great days, those. Great days. I think there are a lot of Unirads today, the young ones especially, who don't realize how much we owe you."

"Perhaps you'd like me to do a lecture tour?"

Browning roared with laughter.

"No, Matt. I think we'll leave it to the historians eh? Look Matt, what I've been trying to do with this film is to remind you of what you once were. It was you who created the modern Unirad Party, Matt. You attack us and slander us, but we're your creation. When I was a lad in my teens and just getting interested in politics, it was you whom I took as my model. You were held up to me as the greatest thing that had happened to this country since Churchill."

"So we have had a nostalgic stroll down memory lane, Prime Minister. With the heat full on. It's been very interesting. I think I must go now."

Browning put on his mock-penitent look.

"I'm sorry about the heat. One of the Psychi boys suggested it. Said it would lower your resistance. Bloody tom-fool idea it sounded to me. I know the only way to destroy your resistance is by reason, Matt, boy."

Matlock again was almost taken aback by Browning's frankness; then he shook his head and sighed heavily, a trifle histrionically.

"You were right, Prime Minister, we don't meet often enough nowadays. I find myself at times tottering on the brink of trusting you."

"Oh you can, Matt. You can. You must. Look, I'll be frank. We're in a spot of bother. Nothing really. Just a bit of shoaly water. But till we get over it I'd like you back in the Government. You can be sitting in the Cabinet tomorrow. It'll take three weeks to get you elected, though. We can't hurry the next by-election. But that doesn't matter. It's a safe seat. They're all safe seats since you got us going, eh?"

Matlock found himself joining in

the man's laughter. There didn't seem anything else to do somehow. Browning stopped first and Matlock found himself laughing alone. The sound seemed thin and reedy beside the echoes of Browning's deep-throated guffaws.

"So you'll do it?" said Browning.

"No," said Matlock. "But I'll stop till the end of the show. You've got me that interested."

"That's a start. What are your terms?"

"What's the hurry? Indeed, why do you want me at all? I find it flattering, but it encourages me to oppose you rather than support you. I must be more successful than I thought."

"I thought you might argue like that, Matt. Don't fool yourself. Here's the truth. We're in pretty deep, Matt. I've been to the Swiss more than once in the last five years. I've got to go again. But they want reassurances. They want evidence of good faith. They want all kinds of things. One of them is a cut in the E.O.L. A drastic cut."

Matlock began to understand. He had suspected the country was mortgaged up to the hilt with the Swiss but was horrified to learn that they were in a position to be able to command an Expectation of Life cut. Outside influence on the E.O.L. was a possibility he had always strenuously denied when he was in office. But so many other reassurances he had given had proved false in his own day that he forced himself not to feel indignant at this.

For many years now the Age Rate had been the outward and visible sign of the state of the country's economy. He had never intended this, but somehow it had come about. In a good year when the economy could support a heavy load at the top, the Age Rate remained high, 84, 85 years perhaps. During the great boom of the previous decade it had twice topped ninety. But the last few years had seen a frightening decline, till at 76, the country had the lowest E.O.L. in Europe (only Switzerland was not now a heart-clock economy).

Now it was to come down still further. Browning went on speaking.

"We'll have to cut it. We can't afford not to. It'll be in the Budget, of course. I'd like you beside me when I present that Budget, Matt."

"How big's the cut?"

Browning grinned and laid a finger by his nose.

"Now that'd be telling. But big, Matt."

"It can't be too big. You're getting a bit near the Bible Barrier."

As he uttered the words, he heard again briefly his own young voice sententiously proclaiming. "Three score years and ten we are promised in the Good Book. And three score years and ten we shall have whatever happens. But more than that, I promise you, much more. Eighty, ninety, eventually one hundred years can be ours if we put our house in order now."

Thus the Bible Barrier had been born and though it was mentioned nowhere in the Act itself, the concept was one of peculiar force.

"Look, Matt. Even if we drop just a year, it's a year too much for you. You can't afford a year at your age. But come back in out of the cold and you can have another quarter of a century. You're in great trim, I can see that. And we've got drugs that'll keep you that way."

"I've never heard of any."

"For God's sake, Matt, be your age, if you'll forgive the phrase. What's the point of releasing new drugs when the E.O.L. is seventy-six? But once in the House nothing can touch you. It's Sanctuary, Matt. You should know. You built the bloody cathedral, eh?"

Yes, thought Matlock, I built the whole hideous edifice. Not that the House had taken much persuading to agree that M.P.s should be outside the scope of the Act on the grounds that considerations of one's own age should not be allowed to become a factor in the way an M.P. voted on age cuts.

"I'll think it over," said Matlock and turned to the door. I really will think it over, he thought. I must think it over to discover why he is really offering me this job. There can surely be no real danger to him in this Budget. He'll get the vote — Jesus, he has a majority of hundreds and there's no election for two and a half years. In any case, he has the electoral system sewn up tight, the police and the army are in his pocket.

Why has he offered me this deal?

"I'll think it over," he repeated.

65

"No, Matt," said Browning. "Don't think. You might think yourself to a wrong answer. What's holding you back?"

"It's a big step," said Matlock lightly. "Turning my back on twenty-five years and publicly reversing all my beliefs."

"You did it once before, Matt," said Browning with a trace of a sneer. "Look."

He raised his index finger. The lights dimmed but did not go out, the poro-screen shrank to its normal size and the film began to race through. The voice was a mere gabble but Matlock needed no voice to interpret the ludicrously rapid scenes which unwound before him. He saw the Age Bill being put into effect, saw himself talking, talking, always talking, the lower jaw rattling up and down at an ever increasing speed till the whole thing became a blur. When the film finally decelerated to a viewable pace, he was still there but he was no longer talking. He was sitting with his head between his hands, listening.

The voice which settled out of the high-pitched swirl was his wife's. Edna.

Dead now for eighteen years.

"You can't do it, Matt. You can't. It'll finish you. It'll be the end of father. But you can't destroy the Party. That's too strong now, because of you. But it will never forget, never forgive. The Party will destroy you."

Matlock raised his head on the screen.

I look older than I do now, thought the spectator Matlock.

"I must do it, Edna, even if I am destroyed. It's gone sour, all sour. This is not what I meant, not what I meant at all. I must resign and speak out."

"Speak out! What chance do you think you'll get to speak out? Do you imagine they don't know?"

"You forget that I am still 'they', my dear."

Edna looked down at him.

"You are still rather touchingly naive, Matt."

She was right, thought Matlock. I knew soon enough she was right. But dear God! that they could have been filming this!

"Enough?" asked Browning.

He nodded.

The film froze on his face again, this time lined with weariness and despair. The lights came on.

"I couldn't do it twice, Prime Minister. Not that."

"You once would have said you could not have done it once."

"But I had reasons then that you cannot offer me now. Faith, conscience, a desire for atonement."

"You had believed in what you did. Could you not believe again?"

Matlock shook his head wearily.

"I did an evil and believed in it. But worst, I convinced others. I used no force, no coercion. I made them believe. That's what I have been trying to undo ever since. You can give me no reasons for stopping doing that."

Browning's voice dropped to what in another man would have been a histrionic softness.

"Oh, but I can, Matt. I cannot persuade you to join me, perhaps. But I can give you reasons to stop opposing me."

"Are these threats?"

"Only if the law is a threat. Your law,

Matt. You are getting old. You must be tempted to try to escape the law. Perhaps even now you are arranging to go for Op. But it won't do, Matt. It won't do. You must keep your nose clean. And that means you mustn't be an accessory to any breakage of the Age Law. And that's what you are, every time you preach one of your little sermons, so my legal boys tell me. You encourage evasion. Do you deny it?"

Matlock laughed.

"I say nothing, Prime Minister. Except that in the end you have disappointed me. You threaten my freedom. Perhaps my life. I value both, more than you can know. But they are not negotiable in the long run. I will not bargain with them."

"I expected no less," replied Browning. "Indeed, Matt, I expected a bit more, but that's beside the point. No, the real thing is that you seem to have forgotten what your Law says about the penalties for evasion, or attempted evasion of the E.O.L."

"Hardly. The penalty shall be loss of years and any superfluity in the penalty shall be carried out, at the discretion of the court, on the wife and or children of the offender."

"And you could lose up to one hundred years, Matt. You can afford only six. That leaves a possible superfluity of ninety-four to share out. A stern measure. It had to be stern, remember, to make this law for all people, all classes."

"I remember saying it, Prime Minister. It was a foolish thing to say, but at least you cannot turn it to use against me. My wife has been dead for eighteen years. We had no children. It is me you must deal with. Alone. Good day."

Matlock was almost through the door this time when Browning's voice made him turn again.

"Look at the screen, Matt. Just once more."

The entire wall was filled with the picture. Projected on it were two documents. The lights in the room were too bright to let the writing on them be immediately legible.

"Oh, I'm sorry," said Browning. "Can't you see properly?"

He waved his hand and the lights

70

dimmed once more.

"There we are. Can you see now?"

Matlock could see, but he could not understand. The blood seemed to be bubbling through the veins at the side of his forehead and a line of sweat arched across his upper lip.

The top document was a certificate of marriage, dated three years earlier, between himself and Lizzie Armstrong, Spinster.

The lower one was a birth-certificate dated forty years previously. The parents were named as Matthew Matlock and Edna Carswell. The child was a boy. Named Ernst.

The documents faded and were replaced by two faces. Lizzie and Ernst, smiling out at him.

"They can afford about seventy between them. That's what we're bargaining about, Matt," said Browning. "Off you go now. Just think things over. See you soon."

Matlock stumbled through the door.

3

BY the time he had reached the lift, Matlock had recovered sufficiently to remember the reporters whose attention he had so efficiently drawn to his arrival. They would be waiting below, eager for some meat to clothe the bones they had already given their editors to gnaw.

Matlock had no desire to be faced with a barrage of questions at this moment. His mind was still disorganized by Browning's threat. He knew that this particular section of the Age Law had not been acted upon more than a dozen times since it was passed, and then only in cases when the man concerned had got clean away. The first three times, the escapee had returned and the family had been released. People had begun to call it a bluff.

The fourth time, the man had not returned. His wife and son were executed.

Painlessly, quickly, but killed by law for all that.

Matlock had finger-stamped the execution order.

"Christ, I was certain in those days!"

He had spoken aloud. The sound of the words cut through the turmoil in his mind. He was standing in front of the open lift. Turning away from it, he set off up the corridor to his left.

About fifteen yards along, he hesitated in front of a plain unnumbered door. He glanced back up the corridor and counted the doors he had passed. Three.

This was it. This had been his room for those powerful years.

He turned to move on. But something (not sentiment, he thought) made him press the handle. The door slid silently open.

A man turned from the ebony-inlaid kidney-shaped desk which dominated the room. He wore uniform.

"Good-morning, Mr. Matlock, Sir. It's nice to see you again."

"Hello, Jody," said Matlock with relief. "It's nice to see you too."

The grey-haired figure came towards

him with a pleased smile. A Messenger of the House, already old when Matlock had occupied this room, he must be in his nineties now. He was a peculiar case, a man outside the Age Law. He had a very rare blood disease, one of the few conditions beyond the reach of modern medicine. His doctors had certified that an operation would kill him. They were doubtless right. They had also certified that he had at the outside a couple of years to live.

Matlock, with a single finger stamp (life and death in my finger! he thought) had put him outside the Age Law. But the doctors this time had been wrong. Jody thirty-five years later was as hale as ever. He rarely left the House now, partly because his advanced years were not so noticeable in the one place in the country where old men abounded. Partly because in the straight, smoothly padded corridors of the House which he knew like the back of his hand there was less chance of his meeting with the accident which could mean his death.

"Visiting the Minister, are you, sir?" asked Jody.

"Not really, Jody. Just looking around."

"Oh," said the old man.

"I've been with the P.M.," added Matlock, sensing the Messenger's uneasiness.

"Oh, that's all right then," said Jody brightly. "And you're just having a look-see for old time's sake, eh? Changed a bit since you was here, Mr. Matlock."

Matlock looked at the huge desk, the white nylon-tread carpet, the lazer-cut sculptures welded to the wall.

"Yes, it has. My desk was a bit smaller, eh Jody? And we didn't have these works of art in those days."

"No indeed, sir. We did not. The Minister says they represent the sexual rhythms, sir. I know I'm getting on, but they ain't like what I recall of it, sir. Not a bit. Eh?"

He cackled away to himself. Matlock joined in.

"You're not that old, Jody. And with some of the new drugs, you could go on for ever."

Jody winked wisely.

"So you've heard about them, sir? Are you coming back to join us then? They said you would."

Matlock, who had been preparing to disengage himself from the conversation, now gave his full attention.

"Did they? Who was that, then, Jody?"

He was as casual as possible. Jody was like the Vicar of Bray. Old acquaintance was old acquaintance, but he belonged to the man in power.

"Why, the P.M. was just telling my Minister the other day."

Something in Matlock's expression must have warned the old man for he suddenly became very alert.

"You did say you was coming back, sir?"

"I'm not sure, Jody."

Jody tried to move him to the door, talking quickly and genially, but Matlock stood fast.

"It won't do, Jody. Tell me more. If you won't, I'll go back and ask Browning. Quoting you as my informant."

It was cruel; Jody could not risk official disfavour, but even then for a moment he did not seem able to make up his mind.

Give him another reason, thought Matlock. It's worked with better men for worse deeds.

"Remember, Jody, you're alive because of me. You owe me something."

It worked.

"Look, Mr. Matlock, I've got nothing to tell really. Nothing at all."

"What did you hear, Jody?"

"Nothing really. It was just that I was clearing up some things of mine in the store-cupboard yonder when I caught a few words between my Minister and the P.M. Well, my Minister . . . "

"Sedgwick."

"Yes. Mr. Sedgwick. Well, my Minister said, 'If you don't get Matlock you're in trouble,' or something like that. And the P.M. said, 'Don't you worry about that. I'll get Matlock back. He'll be with us within a fortnight'."

"What were they talking about before they mentioned me?"

"I don't know. Really I don't. I didn't hear that. You'll not say anything will you, sir? Not to Mr. Sedgwick or Mr. Browning."

There was a pathetic fear in the old man's eyes which made Matlock turn away.

Will I cling on to life with such little

dignity? he wondered. Or am I clinging on already?

But there were more important things to occupy his mind than the pleasures of self-analysis.

Budget Day was just under a fortnight away, so this seemed the obvious time-limit referred to.

But his own importance in all this was still a mystery. The official attitude to him for twenty-five years now had been quiet suppression. Nothing dramatic enough to bring him into the public eye. He was never allowed to become a hero — or a martyr. The storm surrounding his resignation was allowed to subside. But his efforts to rejoin Parliament in opposition were efficiently and unobtrusively thwarted. And thereafter he found himself continually and inevitably channelled into obscurity.

Now suddenly power had been handed back to him. He was worth bribing, worth threatening. And he had no idea of the reason why.

"You'd best be on your way then, sir."

The old man's unease showed clearly

through his deference.

"I'll call the lift for you."

"No, don't do that, Jody. I'd rather leave nice and quietly. I could probably find my own way out without being seen, but it's been a long time since I was here and I shouldn't like to give the impression of prowling about. But I'm sure you can find me a nice side exit if you try."

Jody obviously did not like the idea of Matlock 'prowling about'. He stood uncertainly for a moment, then said with stiff formality, "Come this way please, sir."

Five minutes later Matlock was walking across Westminster Bridge.

He paused to peer down at the Thames. The crystal clear water was dotted with hover-taxis and sight-seer craft, though there were fewer of these than had once been the case before travel restrictions had become more stringent. The purification of the Thames had taken place during Matlock's own lifetime. Now it was worth fishing off Westminster Pier.

We have done something worth while. We have made an open sewer into a waterway fit for the barge of a queen.

The romantic thought amused him. The visionary in him had been left a long way behind.

But there is a poem I once knew. About Westminster Bridge. 'Earth has not anything to show more fair.' That's it.

Something of comfort began to steal over him as the lines came back.

Something about 'a calm so deep. The river glideth at his own sweet will. Dear God! The very houses seem asleep. And all that mighty heart is lying still.'

That mighty heart.

What shall I do? rose the great cry in his mind. How shall it all end?

He turned in anguish to continue his walk. Coming towards him from the south, unhurrying, his loose robe flapping in the slight east wind, was the bearded man he had seen outside his flat the night before.

Matlock turned quickly. He wanted no conversation at the moment. His mind was confused, in turmoil. He had to have time to work out the full implications of the morning. This seemed the day for old quotations for now another rose into his mind.

He who hath wife and children hath given hostages to fortune.

To Browning. Hostages to Browning.

He set off at a brisk pace back the way he had come. Once off the bridge he glanced back. The bearded man had fallen further behind. But as he turned into Victoria Embankment his sense of being pursued suddenly doubled and his legs seemed to lose their strength. They felt old, wasted.

Like dry sticks. Sticks with expensive cloth flapping around them. How shall I escape?

He glanced round again. There was no sign of the bearded man. Just ahead was a building he knew well. The Globe Slow-Theatre. He and Lizzie often went there. He did not even pause to look at the posters but strode quickly across the foyer to the ticket machines. Clutching the metallic disc he headed for the escalator. He stepped on and was sucked up into the green-lit dimness above.

Having no idea which dance was being performed today, Matlock had no logical preference for any level. He got off at the third for no better reason than that this had been Lizzie's choice on their last visit, though he had argued in favour of the fourth as giving a more aesthetically pleasing angle for that particular dance.

At this time of day there was little difficulty in finding an empty box. He pressed the button which opened the door.

He entered an ovoid cubicle, sound-proofed to prevent disturbance from or to the neighbouring boxes. The glass shell before him was so clear that, as always he had to touch it to make certain it was there. He leaned back in the ergonomically designed chair and brought his attention to bear on the stage.

The Slow-Dance was the artistic product of an aesthetic theory which had its roots in the orientalization of Western philosophy in the last three decades of the twentieth century. Meditational processes, flower symbolism, the new Hermetism and a myriad of other elements had combined to produce the simple proposition that all art should mirror the great imperceptible movements of life, invisible yet inevitable — the blossoming of a flower, the growth of a tree, the cycle of the seasons.

The ageing of man, thought Matlock.

But his mind was already beginning to react to the scene on the stage below.

Five dancers knelt in a circle. They faced inwards but their bodies were arched back till their heads almost rested between their ankles. Their eyes were closed, the lids painted a matt white so they stared dully, blankly, sightlessly from the circular stage.

In the centre of the circle stood another dancer. He stood upright, heels slightly raised, arms by sides, hands with their palms facing forward. All the dancers looked as if they were resting in perfect stillness but Matlock knew that slowly, inexorably, they were moving. This was one of the classical rising movements and would take at least another three hours to complete. They must have been at it for over an hour already.

He settled back in his seat to enjoy the performance. It was one of the most relaxing experiences he knew. It was the awareness of movement without the perception of movement that drew out time into long valleys of peace, he had decided. Like watching a clock, which moved though you could never see it moving.

How much of the hour had gone, he did not know. But suddenly the performance was horribly, violently disrupted. From the side of the auditorium appeared a man. He staggered across to the circular stage and tried to climb it, but collapsed with his legs trailing over the edge. He was hardly a yard from one of the choral dancers, and the sight of that body heaving with the effort of breathing so close to the exquisite stillness of the dance was an obscenity in itself.

But worse followed. From all sides of the auditorium came the police. Tall dark-uniformed men, about a dozen of them, guns at the ready, moving without haste (though relatively their movements seemed violent, outrageous) towards the stage.

The fugitive looked round wildly, made a final effort and dragged himself wholly on to the stage. He was shouting now, opening his mouth into a cavern of terror and despair. But the whole scene was made even more horrible to Matlock because the glass shell before him kept all sound out.

The police reached the side of the stage. Ten of them stopped there. Two vaulted lightly on to the platform.

The fugitive backed away, crashing into one of the choral dancers and sending him flying. He was old, Matlock saw. Old and terrified. This was no escaped criminal, he knew. This was one who had fled the moment of death. This was a man whose time had come and who had broken under the knowledge.

The police had reached him. They bent down and took him gently by the arms. He screamed silently. Shook them off and flung his arms around the central dancer. The police pulled, the dancer toppled. For a few vile moments they all thrashed around in orgiastic violence. Then Matlock saw one of the police press an anaesthetic disc on the back of the old man's neck and within seconds he was as still as the remaining choral dancers who had held their position throughout the confusion.

The policemen picked up the still body and carried it to the edge of the stage where they passed it down to two others. Quickly the little procession disappeared into the darkness of the auditorium.

Matlock sat back, his mind filled again with turbulence and horror. He could guess what had led to the scene below. When a man's E.O.L. was up, he was invited to visit a terminal hospital (the Death House as they were usually called) where the stopping of the heart clock would take place with the minimum fuss and distress to friends and relatives. Most people went. But some preferred to remain at home to the end, either through love, or fear. Others (a troublesome few) insisted on pretending that the time had not come and went about their normal business — till they fell dead in the street, or at work.

But in addition to these, there were always those who broke under the strain. Sometimes they went quietly mad; sometimes they went berserk. In the early days of the Age Law there had been a great upsurge of sexual and other crime among these soon to die. But this had eased off as it became generally realized that the laws of the land still applied and that any sentence passed on a man (or woman) but unable to be carried out on him because his E.O.L. was up, could be transferred to his immediate relatives. And as the most common form of punishment in the courts nowadays was the time-fine — that is, the curtailing of the guilty man's E.O.L. by a period ranging from a month to several years according to the seriousness of the offence — family supervision was usually enough to keep the old man on the rails.

But always some broke loose and were a terror and a danger to the public as they ran wild in search of an escape that was impossible.

"Not a pleasant sight, Brother Matthew," said a voice behind him.

He turned. Standing in the doorway was the bearded man.

Matlock almost welcomed this diversion from the troubled maze of his own thoughts. In any case, the bearded man was a problem that needed solving. The easiest solution was that he was one of Browning's men. But he had not acted like one the night before. And it seemed unlikely that Browning would have him followed by someone whose appearance cried out for attention.

"Yes?" he said interrogatively.

"Ah. The Abbot said that you were a great statesman. You invite me to speak without promising to reply."

"You read a great deal into a single word."

"Very little, Brother. The whole universe is comprehended in a single word. Would that we could comprehend the word!"

Gradually it was beginning to dawn upon Matlock who, or rather what, this man was. The Age Laws had thrown up many odd minority groups. Some had been banned. Like the Birthday Unions whose members shared the same birthday — and therefore the same E.O.L. Their activities became so wild towards the end that the Government had stepped in.

But there were others, several religious in origin. And the largest of these was the Brotherhood of the Meek. Matlock knew little about them though he did recall a magazine article a few months earlier. They had re-established a community in the ruins of one of the great Yorkshire abbeys. Fountains it was, he thought. There had been rich and powerful connections from the start. Now about a thousand of them lived there under vows of obedience, chastity, and poverty. Their attitude to the Age Law was simple. The Meek would inherit the Earth. The Age Laws did not apply to them. Their heart clocks were fitted and worked all the same. They accepted this, smilingly.

There had been photographs with the article and this, Matlock realized, was where the memory of the bearded man's strange clothes came from.

"What's your name?" he asked.

"They call me Brother Francis."

"What did they call you before they called you that?"

The bearded man lifted his hands as if in awed acknowledgement of Matlock's intelligence.

Matlock thought he detected a touch of mockery and was glad. That at least hinted at an underlying sanity.

"What do you want?"

"What all men want, Brother. Peace and the Will of God."

"Then I'll leave you to it."

Matlock made towards the door, but the man's bulk, magnified by his loose garments, blocked it completely.

"I have been sent to fetch you, Brother."

"Then you'd better go and pray that I will come. Brother."

Matlock reached determinedly forward to thrust the man out of his way, but his hand stopped before it touched the rough woollen garments. From somewhere in its maze of folds, Brother Francis had produced a gun. It was pointing steadily at Matlock's stomach.

"Oh, I have prayed, Brother, and you will come."

Matlock shrugged.

"If God wants me that much," he said.

Outside in the street, he stopped and the bearded man closed right up behind him.

"Do we go by foot, Brother," asked Matlock, "Or is there a chariot of fire?"

Francis did not seem offended, but he did not laugh either.

"Walk a little way, Brother. Just a little way."

In fact he told the truth. A hundred yards away round the corner a car was waiting. Behind the wheel in ordinary clothes was a little wizened man who, had it not been for the law, Matlock would have said was nearer ninety than eighty.

They got in the car which started before Francis had finished closing the door. It was an ancient car. Even Matlock, who had not been used to very luxurious travelling in recent years, could not remember anything older. He did not know whether the external noise it made was within the limits laid down by law, but inside it was the most deafening din he had had to put up with in years.

He looked round in alarm and momentary fear as Francis poked the gun into his ribs, but realized the Friar merely wanted to attract his attention.

"What?" he yelled.

"Sorry about the noise, Brother," screamed Francis. "But we always assume we are being listened to."

For a second Matlock could not understand what he meant, but then it came to him that the racket was merely an apparently accidental jamming device against any hidden microphones.

He was not sure whether this additional evidence of rationality was reassuring or not.

The car was now deep in a Curfew Area. They had passed the neon rings minutes earlier. The psychologists had found none of the long promised answers to criminality and in the end the creation of what in effect were criminal ghettoes was the chosen solution. Every large town had its Curfew Areas. Matlock knew most of them. He had found his meetings channelled there more and more frequently in recent years. Not everyone who lived here was a criminal, of course, but these were the known habitats of known criminals. An hour after dark the Curfew Wagon swept everyone it met off the streets into its iron belly.

Matlock looked uneasily around. It was still only the middle of the day, but he was deep in unknown territory.

Finally the car drew up outside a small undistinguished house. From its dull, unimaginative construction, Matlock reckoned it was a rare survival from the mid twentieth century. There was no value in its rarity. It was just surprising that it had not fallen down long before.

The wizened chauffeur unlocked the door and led the way in. Matlock followed and Francis came carefully behind.

The inside was as drab as the exterior.

"Why are we here?" he asked with distaste.

"Please lead on," said Francis motioning to a door in the wall which faced them.

"Why are we here?" asked Matlock firmly, standing still.

Francis walked by him, keeping far enough away to be safe from any attack, and pushed open the door.

"We've come to see the Abbot," he said. "Please go in."

He motioned politely. The gun had re-appeared. Matlock went through into the room.

If he had expected improvement, he

was disappointed. The walls were scarred and cracked and of an undeterminable colour. Two hard chairs stood on either side of a small television set. Otherwise the room was empty.

Matlock turned to the door where Francis still stood.

"Where's your Abbot then?" he demanded.

"Why, here I am, Mr. Matlock. I'm sorry you have been kept."

Into the room smiling with what appeared to be genuine pleasure came the wizened chauffeur. He extended his hand and Matlock automatically grasped it. It felt firmer and stronger than he had expected.

"You look rather surprised, Mr. Matlock. I'm not a very distinguished figure out of uniform, am I? But I look fairly formidable when I'm dressed up. Oh yes. Here, let me show you."

He leaned forward and pressed a switch on the T.V. The screen lit up almost instantly into a rainbow swirl of colour which quickly flowed and formed into sky and trees and buildings. The picture held for a moment while Matlock pried into his store of memories. This had to be Fountains Abbey. He had visited it once in his late teens and he could just about re-create a picture of the majestic ruins in their splendid natural setting.

But the picture he looked at now was of no glorious ruin. The broken cloisters were whole again; the once empty frame of the great east window glowed with light and colour even though the afternoon sun cast the shadow of the great buttresses across it.

The Abbot adjusted a switch with an apologetic smile. The picture faded, the colours swirled and re-formed into an interior. Matlock realized they were now looking at the east window from the inside.

Slowly the camera panned down until they were looking straight up the main aisle of the Abbey. A service was in progress and the telescopic lens of the camera carried them swiftly over a forest of long-haired heads towards the sanctuary where on the third of the five altar-steps stood a solitary figure.

"Now, there I am," said the Abbot with a note of self-congratulation in his voice. "Is that impressive enough for you?"

By the pressure of a switch he held the figure full length in the picture.

Matlock had to agree that this *was* impressive enough. The flowing white robes shone with a startling radiance against the dull gleam of gold from the altar rails and table. At his breast on a simple silver chain hung a gleaming blue stone.

Now the camera swooped their gaze under the bowed forehead right into the face.

Matlock found he was looking at the features of the man who stood beside him.

"I told you it was me," he said triumphantly, then added, in response to Matlock's unspoken puzzlement, "Oh, no. It's not a recording. That's happening now."

Another switch. A grey-bearded face appeared and nodded at the screen.

"All is well, Brother Gareth?"

"All is well."

"Good."

The picture faded and the screen went

blank. The Abbot sat down on one of the hard chairs and motioned Matlock to the other.

"You see, Mr. Matlock, either I had to come to you — or you had to be brought to me. Now, while it was impossible, of course, to prevent them from knowing we wished to contact you . . . "

"Them?" interrupted Matlock.

The Abbot raised his eyebrows a fraction.

"Why, anyone who *wants* to know such a thing. As I say, it was impossible to conceal the desire, even the attempt. But it did seem possible to keep the fact of a personal meeting a secret. That could be important, you know."

"Why not take me to Yorkshire?"

"Time, and secrecy. We can't keep you out of sight for very long without someone noticing. Whereas, as you have seen, I can stay away almost indefinitely."

"That other's an actor?"

"Of course. In fact, he really *was* an actor before he joined us. He is also a much loved and respected member of the inner circle of the Brotherhood."

"Do the others all know?"

97

"My dear Mr. Matlock, what do you take me for? Some naive curate with a touching faith in his fellow men? I know at least half a dozen of my Brethren who have been planted there by Browning. How many others there are, God alone knows."

"And hasn't yet told you? So now you wish to talk to me, Abbot — I should call you 'Abbot', should I?"

The Abbot was amused this time.

"There is no need, if it offends you."

"Only pointless mysteries offend me."

"You are right. I will be naive, Mr. Matlock, and take your puzzlement at its face value, though as you have already been approached by the Prime Minister, and will be soon by the Scottish Ambassador, you can hardly be totally ignorant."

Matlock's training made it fairly easy for him to take the reference to the Scottish Ambassador without reaction, but his mind buzzed with conjecture. There had to be a common denominator somewhere.

"Go on," was all he said.

"Well, now. I will accept, however,

Mr. Matlock, that you probably are ignorant about certain areas of importance."

"Geographical or political?"

"Both. You have, in fact, led a very sheltered life for many years."

Matlock half rose from his chair.

"Do not be offended," said the Abbot. "I do not mean to denigrate you or understate the valiant efforts you have made to establish contact with the people. But you must have been aware yourself of the rigid limits of activity and influence permitted to you by your former party."

"I have been aware," said Matlock slowly. "But I have met with some success in stepping beyond them."

"Less perhaps than you think. A rebel must be given some encouragement if he is not to be driven to desperation. This is true, is it not?"

Matlock remembered bitterly his own growing sense of uselessness, of outside control. It was no comfort to have his fears confirmed.

"It is true."

"Good. You would not be the man I think you are if you did not know it. Less obvious to you has been the interference with your own few channels of information and communication. You have had to rely on others as your eyes and ears for a long time now. You have been a man without friends for almost as long."

This time Matlock did rise, his chair falling behind him.

"What do you mean?" he demanded, leaning over the small seated figure of the Abbot.

The door opened a fraction and Brother Francis appeared. The Abbot motioned him away.

"Perhaps more, perhaps less than you think. Do sit down."

Matlock passed his hand over his forehead and swayed slightly. He reached out a hand and steadied himself against the wall.

"Won't you sit down, Mr. Matlock?" said the Abbot. "This has been a very distressing morning for you, I know."

Matlock wondered how much he did know. His head was quite clear now and he felt more alert than he had done since leaving Browning. But he shook his head again.

"No, I'd rather stand for a moment or two. You were making certain implications. Please continue."

The Abbot frowned and the terrible sternness which settled on his face for a moment gave Matlock some indication of the man's real quality.

"I imply nothing, Mr. Matlock. I was about to give you some facts. Here they are for what they are worth. You were I think threatened this morning with a forged family link between yourself and your secretary Miss Lizzie Armstrong, and your assistant Mr. Ernst Colquitt. Right?"

"If you say so."

"I do. This is a threat you would do well to disregard."

"Why?" asked Matlock, knowing already the answer he was going to hear.

"They are Browning's creatures."

Ready though he had been, Matlock could not hold in an outcry of protest.

"I won't believe it. I know them too well. No one could . . ."

He tailed off as he regained control of himself.

"You are involved in a confusion I find

hard to understand in a mind of your calibre. But it's an old confusion. You don't really believe all Unirads should have horns and tails, do you? You don't really believe that you and your few supporters have a monopoly of virtue, of honesty, of pleasing personalities, do you?"

"No. But these are my friends."

"And their friendship is, I am sure, sincere. It has built up in the years they have known you. It may even have developed to the point where there is a dangerous tension between their beliefs and their friendship. Though I'm sure Browning has kept a careful check on that. But to them, their friendship and their party's policy have long had the same aim — to keep you out of the public eye — to let you indulge in activity without effect. You trouble no one, so the Party is pleased. You are in no danger, so their friendship is pleased."

"Prove this," said Matlock as dispassionately as he could. "Prove it."

The Abbot's eyes looked at him sympathetically from the small wrinkled face.

"How can I prove it? What proof would you accept? You have seen 'proof' already today that you are a married man with a son. What proof can I offer strong enough to overcome the memory of that?"

"Forget it," said Matlock. "True or false, you have tried to reduce me to a cypher. But this is not the end. I know I have done little in these past thirty years. I know I have been out of touch. I know, whatever the details may be, that I have been spied upon, and manoeuvred, and suppressed, and misinformed. But I know also that I can have a seat in the Cabinet tomorrow. I know that I can be the cause of a complicated religious charade two hundred miles away. I begin to suspect that there may be others, silent as yet, who wish to speak soft words in my ear."

"Oh, there are. There are. There's an invitation from the Scottish Ambassador being delivered to your flat even now."

"For a cypher, I am doing well. I've had the Browning version of the reasons why I'm suddenly in demand. Now let's have yours."

"Mine is no version, Mr. Matlock.

Mine is the simple truth. Or rather, the complicated truth, for it was only recently that I myself came to understand it. The point is this, that there is in the North a highly complex and organized Underground resistance movement, which is on the verge of open war."

Matlock was stunned. This was such arrant nonsense that he could hardly believe he was hearing it.

Finally he laughed contemptuously. "Don't be stupid, Abbot. This is a dream. My lines of intelligence may be suspect, but if such a thing existed on such a scale, I must have heard of it. It is impossible that I should not have heard of it."

The Abbot leaned forward thoughtfully. He produced from an inside pocket a packet of long herbal cigars one of which he lit. The yellow smoke drifted across to Matlock and the sweet smell rubbed itself against his nostrils.

"I find it strange that you should say that about this Movement," said the Abbot slowly. "Especially in view of the fact that you are its most honoured and respected Leader."

4

IT was after four when Matlock returned to his flat. The door was flung open as he approached and Lizzie rushed out to him, her face pale with worry.

"Matt," she said, "Matt. Thank heaven you're back."

She pressed her head against his chest and dug her hands into his back. Automatically he rested his hands on her shoulders. Over her head and through the door he could see Ernst and Colin, their faces alight with relief also, but hanging back in the face of — or rather, the rear of — Lizzie's emotionalism. He forced a smile and they came to him.

"Are you all right, Matt? For Godsake, where have you been?"

This was Ernst. Relief, with a hard core of curiosity. The friend and the heir apparent both on show.

"I'm fine," he said.

Colin said nothing but reacted just

as typically. He prised Lizzie loose and led Matlock into the room. His eyes, Matlock knew, were unobtrusively but efficiently examining his face and head for damage.

He sat down, took the glass which Ernst offered him and sipped a little of the drink. He wrinkled his mouth in distaste at the comparison evoked with Browning's Scotch.

"I'm sorry I'm a bit late," he began. "But I see no reason for you all to get in a panic."

"But Matt, we got your note about Browning and waited for ages. Then Colin made some enquiries at the House. All the reporters there had seen you go in, but no one saw you come out. We were worried sick."

"My dear Lizzie. What did you imagine had happened to me? That Browning had whisked me off to some dungeon under the Thames where I was being put to the test on the rack?"

Lizzie flushed violently enough for something like this to have been her actual fear.

"So what did happen, Matt?" asked Colin.

"Why, Browning offered me a seat in the Cabinet and I slipped out by a back way and went for a little walk to think things over. I was rather abstracted, I'm afraid, and quite forgot to telephone you. I am very sorry."

He sipped his drink slowly and through half closed eyes watched their reactions closely. Lizzie and Ernst looked at him in disbelief, their amazement at the news aggravated by the casual way it had been offered. Only Colin looked unperturbed and nodded slowly as though confirming something in his own mind.

"You're joking, Matt," said Ernst.

"No," said Matlock. "Fill me up again will you?"

He handed over his empty glass. It made a useful stage-prop. From now on, he realized, he would be acting all the time, never knowing who was acting with him. He was faced by a bewildering complex of possibilities through which the straightest way seemed to be to assume that he could trust no one, that everything he said would be reported back to Browning.

"I am nearly seventy years old," he had said to the Abbot. "And you are asking me to be without friends. You are telling me that in seventy years all I have collected round me are my enemy's spies."

"No," the Abbot had replied, "they are your friends. But to love a man does not mean to love his beliefs. Just as to love a belief does not mean you must love those who share it. In any case I have spoken against only two people. Of the man, Peters, I know nothing damaging. Nor of the great mass of your sympathizers."

Perhaps the straightest path, he thought now, would be to tell them everything. But Colin's slowly spoken question made him realize he had not the right to do this.

"Why," he asked, "should Browning think you dangerous enough to be offered such a bribe?"

Matlock imagined he sensed a tensing in the other two as they waited for his answer.

If what he said now was going to be reported back to Browning, then his

108

answer must ring true. But the crux of the matter would be whether or not Browning knew of his contact with the Meek. Twenty-four hours earlier he would have said that he was not important enough to be shadowed everywhere. Now he was certain he was, but whether his exit from Westminster had been surreptitious enough to throw them off the scent, he did not know.

He decided to sit on the fence. To hint knowledge, but not its source. Let Browning take it as he liked.

"I'm not sure. That's what I've been trying to work out in these past few hours."

"And?" It was Ernst, his face eager. Too eager? Or was it just that his own importance must swell in direct proportion to Matlock's?

"I'm not sure. There are too many factors."

"But you have an idea?"

Lizzie this time. Dear God, once you started thinking of spies, how conspiratorial everyone looked!

"Yes. An idea. But nothing of that yet. I want more time to work things out."

"This could be the beginning of a break-through," said Ernst. "You remember what I suggested about Percy's death, that this might be in the way of a warning? And things have been made progressively tougher for you, in the North in particular, in the past couple of years. Perhaps we've been making more progress than we thought."

"With the kind of attendances we get, that hardly seems likely. Two members of the police-force for every member of the public!" said Colin.

Ernst snapped back, "Well, you explain why Matt has become important enough to warn off, to threaten, to bribe."

"No one has threatened me, have they?" said Matlock mildly.

"Of course not," said Colin. "Look Ernst, I can't explain it. All I am saying is that if we've made progress in the North or anywhere, it's been invisible progress, not measurable in any terms I can understand yet."

Matlock looked at Colin and nodded his head as though in agreement. What he was thinking about was a coincidence of wording. 'Invisible progress' had been

110

the very phrase the Abbot had used.

"You see," he had explained, "it cut two ways, this pleasant scheme of Browning's to keep you out of harm's way. He very efficiently shut you off from public view and shut the public's views off from you. But oddly enough, by decreasing your influence and authority on a public, political level, he increased it in another way. He cut off your power, but your charismatic value increased enormously. Charisma. Yes, that's the word. That attracting force which bears little relationship to objective factors. Don't feel too proud, Mr. Matlock. This cult was not altogether spontaneous, not altogether due to your own many virtues and attractions. No, like the cult of Guevara in the late sixties of the last century, it was a controlled spontaneity. It was in the interests of certain factions that there should be a leader, a focal point, beyond the reach of internal squabblings and politics. You were that man."

"Why? Why me? After all, Abbot, I was the man who created the Unirads and the Age Law."

111

"All the more reason, my dear Mr. Matlock. The convert, or the apostate, depending on how you look at it, is very frequently the most useful and respected member of his new-found faith. One does not have to look much further than the case of Saul of Tarsus. Or Lucifer."

"That's quite a bit further."

"I meant nothing personal in either instance. The point is this, Mr. Matlock, that you are possibly the single most influential name in the extra-Parliamentary opposition group which is at its strongest in the Northern counties."

Matlock had listened with growing disbelief.

"No," he burst out now, "no. This can't be true. I have gone up there to meeting after meeting. I would have seen some sign. Instead, the attendance has grown steadily smaller."

"You could have had thousands there, Mr. Matlock, thousands, had you not given the word that you did not yet desire a show of strength."

"I gave the word?"

"It was given for you, I'm afraid. Just

as your followers were also informed that these pathetic meetings which always degenerated into brawls followed by your ejection back to London, were merely covers for the passing by you of information and instructions to your lieutenants. It was a plan much admired."

Matlock had taken a few moments to sort this welter of assertion into some kind of acceptable order.

"All right," he said finally. "Suppose I accept this. Suppose I accept that I am the revered leader of an underground movement, why at this particular time have I become so popular with Browning? I presume he knows all you tell me. Why not just have me arrested?"

"You are determined to be naive, Mr. Matlock. Browning's intelligence service has, of course, penetrated this underground of yours. He knows much, though by no means all. He is not really certain how much you know. And he is not yet ready for a confrontation. But he knows that Budget Day will bring matters to a climax. Yet he is a man of insight and of cunning. He has seen how his own plan for your suppressal has been turned against him. To arrest you now would be to martyr you. But he hopes to be able to turn the tables once more. Your charisma has been so carefully cultivated that it is now self-propagating. It has gone far beyond the original intentions of the Underground organizers. It could not be killed with your death or disappearance. Only by your betrayal. If you join the Government before Budget Day, the effect on morale and internal discipline within the movement will be so disruptive that his new measures will pass with no more than a whimper of protest."

"And this is what you have come to tell me. You have come to tell me that unwittingly I have been used in a battle I would willingly have joined had I known it was being fought? You have come now to invite my blind co-operation in plans I know nothing of? Why this is almost as bad as Browning's threats."

"Worse, Mr. Matlock. He does not want your death. We don't mind. In fact certain elements in our midst feel that your influence should be given the permanence of heroic memory. They have been outvoted. But be sure, Mr. Matlock, that if you show any signs of capitulating to Browning's request, you will be killed instantly. It will look like Browning's handiwork, of course. But you will be dead. That's the burden of my message."

The two men had sat and stared into each other's eyes for a long moment, both mask-like in their expressions. Then the Abbot had relaxed, leaned forward, tapped him familiarly upon the knee and said in a much more ordinary everyday kind of voice, "Well, that's the official business. Now let's have a little unofficial chat, shall we? There's plenty of time. After all, your job is best done from a position of invisibility, eh? You're making invisible progress all the time!"

"Invisible progress." Matlock realized he had spoken the words out loud. The others were looking at him. He would have to make a greater effort to control these fits of abstraction. More and more he was withdrawing in upon himself lately. It must be age. Or the awareness of age entailed in the Age Law.

"You're right, Colin," he said. "We must have made some kind of progress, it seems, but in what direction I'm not sure. But I apparently have some value. Great value if it is to be judged by Browning's offer, though we must remember that what he can so easily give, he can as easily take away. In many ways, I am tempted to accept."

He sipped at the new drink Ernst had brought him and watched their reactions once more.

He saw in Colin's face a look of blank bewilderment, turning to indignation.

Ernst too looked puzzled, but some other emotion — certainly not anger — was there too.

Only in Lizzie's face did he see the brightening of hope and he closed his eyes at the sight of it. He longed to ask her how much was hope for Browning and how much a woman's hope for some years of peace with the man she loved.

Matlock was suddenly very tired of all three of them. Or rather, he was tired with the events of the day and could not face the thought that here where he should have been most at ease, he had to be most on his guard.

"Look," he said. "Of course I'll do

nothing without discussion. But I must be my own master. I do not claim to be yours, Colin, or yours Ernst, or yours Lizzie. Now I'm rather tired. Let's leave this till tonight, shall we?"

"Anything you say, Matt," said Ernst with his ready smile.

"Not tonight, Matt," said Lizzie. "You're suddenly in demand. A late invitation to a little 'do' at the Scottish Embassy. With a most cordial handwritten 'do hope you can make it' from the Ambassador himself."

"Oh yes. That," said Matlock.

Lizzie looked at him quizzically.

"You knew?"

"Well, half-knew. Let me see."

He glanced at the ornately printed card with the great red lion running along the top of it. On the back in writing just as ornate was the note. If he had not known the Ambassador's name was Fergus McDonwald, he would never have guessed it from the signature.

"I suppose I must go," he sighed.

"What's he after, do you think?" asked Ernst, pausing on his way to the door.

"A chance to demonstrate his literacy,

I shouldn't wonder. Good-bye, Ernst, Colin."

The door closed behind the two men and Matlock found himself in the situation he had hoped above all to avoid. Alone with Lizzie.

He strolled through into his bedroom and stood at the window moodily twisting the poro-control. The window changed from its normal translucency to utter blankness and the room darkened.

"Where did you go this afternoon, Matt? Something happened, didn't it? What was it?"

He half turned. Lizzie was framed in the daylight of the living-room as she stood by the door.

"Nothing."

She did not pursue the question but took a step into the room.

"Do you want me to stay, Matt?"

"No!"

The violence of his reply surprised him. At the same time he thought with alarm that perhaps the darkening of the room had seemed like an invitation.

"No thanks," he said, gently trying to disown the previous negative and at the same time twisting the poro-switch to full transparency. As the light poured back into the room, he saw the effect of his denial on Lizzie's face. It was as though he had struck her.

I will not believe she is a spy, he cried inwardly, and "Lizzie", he began, stepping towards her.

Behind him the guaranteed shatterproof window blossomed violently into a multi-faceted rose, and the wall beside Lizzie cracked crazily under the plastic paper even before the fragments of glass showered over his shoulders.

His loving move towards her turned into a terrified dive, his shoulder caught her in the stomach and they both tumbled through into the living-room as the wall trembled under another impact.

"Matt!" cried Lizzie, trying to struggle into a sitting position but unable to shift the downpressing weight of the man's body. "Matt! Are you hurt?"

She managed to raise herself up on her elbows, but Matlock thrust her savagely back.

"Lie still," he snapped.

He himself rose to a crouch, his right

hand pressed painfully and obliviously to her breast. Then, his head held low, he scuttled around the room darkening each window in turn and pulling shut the bedroom door. His face was white as chalk, though whether for her or himself Lizzie did not know.

Finally when the room was in utter darkness he switched on a small table lamp and came across to where she lay.

"Are you hurt?" he asked abruptly.

"Well, I've probably got a few bruises and fingermarks. Matt, what was it?"

He helped her to her feet and for a moment she rested trembling in his arms. Then, without answering her question he went across to the 'phone and called the police on the emergency beam.

"It must have been a force-gun," he said. "Those windows will resist up to a hundred pounds of pressure."

Lizzie raised her hands to her face in the classic gesture of horror.

Is it just a gesture? Matlock asked himself. How can I tell?

Inside him a thousand nerve ends were jangling. Nothing that had happened so far that day had prepared him for this.

"They were trying to kill you!" gasped Lizzie.

Matlock looked at her in real surprise.

"You didn't imagine it was merely a blown circuit, did you? A domestic accident?"

Lizzie's head moved from side to side as though of its own volition. Her face belied the gesture.

"Who, Matt? Who?"

"I don't know."

He poured himself a long drink and disposed of it like a short one.

"Whoever it was seemed to have plenty of time. Time to fire another shot before packing up and going home. Where are the police?"

He strode up and down the long room. Inside he was almost back to normal, but this display of nervous anger postponed the reassertion of the old relationship.

I was going to tell her, he thought. I would have told her. But not now. Not now.

"Could it be Browning?"

That's a good question, Lizzie my girl. It deserves a good answer.

"It might be. He'd like me dead, and

121

it's easier than having me in the Cabinet. More final."

That's an answer which would interest Browning if it ever reached him.

There was a short ring at the doorbell followed by a fusillade of knocks.

"That can only be the police," said Matlock.

He flung open the door.

"You took your time," he said.

An hour later they had gone. At first their attitude had been rather overbearing. They obviously had some official knowledge of Matlock and the implication of their casual approach to the case was that a trouble-maker must expect trouble. Matlock had wound himself up to give the Inspector in charge a tongue-lashing when the 'phone rang. It was for the Inspector. He did little talking, but a great deal of listening. When it was over, his whole attitude had changed to one of courteous, almost deferential efficiency. A full-scale investigation was initiated and by the time they had left, Matlock had been assured he would receive every protection the police could give.

Lizzie had noticed also.

"Who was behind that call, Matt?" she asked.

He shrugged his shoulders, as much for the benefit of the little man who was whispering caution in his head as for Lizzie.

"Browning. Who else?"

Who else indeed. She must have guessed as much herself if she did not know for certain. A report on his call must have gone straight to the Prime Minister. And Browning, if the Abbot was to be believed, had every reason to want him alive for a while.

Which meant that Browning could not have been behind the shooting.

"But why should he arrange protection if he wants you killed?"

A good question. Lizzie had a quick mind. He had lost his desire to tell her everything, but he was in no mood for further fencing.

"Look Lizzie," he said, allowing his very real irritation to show through. "It's nearly six. I'm going to have a long soak, a short sleep and then get myself ready for the McDonwald of McDonwald or whatever he calls himself. So let's just add this to all the other problems we've got to sleep upon eh?"

She began gathering her things together with an attempt at a smile.

"All right, Matt. Don't forget to brush up on your Burns."

He did not feel he dared respond to her lightness, but watched her to the door in preoccupied silence.

She turned in the open doorway.

"Matt," she said, "take care."

Then she went leaving Matlock staring at the door wondering whether it was just concern he heard in her voice.

Or warning.

5

THE Scottish Embassy was aggressively Scottish in everything from the décor up. Or down. Matlock saw the profusion of tartan hangings, stags' heads, claymores and thistles for what it was — a very basic gesture at English 'refinement' and 'taste'. He enjoyed the joke, especially as it was being washed down with such excellent whisky served in heavy hand-chiselled crystal glasses. But others didn't.

He was surprised, in fact, to realize how much he *was* enjoying the evening. His long soak and short sleep had done the trick marvellously well. And the drink helped.

He was standing two thirds of the way down a long reception room brightly lit by three scintillating crystal chandeliers. Young girls in national costume were walking round with trays of drinks. Three of scotch for every one of anything else. A long table at the far end of the room was covered with a profusion of Scottish confections and produce, from smoked salmon to black bun.

In the centre of the room as of right, and in the centre of the largest and liveliest group, was his host, Fergus McDonwald, His Excellency the Scottish Ambassador to England. Matlock could dimly remember his first appearance in London. "My dear," a Foreign Office acquaintance had said to him, "there's no such man. It's a character actor they've hired for the part. It must be. And such a ham! That voice and that beard!"

That voice, roughly burred, with a guttural lilt to it, was booming out from above *that* beard, rich red just lightly flecked with the silver which told the man's age. He was an imposing figure, nearly six and a half feet tall with breadth of shoulder to match. He wore the dress kilt of his clan and looked in no way ridiculous despite the malice of many of his guests. A good story about him (there were many) related that a particularly strident lady columnist had asked him what he wore under his skirt. He had instantly raised his kilt and shown her.

Then advancing on her he cried, "And what d'ye have hidden under yer ain, my dear?"

She fled.

Those who met the man realized that if the story were not true, it was still necessary to invent it.

McDonwald's pale blue eyes caught Matlock's gaze upon him and he paused in his conversation, or rather his monologue, to wave genially across the room, the delicate white lace at his wrist falling back from the huge deep-lined hand.

Matlock waggled the heavy glass back and some of the contents slopped over his hand. He transferred the glass to the other and shook the drops off energetically.

"I say, steady on," said a tall young man turning to see what had dampened the back of his neck. Matlock recognized Browning's aide who had called for him that morning.

"Hello there! Clive, isn't it? How are you, Clive? And the master, Clive? How's the master?"

Others of the group turned and looked at Matlock. I must be a bit drunk, he

127

thought. Clive stared at him coldly for a moment, opened his mouth as if to speak, then turned away without saying a word.

He was going to put me down with a sharp quip, thought Matlock gleefully, but he changed his mind. They must still be hoping I'll play.

"Ladies and gentlemen!"

An unmistakable voice was bellowing from the centre of the room. Fergus McDonwald used no M.C. He did his own shouting.

"I just want to say how glad I have been to have you all under my roof tonight. You know I'm not much of a hand at standing in a draught, shaking hands and saying good-night, and anyway I hate to stop people enjoying themselves. But I must be off to my dinner just now. So if you'll excuse me, I'll leave you to it. Stay as long as you want. The scotch will last longer than you lot, eh?"

He gave a laugh then ploughed his way through the guests towards Matlock who watched his approach with a fixed smile on his face.

"Matt Matlock!" cried McDonwald in

a voice which was audible in every corner. "You'll be stopping for a wee bite with us? Come along, eh?"

His great arm rested like a yoke round Matlock's shoulders and he was steered unresisting towards the door. Before they left the room Matlock caught a glimpse in a mirror of the crowd of wildly surmizing faces they left behind. In their centre was Browning's man, his face impassive.

"The world will know," he said as the door closed behind them.

"Know what, eh?"

"That we're just good friends."

The red-haired man laughed immoderately but did not pause in his progress down the long corridor which lay before them. Matlock was almost trotting to keep up with the man's powerful strides.

"What're we doing? Working up an appetite?"

"Oh, how I love your English wit."

They reached the end of the passage and as they did so the door facing them opened. McDonwald swept him in without pause.

"Sit," he said, pointing to one of two

uncomfortable looking chairs which were the room's only furnishings. The total effect, despite the better state of the walls and ceiling, was much the same as that of the room where he had talked with the Abbot.

"No thanks," he said.

"The Laird said 'sit'," said a voice so deep and accented it made McDonwald's sound like a middle-class drone. From behind the door, shutting it with his shoulder as he stepped forward, came a figure not much more than five feet high and just as broad. His head was shaped like a cottage loaf, wide-jawed rising to a low peak at the black-thatched crown. His nose looked as if it had been added as an afterthought in plasticine and his eyes were tiny and blankly evil. Brother Francis seemed a happy memory.

"Sit," he repeated jabbing Matlock in the chest with a finger like an iron rod.

Matlock staggered back, the creature advanced. McDonwald said in a mildly admonitory tone, "Now Ossian," and Matlock brought his right hand round, fully expecting to break his wrist.

He was still holding the whisky glass.

It shattered with a mild explosive noise as it crashed into Ossian's head just above the left ear. His face registered little change except for the superficial embellishment of a great ribbon of blood which flowed swiftly from his temple to his nose, and he sank to the floor without a murmur.

Matlock looked at his hand which still clutched the solid base of the glass. The broad silver ring he wore on his middle finger had a drop of blood like a ruby perched upon it. He dropped the base and looked intently at his open palm. It was unmarked. He bent down and wiped the ring carefully on the unconscious man's jacket.

"Now," he said, "What about dinner?"

"What do you think this is?" asked McDonwald. "A bloody fight behind the fives court? Just because you're drunk enough to knock this bungler out doesn't mean you impress me, Matlock. You'll sit for me now."

Matlock sat, wearily.

"What about him?"

"Succour for the fallen foe, eh? He'll be all right just now. I wouldn't be around if I were you."

"I'd like that."

"In that case, just tell me quickly what I want to know. What was Browning's offer?"

"A seat in the Cabinet."

"You accept?"

"Not yet."

"And that bloody rambling priest?"

"He wasn't as generous. He merely threatened to kill me if I came to terms with Browning."

"That all, eh?"

"Oh yes."

"Nothing about me."

"Oh no."

Oh yes — a great deal about you, my kilted Celt. Enough to have made me more careful.

"Now listen to me, Matlock. We don't like you much in Scotland. We have long memories there."

"Then you'll remember that it was me who made you independent."

"Aye. And we remember what you said."

The Scots had been agitating for decades for some form of independent government. The Age Law proposals were used as the basis of yet another great wave of patriotic protest. People were taking to the hills in droves. Matlock was badgered day and night in and out of Parliament. A militant group in Edinburgh occupied St Andrew's House and proclaimed secession. Their broadcast statements were so anti-English in tone that Matlock was urged from all quarters to send the troops in. He didn't. He accepted the secession, gave two days grace for transference across the border either way, required all Scots domiciled or wishing to remain in England to register as aliens, deported those who wouldn't, including the entire Scottish Nationalist Party in Parliament, and threw a line of barbed wire across the border which was later replaced by what the papers called a prefabricated version of Hadrian's wall.

"You said that it was like cutting off a dead branch, noisome with fungus and riddled with worms. You said that the decline of England began with the Act of Union."

"Did I say all that?" asked Matlock as if surprised. "Perhaps I was a bit extreme.

I do recall, however, saying that if we looked at the European boundaries of the Roman Empire, we would see to this very day the boundaries of civilization. The barbarians are beyond. I see no reason here to change my opinions."

McDonwald's large fist crashed into his rib-cage just below his heart. The red beard thrust close to Matlock's face as he leaned forward in pain, and the harsh voice hissed fiercely, "Don't try to be bloody English with me, Matlock. I'll have a drop of your blood with every drop of your bloody false condescension."

"What makes you call it false?" gasped Matlock.

"That," said McDonwald, repeating the blow.

It took Matlock longer to recover this time. Even now he felt the same stupid urge to counter with some ironical comment but held his tongue. Two punches from this man were enough. And in addition Ossian was beginning to stir.

"What else do you want?" he croaked.

"That's better. Much more sensible," said the Scot. "Matlock, I'm not sure how much you know, how much you're just a pawn. I could find out or Ossian here could find out for me. But this much is certain, you're very important to a lot of people. And if you're important to them, you're important to me. So listen Matlock. It doesn't matter much whether you have power, or are having power thrust upon you, or even if you're just the bloody messenger boy. No insurrection in the North can succeed without us. That much is certain. You've come to us for aid enough already. Now, if you want our help, you'll do things our way. Understand? I said I don't like you, Matlock, but I think you're a man I can deal with. I want to see that Bible-weevil cracked open before we move another step. Then we can get down to some serious talking."

Matlock shook his head.

"I'm sorry," he said, in a voice he tried to keep quietly sincere, "I just don't understand."

"Don't play with me, Matlock. I'm offering you the Governorship of the Northern Counties when this thing comes off. You've got a big organization there, but there are too many groups; it's too bitty. They'll be at each other's throats sooner or later unless there's a top man. That's you. You've got the name, got the reputation. You just need the organization. That's me."

Matlock rose to his feet and took a couple of steps towards the grotesque figure of Ossian who had now raised himself up on his elbow and glared balefully up at his attacker. The blood on his neck was beginning to congeal, so obviously (more's the pity, thought Matlock) no major vein had been severed. As the man moved his head, the light struck off several minute fragments of crystal still set in the brown band which wound over his face. The effect was rather pretty in a way. But not in any way that brought present comfort to Matlock.

"Listen McDonwald," he said. "I'm not being funny, nor even particularly evasive. I've had a long, hard trying day. I need time to digest both your drink and your offer. I must have more details, more information. And I would prefer to continue our talks out of the company of this creature."

The Scot came towards him and he stepped back instinctively expecting another blow on the chest. It was not offered, but Ossian suddenly grappled with his left leg. Fortunately he had made his effort before he had fully recovered his strength and Matlock had no difficulty in keeping his balance and bringing his right leg round with a vicious kick to the stomach. The servant groaned bubblingly and subsided again.

"You're not storing up riches in heaven, Matlock," said McDonwald. "None the less, you may be right. Let it not be said that a McDonwald did not know how to treat a guest. You mentioned dinner before. Come away then and we'll try to restore your precious equilibrium."

"Lay on Macduff," said Matlock with relief. "And damned be he that first cries, Hold! Enough!"

The Ambassador squinted at him suspiciously, then decided to accept the remark as a compliment and bellowing with laughter he led the way back along the corridor, turning into a more noble and dignified door which proved to open into the dining-room.

137

Matlock never forgot that dinner, though everything about it, from Freud's theory of the selectiveness of memory to the alcoholic base of apparently every dish, seemed to consign it to oblivion.

There were two other guests — an Oriental from some anonymous Embassy who sat all night as inscrutably as folklore demanded, and another Scot whose status was not revealed. He was a small wiry man who looked as if he was used to the outdoor life. His face was brown with the blowing of winds, not the bombardment of infra-red from artificial suns which Matlock had seen on Browning. Only a curious hollow on his right temple, as if the bone had been crushed in, had proved impervious to the blast of weather, and the skin in the nadir of this cavity gleamed palely.

No introductions were made, not even to the small impressively still woman who sat at the foot of the long polished table and whom he assumed to be McDonwald's wife. She it was who by small gestures of the fingers of her left hand controlled the entrance and exit of the courses. McDonwald's part seemed to be to produce drink which he did in profusion, not letting himself be confined by any jingoistic considerations. Matlock at one stage found his plate surrounded by half a dozen glasses including one of Tokay and one of Danish Lager, almost as rare in these insular days. He could not have survived the meal had not McDonwald followed his frequent toasts by hurling his glass into the fireplace. Matlock followed suit with enthusiasm. He was sitting at the west side of the table (he gauged north by the direction in which his host normally turned when toasting Scotland) and the fireplace was on the east side of the room. His glasses had to be hurled across the table between the Oriental and the other Scot and Matlock's half-full glasses spattered them as they passed. Neither moved.

Somewhere along the trail of courses a piper had appeared and was walking majestically round the room playing a music whose few tonal variations did not seem to correspond with any known melodic system.

"Is he miming to a record?" Matlock asked very clearly but no one seemed to understand him. McDonwald probably did not even hear him as he was on his feet again proposing another toast to the Immortal Memory. Matlock joined in. His glass took a small nick out of the Oriental's left ear as it whistled towards the fireplace. Smiling, the man rose, bowed politely to each member of the company and left. As he did so the panelled wall at the north end of the room folded smoothly back, the piper stopped playing, a trio of two violins and an accordian struck up in his place and the long polished floor revealed by the removal of the wall was invaded by eight kilted men.

They began to dance. They danced lightly, athletically, with muscular grace. Matlock was enchanted. The Scot with the hole in his head disturbed his concentration by thrusting another drink into his hand. He tried to put it away from him, but the man insisted. Finally he tossed it down for the sake of peace.

It bubbled down his throat and into his stomach. For a second he felt very sick, then it passed and he was cold sober.

"Now," said McDonwald who did not

seem to need any artificial restoratives, "perhaps we can talk."

In fact it was McDonwald who talked, for which Matlock was very grateful. His sobriety was confined to his immediate neighbourhood. Outside a circle of about six feet in radius from his mind, everything was still gloriously, drunkenly hazy. He watched this boundary with suspicion while McDonwald rambled on, with what sounded like an official lecture on Scottish History since Secession.

"You did us a favour, Matlock," he said at one point. "By making us an agricultural economy again, you gave us back our greatness. We've got space and to spare up there. There's fish in the rivers and lochs again, grouse on the moors, and the red deer on the mountain slopes. We're a nation of farmers and fishers again, of herdsmen and hunters."

Matlock took time off from his watch on the hazy middle distance to laugh and say, "I think one of the funniest things I ever heard was when you accused the English of coming across the Border to steal your sheep. One of History's little ironies."

McDonwald's eyes smouldered redly.

"Ironical perhaps. But more than irony for those we caught. There was another raid last night. Fifty of your thieving countrymen died."

"It cuts both ways, McDonwald. The Border's no barrier to your own men."

"Do you blame them?" said McDonwald with a smile. "Provoked, that's what they are. And admittedly we may be a wee bit short of manufactured goods. Not that we need them, you understand."

"They bring enough on the black market, I hear."

"Now where would you hear a thing like that? It sounds like Browning's propaganda. I'm surprised at you, Matlock."

The circle of clarity, unsupported by his watchfulness, was beginning to contract rapidly.

"Let's stop fencing," he said wearily. "What do you want of me?"

"Nothing. We want to give you our help. You need it. Listen, man. The North of England, geographically, economically and, I believe, culturally forms a unit with the Scottish Lowlands.

142

The boundary has been an artificial division since Hadrian built his bloody wall. Now there's a chance to right a great historical wrong at the same time as you right a great social wrong. Once we link the manufacturing power of your Northern Counties to the natural and agricultural wealth of Scotland and we're embarking on a new era of greatness for this island. Man, you're a Northerner yourself. This is where your destiny lies."

"Again I ask, what do you want of me?"

"I'll put it simply if you want it simply, Matlock. We're willing to help. But if we commit ourselves to an Act of War, we want certain guarantees. To date, we haven't found a man able to give us those guarantees, or at least one we would be willing to accept them from. Now once this thing gets going, you'll have it in your power to come, like Lenin, from a great distance if necessary and take over all control. We provide the machinery to get you there, to get you heard. But there are others who won't want you to take charge, at least not in any capacity other than that of a figurehead. The Abbot of Fountains is one of these, perhaps the most important. This is the first agreement we must make with you. He's a key figure, so we can't take care of him too early. He's well protected in his own den, so we can't get too close to him. But he has to go, the minute he has served his purpose which will be the minute you arrive on the scene. As I say, there are others. But the Abbot is the first."

The circle of clarity barely included McDonwald now. Matlock stood up and by a great effort of will pressed it a little further back.

"What you are saying then is that you know you are not strong enough to take on England alone. Equally you realize that if you make a move to take over control of an internal revolt without co-operation from its leaders, you will fail and probably the revolt with you, and Browning will have a perfect excuse to invade you."

The Scot with the hole in his head spoke for the first time.

"That's about it," he said.

"So you want me."

"Yes."

"I'll think it over. It's been a great day for offers."

"You can have till tomorrow. Think wisely, Matlock."

"Not more threats!"

The circle rushed in on him with frightening rapidity.

"You didn't try to kill me today, did you?"

"No. Why should we?"

"Why not. Why why why not?"

The circle no longer existed. The euphoria of the alcoholic haze was back. The two fiddles and accordian were still rattling away and the kilted men sped unerringly along the maze of their dance, hands raised high, mouths set in formal smiles or opened to emit nape-bristling shrieks.

"Eech — ha!"

The sound was so near it was almost deafening. Suddenly Matlock realized it had come from him. He smiled slackly.

"I'm sorry. Perhaps I had better go home."

"Perhaps you'd better. Matlock, were

you serious? Did someone try to kill you?"

"Oh yes yes yes. Ver very much."

Deep inside him he felt stirrings of the giggling shame of the drunken man in sober company. The weather-beaten Scot said distantly to McDonwald, "Put a guard on him. We must give him protection." A small area of his mind noted with interest that the slight man was giving orders to the great McDonwald. Suddenly he sat up and looked gravely down the table to where Mrs. McDonwald might or might not have still been sitting.

"Thank you very much for a splendid evening."

Out of the mists a figure moved. But no female this. It was a troll, a mountain-troll with his face patched leprous white.

Ossian. Bandaged but not soothed.

I hope he's not my protection, thought Matlock sleepily. Protection.

He began to laugh.

All those who are not protecting me are trying to kill me. And all those who are not trying to kill me are protecting me.

Laughing still, he fell asleep as the

fiddles struck up a slow, lilting melancholy waltz and the kilted men moved silently off the polished wooden floor.

★ ★ ★

He awoke in his own bed feeling remarkably fresh. Someone had obviously been kind enough to pop a Cleerhed capsule into his mouth last night before bedding him down. He had no recollection of his return.

He stretched luxuriously and his right hand came in contact with something soft and warm. For a moment puzzled, he let his hand stray this way and that. Then he turned round.

"Lizzie," he said.

She was leaning on her elbow looking down at him. She smiled and made a slight movement forward so that her right breast brushed his shoulder.

"Good morning," she said. "I came at my usual time and when I found you here I thought that what's good enough for the boss is good enough for the secretary."

He sat up and looked round the

room. The window had been repaired he noticed. Quick work by someone. Though the blast marks still remained in the wall.

His clothes he noticed were neatly arranged on a hanger in the open wardrobe. Lizzie's on the other hand were strewn over the floor in uncharacteristic disarray. She followed his glance and said, "I was in a hurry. In case you woke up and stopped me. It seemed the best opportunity I'd had in ages. Matt, what's the matter? Why have you been putting me off?"

"Lizzie," he began despairingly, but she did not let him continue.

"No; wait, Matt. Explanations after. Let's remind ourselves what we've been missing."

She put her arms round his neck and drew him back down beside her. He tried to speak once more, but her mouth pressed hard against his. After that he didn't try again.

Later she lay on top of him like a wrestler who has just made a pin-fall.

"Now," she said, "talk."

He could find nothing to say. Lizzie,

Lizzie, he thought in anguish, I cannot believe you false. Or at least I cannot bear to find you false.

He crushed her to him with unconscious violence so that she gasped and struggled free.

"Who'd have thought the old man had so much blood in him?" she asked, twisting round to massage her back.

"I'm sorry," he said.

"Don't be sorry," she said and ran her finger gently down the scar on his chest. "Is it this, Matt? Is it wondering what to do? Wondering when a man can say 'to hell with it' and start living for himself instead of others?"

She paused a second, but when he still didn't speak, she went on.

"Listen, Matt, I don't care what you do. Take Browning's offer. Go for Op. Or just sit it out. But whether you live one year or forty, make a place in it for me, Matt. I'm not saying you owe me it. I'm not an old woman debt-collecting. I don't need to, Matt, do I?"

She flung the sheet back and knelt upright so he could see her mature but beautifully firm nakedness.

"But I believe that there's a place for me with you, Matt. I won't try to persuade you what to do, but don't shut me out. I'm in. I've been in for twenty years. I won't go now."

"I don't ask you to, Lizzie."

Matlock felt a happy calm spread through his being. He had made up his mind. He got out of bed, caressing her long flank as he did so. Then he moved purposefully and unselfconsciously across the room and opened a panel on the wall. Reaching in he pressed a button and looked closely at a couple of dials. This little toy was known as his bugswatter. Any electronic eavesdropping device within a range of fifteen yards was now jammed. He knew his flat was well bugged. Indeed he knew the location of several of the mini-mikes. But how many more there were he could never be sure, so it was pointless digging them out. Instead he jammed them.

He paused in front of the long mirror on his way back to the bed, drew his stomach in and puffed his chest out.

"I'm really not so very old, you know," he said.

Lizzie watched him with delight and was obviously eager to start all over again when he got back to bed, but he held her at arm's length.

"Later," he said. "Listen to what I want to tell you."

Then coolly, dispassionately, he proceeded to recount the events of the previous thirty-six hours.

She listened as a good secretary should, attentively, without interruption. Her silence stretched into his own when he was finished.

Finally she asked, "What made you make up your mind about me, Matt?"

He grinned widely and made a gesture which encompassed her breasts and belly.

"This, of course."

"Seriously."

"Seriously I never doubted you for a moment. Oh, I know I didn't fall over you when I got back yesterday, but do you blame me?"

"Yes."

He put his hands on her shoulders and looked into her face.

"Lizzie, what I believe in is based on individual faith and trust and hope. If I

151

lost that in you, then I lose my worth, my purpose. I'd have taken Browning's offer if I had believed the Abbot."

"I still don't understand why he told you those lies."

"Simple. According to his logic, it negated the power of Browning's threat against you and Ernst through the forged documents. He didn't realize what dangerous ground he was treading on."

"What happens next, Matt?"

In Matlock's mind things were beginning to sort themselves out with crystal clarity. He recognized that the doubts and self-searching of the past day had been much graver than he had told Lizzie. He knew that deep down inside him, in the caverns of his mind, was an area where his surface certainties were shifting, shadowy. But he knew himself well enough to recognize how unfitted he was to deal with any change of personal loyalties. He had done it once. Old friends had felt themselves betrayed and turned from him with disgust which he himself had felt like treachery. His wife had moved out of their bedroom, then out of their house. A few months later a burst spleen had moved her out of his life. (It had been an irony of fate that an anti-Matlock protest strike by one of the big Unirad-controlled Unions had cut off the power supply to her flat and prevented her from summoning help.) Her father who outlived her by five years, when he was replaced by Browning, always said she died of a broken heart. Adding, "As I shall too."

Matlock knew he could not take this again. *Even if my beliefs change, I cannot change my friends, those I love.*

"First," he said, "call Ernst and Colin."

Lizzie looked surprised.

"Matt, are you sure?"

He raised her gently from the bed and pushed her towards the door.

"As sure as I am of you, Lizzie. They do not give me the same pleasure, but I love them too."

He dressed swiftly while Lizzie was on the 'phone and joined her in the living-room as she hung up.

"My, are we finished then?" she said. He smacked her behind vigorously.

"Get dressed. There's work to do. First, breakfast."

Thirty minutes later as he sipped a mugful of black coffee, Ernst arrived. Matlock waved aside his questions till Colin had appeared also. Then as swiftly and accurately as he had talked to Lizzie, he revealed the course of recent events to them. When he had finished he looked from one to the other.

"How surprised are you? Did either of you have any knowledge, suspicion even of the situation? I have to ask. There've been too many false assumptions, concealments, deceptions already."

"What do you mean?" asked Ernst.

"Not a whisper of my own plots and schemes in the North has reached me in any of our lecture trips. But our contacts must have known. They must have been supremely well drilled not to show any awareness of what was going on."

Colin shook his head. "Surely, the thing is, Matt, that even if they had done, you wouldn't have recognized it as such."

"My God!" Ernst again. "Matt, Percy. Percy said something when he was dying, something like 'till the Day'. Then he smiled. It seemed a happy thought somehow."

154

Matlock remembered his friend's peaceful face on that dingy stage. The Day. Budget Day.

"But Percy would have spoken. *Must* have spoken to me about something like this. He was the closest of all our Northern Contacts."

"And therefore likeliest to obey absolutely any injunction to silence he thought came from you," said Ernst.

"Anyway, that's immaterial now," replied Lizzie. "The thing is, where do we go from here?"

"Look," broke in Ernst, "what I don't understand is the Scottish situation. I don't see why they should need you, Matt, if they're in as close contact with the Organization as McDonwald claims."

"They are in contact, Ernst. Get that straight. The Abbot told me. He also told me a little more in what he termed our private chat. I haven't mentioned this before because it was immaterial to the main drift of events, but central perhaps to our choice of action. With Browning controlling the papers, it's as difficult to get a true picture of the state of affairs in Scotland as it is anywhere

155

else. McDonwald tries to give the impression of a happy, stable, democratic, agricultural community. Arcadia, so to speak."

"Couldn't you have got more out of him?" asked Ernst.

Matlock grimly rubbed his ribs and winced. He hadn't noticed the pain when with Lizzie but now it came back.

"No. He had a rather touching sensitivity about his country. The other side of the coin was shown me by the Abbot and it's rather more in line with the kind of anti-Scottish propaganda Browning's been pumping at us for years. Though it has slackened off, of late."

"A deal?" asked Lizzie thoughtfully.

"Who knows? Anyway, Scotland according to the Revised Version is indeed almost a self-supporting agricultural economy. But it's full of cracks. On a local level, the people have reverted to the old clan system with its tight-knit code of loyalties. On a national level, the old urban rivalry between Glasgow and Edinburgh has become a desperate political struggle between opposing clan-based factions for national domination, with a third smaller but very militant group up in Inverness waiting for its chance."

"Yes, but how is it that they've managed to get by without Age Laws for nearly thirty years? Their problems must have been as grave as ours when all this started."

"Not quite. There was more room for one thing. But yes, of course they had basically the same population problem as us. Worse perhaps. But the Abbot assured me yesterday, that the population of Scotland is smaller today than it was thirty years ago."

Ernst whistled.

"But how?"

"Two things. They had no Age Law. But in those early days there were many things they didn't have. Among them was an efficient Health Service. We'd cut off its head. It's so hard to die in England that we had to invent a new way to do it. But Nature provided ways in plenty for the Scots. There were no outbreaks of plague or anything like that, you understand. It was just that people began dying from things no one here has

157

died of in years. Infant mortality rate shot up, expectation of life dropped down."

"But that alone can't have accounted for a total drop after thirty years!"

"No. I said there were two things. The second was the struggle for survival before central, or bi-central government was effectively established. The new clan wars."

"You mean, they fought?" asked Ernst incredulously.

"Oh yes, they fought. And died. Many thousands. There are still outbreaks. The Central government which is Glasgow-based at this moment doesn't discourage it. It keeps the population down. Keeps the people on the alert. The Border Scots in particular have reverted to type and foraging raids into Cumberland and Northumberland are fairly common. They act as a cover for the full-scale smuggling organization which is almost certainly run by McDonwald's mates, if the Abbot is to be believed. There are crippling tariffs on all imports from England. But a constant stream of stuff is crossing illegally by helicopter and boat."

"But why doesn't Browning just move

in? Why play at shots across the Border when you could wipe the Lowlands half off the earth in a couple of rocket attacks?"

"The Scots have got sentimental friends all over the world. America in particular. There are lots of other countries from France up who would welcome the chance to walk into England. We must not appear the aggressor. In any case, you can't raze a mountainous country with ordinary missiles. And that's where they'd be, up in the mountains. And you don't drop nuclear bombs on your own doorstep."

"Anyway," said Lizzie impatiently, "we're wasting time talking about what Browning can or cannot do. The point is, what are we going to do? What are you going to do, Matt. You're the man in demand."

Matlock looked round the tiny circle. Lizzie, her eyes fixed on him, her face full of life and hope. Ernst, relaxed in his chair, regarding him rather quizzically. Colin, seated a little further back than the others, his thin face shadowed and brooding.

159

"This is what I've called you here to decide. I'm faced with a set of rather curious alternatives."

"There's only one choice, Matt," interjected Ernst leaning forward in his eagerness to talk. But Matlock held his hand up, a strangely rhetorical gesture for him.

"Wait a moment, Ernst. Colin, you haven't said a word since we started. What's on your mind?"

Colin slowly shook his head as if to clear it. "I'm wondering if any of us have really faced what we're talking about," he said. "I mean, *really* faced it?"

He was very agitated and stood up now as if to brace himself more firmly to hurl out his words.

"Matt, listen to me. This country of ours is in a mess, we all know that. There's something rotten in the way it's governed, in some of those who govern it. And we've opposed them together for a score of years. We've worked hard, all of us, in that time. We've used every means possible. But we've always worked within the law. But this thing you're talking about now, Matt, talking about as if you accept it without qualm, this situation which has suddenly sprung up overnight, this has nothing to do with persuasion, and education, nothing to do even with political scheming and chicanery. This is open revolution you're talking about, Matt. This is civil war."

There followed a long silence. Colin, as though his words had been the strings which pulled him upright, slumped back into his chair and looked stonily at the carpet. Ernst turned away in mock exasperation and pursed his lips in a soundless whistle. Lizzie half leaned over to Colin, then turned back to Matt, then leaned back over to Colin and placed her hand on his forearm.

"Thank you, Colin," said Matlock. "Now, Ernst."

The words came tumbling out, bumping together in their eagerness to take to the air.

"There's no question what we must do, Matt. For Godsake what's the matter with you, Colin? This is an opportunity to do something meaningful. This is heaven-sent. Here on a plate is being handed to us the power and authority we've been striving for for years. We've got to take it."

In his turn he subsided, slight beads of sweat along the one deep furrow in his forehead. Looking at it, Matlock was reminded of the quiet Scot with the pale hollow in his temple.

"Lizzie," he said.

"I could argue and debate," she said quietly. "I could throw accusations of disloyalty at Colin. I could ask Ernst if power and authority are really what we've been striving for. But what's the point? I cannot help you make up your mind, Matt. In fact I don't think any of us have ever really been able to do that despite what you might have let us think. All I will say is that when you've made up your mind what to do and start counting the heads of your followers, you should always start at two. I'll be there."

"Thank you, Lizzie," said Matlock without any reciprocal show of emotion. "You're quite right, of course. I have made up my mind. Colin, I respect you for what you say. I could reply that this civil war is going to take place anyway and that I must do what

162

I can to make gentle its course. But that would be Jesuitical. No, I embrace this chance without reservation. We have moved beyond the realm of political action. We moved beyond it when I resigned all those years ago though I never realized it till yesterday. And once we move out of the area of political possibilities, we have moved out of the realm of democratic government. As for you Ernst, I wish to give you no offence but this I must say. You are very dear to me and you are my legally appointed successor. But the laws under which you are so appointed are the laws we will fight to overthrow. What I may become and what you may inherit will then be in no way connected other than by my own feeling for you, which not all may share."

Ernst rose angrily.

"Is this what you think of me?"

"No, it is not. But I am speaking publicly now. I have not been a public man for many years despite my campaigns. You may not find me always to your taste."

"Can you speak publicly to me, Matt?"

asked Lizzie challengingly.

"Yes, I can. I will make you in public what you have long been in private. My wife. We will make at least one of Browning's forgeries true."

"Matt!" cried Lizzie, her face a-gleam.

He took her in his arms.

"Perhaps we can adopt Ernst and make the other true also."

Ernst looked as though he were going to resent this for a moment, then his face reluctantly unfolded into smiles and eventually laughter.

"You do that," he said, "that way at least I'll get your money."

The three of them now all looked at Colin who got to his feet and moved away. For a heart-jolting moment, Matlock thought he was going to leave. But he only went as far as the drink cupboard and started to fill four glasses.

"What the hell," he said bringing them over to the others, "if there's going to be a civil war, I might as well be on the same side as the people I like."

Matlock gave him a narrow glance as he made this oblique pledge of loyalty, but Lizzie flung her arms round his neck and nearly sent the drinks flying.

"Oh, Colin. That's marvellous. That's lovely. It wouldn't be the same without you. Now it's the four of us. The same as before. As always. Isn't it, Matt?"

No, thought Matlock, no it isn't, my darling, and I doubt if it ever can be again. But it's better than it might have been.

And with a slight contraction of his forearm muscle he eased back up his sleeve the hand force-gun which the Abbot had pressed upon him the day before. He had not taken it to the Embassy the previous night. Now he would not be without it again.

"Thank you, Colin," he said as he took his drink, and pushed to the back of his mind the thought that Colin might have noticed the small but menacing arm-movement as he set off across the room.

Would I have fired? Matlock asked himself. Who knows?

But he realized he knew very well and his glass was the longer at his lips because of the sudden knowledge.

It was nearly lunchtime so they made

a rapid meal out of the contents of Matlock's fridge, then settled down to work out a plan of action. As their normal discussion pattern unfolded — Ernst the lover of words; Colin the thoughtful and analytical one; Lizzie the recorder, and the realist; himself the chairman — Matlock began to realize just how conditioned they had been by the environment provided for them for so many years. His own growing uncertainties must have stemmed in part from a feeling of repetitiveness, of substituting activity for action. Now they were finding it strangely difficult to make any headway along the new avenues which had opened up. Ernst and Colin were soon locked in a disagreement which became progressively more theoretical, less particular.

Lizzie said nothing but watched Matlock who sat with a strange and complete stillness that was not unfamiliar. She recalled with a slight shock that this had been a characteristic of his in the days when she first knew him, before his separation from the springs of power had been complete.

Now the wheel has turned she thought. It pulled him under, but now he's up on the other side, still clinging, and rising again. It's a long circle to make twice.

Matlock turned his gaze on her as if he had caught her unspoken musings.

I wonder what has changed in me, she thought. And whether it can change back. Whether I want it to.

She smiled at him, but he did not accept the invitation to intimacy. Instead he turned and, in a perfectly normal tone of voice, he cut right through the heated discussion which filled the room, halting it in mid-sentence.

"Here's what we'll do," he said. "We must for the time being come to terms with the Abbot. He is the only contact I have so far with this alleged underground movement whose spiritual leader I seem to be. I do not trust the Scots, begging your pardon, Lizzie. And I cannot know how much we need their help till I have some better idea of our own strength. The only other group we've had any positive contact with is the anonymous lot who tried to kill me yesterday. At least my relationship with them is straightforward."

"What about Browning?" asked Lizzie. The other two were sitting very still.

"Browning is still waiting for my answer. I'm surprised he hasn't contacted me already. But he will do soon if I don't contact him first. I have no illusions about the man — once he knows I haven't accepted his offer, he'll carry out his threats against all of us. He hasn't got where he is by meaningless promises."

"So what do we do?"

"I accept. Or at least indicate I will accept when I meet him tomorrow afternoon."

"That'll get you nowhere, Matt. He'll have you in front of the television cameras in thirty seconds. Whatever standing or influence you have in these revolutionary circles would be wiped out in a moment. This is something you can't bluff over."

Matlock looked approvingly at Ernst.

"You're right, of course. But I've no intention of trying to bluff, at least not longer than tomorrow morning. Browning cannot see me till tomorrow afternoon, he's opening a trade conference in Manchester in the morning, that's a piece of useful information I picked up last night. But the Abbot can see me in the morning. We have an arrangement. He foresaw that this might be necessary. We're going to go underground, all of us."

They took the news with a pleasing calmness, though whether this was due to the inevitability of the decision or their slow recognition of all its implications Matlock could not tell. Abruptly he stood up.

"Meeting's over. Go your ways now. Act normally, but stop by your 'phones tomorrow morning till you hear from me."

"Matt," said Colin slowly, "you mean we're going to go into hiding, just turn our backs on our lives? For how long, Matt, how long?"

"Till Budget Day, you fool," laughed Ernst who seemed to have been elated by the prospect of action. His eyes were sparkling and a smile played constantly around his lips.

"That's right," agreed Matlock. "Till Budget Day. Till Browning takes the step which will instantly unite all the forces of discontent, strengthen the waverers, confirm the doubters. He has to do it or the bottom falls out of the Economy. He has to lower the E.O.L. a couple of points at least. Then it all starts, Colin, and we have to be there. This is the only way to make sure."

Colin said nothing in reply, but his long frame was stooped with melancholy as he unfolded slowly from his chair.

"I see how it is, Matt. I'll expect to hear from you in the morning. Good-night now."

"Night?" laughed Ernst. "It isn't four o'clock yet."

"No, it isn't," said Colin. "Of course. Good-bye, Matt."

He shook Matlock's hand, a formal and uncharacteristic gesture.

Ernst followed him to the door, talking excitedly all the while.

"Matt," he said, "you're right to do it this way. This is the greatest thing that ever happened to us. We'll take Browning apart."

Lizzie said quietly underneath Ernst's chatter, "Take care, Matt. I know I don't need to tell you not to underestimate

Browning. If what you say of the man is true, he'll have every contingency covered as well. Possibly, including this one."

"I'm sure he will," smiled Matlock. "Off you go too, darling. Buy something for your bottom drawer. You'll probably be watched, so make it something that would suit a Cabinet Minister's wife."

"I wouldn't know where to start looking, Matt."

After they had all left, Matlock sat in deep thought for a while. Then he looked at his watch. It was coming up to two minutes to four. He picked up his 'phone and dialled a number. He heard the automatic linkage connect and the buzzer at the other end sound. He let it sound twice, then replaced his receiver.

So much for the Abbot, he thought. This next one requires a little more skill. Carefully he dialled again. "Matlock," he said shortly when the answer came. A second later he felt the amplified resonance of Browning's heartiest greeting vibrating in his ear.

"My dear Matt. I'd just about given you up. How nice of you to 'phone. Now what can I do for you?"

"I'd like to see you, Prime Minister."

"But, of course. Now let me see. Can I fit you in tonight. Or would tomorrow do? Eh?"

He knows, thought Matlock. But he can't. Remember, that's part of his strength. Apparent omniscience.

"As you wish, Prime Minister."

"Then tomorrow let it be, eh? It'll have to be after lunch. I'm off North in the morning. Shall we say two-thirty here? Shall I send you another car, Matt? But you must promise to ride in it this time."

"That would be kind of you."

"Think nothing of it, old chap. Well, see you then. Cheery-bye."

The 'phone went dead. Matlock nursed it on his shoulder as he considered the interchange.

No curiosity. Not a trace. He had shown no curiosity at all. Supreme confidence? Or bluff? Or genuine unconcern?

Analysing Browning's thought-processes was a pointless exercise, he had long ago decided. But it was with difficulty that he put it out of his head, and after a quiet evening spent listening to records and making certain small preparations for the next day, he needed a small hypo to put him to sleep and out of reach of the troublesome thoughts which pattered round the dome of his mind.

Tomorrow will tell, he thought banally as he fell asleep.

He was right. Tomorrow told.

He awoke with a thick, heavy head and glanced at his bedside clock. Instead he saw a pair of elegant shoes resting on the table. They were occupied. He followed the sweep of the neatly-trousered leg, the white shirt, the blue tie with the thin silver line. He ended by looking into the face of the police inspector who had called to investigate the force-gun shooting.

The man was sitting in an armchair and seemed to be asleep. Matlock began stealthily to edge to the side of the bed, his eyes fixed unblinkingly on the sleeping man's face.

There was a cough from elsewhere in the room. He looked round. Seated on an upright chair by his dressing-table was a uniformed policeman with a gun resting in his lap.

The Inspector opened his eyes at the cough.

"Good-morning, Mr. Matlock. Now what the hell am I doing here, is the question you're about to ask. Or how the hell did I get in? Well, technically we had to force an entry, but you'll be pleased to know that we had keys and no damage has been done. As to why I'm here, Mr. Matlock, the answer's simple. To protect you. And at ten a.m., which is now, to conduct you to the telephone. Better still we can conduct a telephone to you."

He clapped his hands, the door opened and a constable came in bearing before him, like a butler with a tray, the telephone. Matlock saw through the open door that the living-room was full of cigarette smoke. And men.

The telephone was put down beside him, the Inspector rose and with a curt nod dismissed the constable and the man with the gun. He himself followed them, turning as he went through the door to say reassuringly, "Don't worry. We'll just be next door."

Matlock slowly picked up the receiver.

"Matt! I hope I haven't woken you. I'm just ringing to say don't bother to come this afternoon. I'll be a bit busy. Though actually I might have fitted you in this morning sometime. I didn't go North after all. There's been a bit of trouble up there. A lot of arrests; so I was probably better out of it. In any case, something came up, Matt. I've just come from the House. We've been in emergency session for a couple of hours. Incredible eh? They managed things better in your day. Well, the long and the short of it is, Matt, that as things turned out, I've had to bring in an emergency budget. Mind you, I often think that's the best way. It cuts out speculation. But the really important thing, Matt, is that I've had to cut the E.O.L. Well, you knew I'd have to do that, didn't you? So I did it. And I thought I'd let you know in case you missed it on the News."

Matlock's mouth was drier than even a drugged sleep warranted.

"What's it down to Prime Minister?"

"In for a shilling, in for a pound, Matt. We've broken all records. We're down to seventy. We've reached the Barrier, Matt. Are you listening, Matt? Hullo, are you still there?"

Matlock had no difficulty in drawing out the silence into the long dumbstruck pause he felt Browning expected. No difficulty at all.

Then, "I'm still here," he said. "For a while. I'm still here for a while."

"For a while, Matt? What do you mean? Oh yes. Of course. Your nearly seventy yourself, Matt, aren't you? Two weeks time, I think. Or is it one and a half? I'm sorry about that, but we politicians can't allow personal considerations to bend us from public duty. You should have accepted my offer the other day. But there it is. I'm afraid the post isn't vacant any longer."

"I thought that you were of sufficient stature not to gloat."

There was an indignant snort from the other end of the line. Matlock was pleased to find he had recovered sufficiently to be able to admire its perfection.

"Gloating? Over what? No, what I rang to say was that I've been very worried about your safety since I heard someone took a shot at you. So I've decided to increase your protection and extra men have been detailed. They should be there now. Don't worry about a thing, they'll be keeping a very close watch. You deserve to live out your life in peace, Matt. The country owes you a lot. And by the way. Don't bother to go down to the Heart Centre for your adjustment. I'm sending my own doctor round. You've earned a bit of privacy. Cheery-bye for now Matt."

Matlock put the 'phone down and stared at the wall. The impact dents from the force gun looked like a pair of breasts, he thought. Perhaps I won't have it repaired, just paint around them.

"I think you had better get up now, Mr. Matlock," said the Inspector briskly from the door. "Have your brekkers before the Doc. comes."

Matlock got up.

6

AN hour later Matlock was fastening his shirt and the very young-looking Doctor was packing his portable adjuster.

"A lot of people would give a lot of money for one of those, Doc.," laughed the Inspector who had watched the brief operation with keen interest.

"They would," agreed the Doctor. "But there's not much chance. They'd need me with it, and I have a wife and family. Or they'd need to cut this chain," he indicated the fine silver thread which ran from the box to his wrist, "and then the whole thing blows up. Or even if they surmounted these obstacles, the thing can be blown up from the Heart Centre by radio. Shall I do you while I'm here, Inspector?"

The policeman drew back.

"I haven't got my card with me."

The Doctor tutted with disapproval.

"That's an offence, you realize. Still

178

you've got another day. I'll be off now."

As Matlock finished dressing he thought of the similar scenes going on all over the country, but mostly in the big Heart Centres. Everyone had to report within forty-eight hours to the nearest Heart Centre for readjustment, taking with them the simple metal card which had magnetically imprinted on it full age details of its owner. This was fed into a computer as the Master Adjuster Clock rapidly deducted the requisite number of years from the individual heart clock. The new information was printed on to the card, and the computer meanwhile checked the card against the previous information it held on the owner. If this tallied, the name was marked in its information banks. At the end of forty-eight hours, unmarked names were spewed out and the police went to work looking for those who did not report.

There were surprisingly few. The penalty for not reporting was a five-year cut in E.O.L. for each day's lateness. After a week, the penalty was transferred to the next of kin.

But after a cutting Budget there was

always unrest even if it was only atmospheric. There were more policemen than ever around the streets, temporary curfews were suddenly imposed, the Curfew Wagons tolled their way in sinister profusion through the scarcely dark streets.

After a cut like this, thought Matlock, they'll need a general Curfew for a while. I should have foreseen it. Browning's been a step ahead of everyone as usual.

He had viewed the news briefly. The main item had naturally been the emergency Budget. But there had also been a lot about the arrests in the North. No details were given, just references to a pool of insurrection. The implication was clear, however; only rapid action by the police had prevented extremists from full-scale outbreaks of violence. Things were under control at the moment, but close surveillance of the situation would be necessary for several days. Citizens were asked to go about their normal business, but to avoid going out more than was strictly necessary. God save the King.

It was good, decided Matlock. It was very good. Just how many important arrests had been made, he didn't know, but probably enough to throw a sizeable spanner in the works. But the master-stroke was to use this threat of violence from extremists as a way of getting the man-in-the-street to accept the Budget without too much outcry. Anything was better than bloodshed. The Brownings of the world had thrived on this credo ever since the capitalist system had burped up the middle classes.

Matlock was hardly at all disturbed to discover he had left it lying around somewhere in the debris of the past few days. What had happened this morning merely confirmed what was already certain in his mind — he had reached the point where he had to stop and say, "No further — no matter what", or be swept into oblivion.

He left the bedroom and walked into the living-room. The Inspector ironically waved him ahead through the door. Matlock did not respond to the humour.

The number of policemen in the room had been reduced to three, with a further two stationed outside. The inside three were sitting at a table playing cards, but he was not deceived by their casualness. The drawn guns resting on their knees were not there to settle gambling quarrels in the old Western tradition. They were for him.

He indicated them with a gesture slight in itself, but enough to send three hands sliding under the table.

"Am I expected to feed them as well?"

"Don't you think the State can afford to feed its loyal servants?"

"I doubt if this State can afford any kind of loyalty."

The Inspector sank luxuriantly into Matlock's favourite chair.

"I adore epigrammatic conversations. I'm going to enjoy these five weeks."

"Five weeks?"

"Oh yes. I've been instructed to afford you every protection. No one is going to harm you, Mr. Matlock, be sure of that. But after five weeks you're not going to need me any more. Unless there's a boom. That's the thing. You must put your hopes in greater productivity."

Matlock moved across the room. The card-players stiffened again. The Inspector sighed.

"It would be more comfortable for us all and cut down the chances of an unfortunate accident if you would announce your proposed movements in advance."

Matlock shrugged his shoulders.

"If you wish. I am going into the bathroom. I would prefer to be alone."

The Inspector raised an eyebrow at the oldest looking of the three card-players who nodded. Matlock took this to mean the bathroom had been searched and declared safe. No hidden weapons. No escape route. He could have told them that himself. But he felt the need to be alone, to think.

"Of course," said the Inspector.

Matlock was not surprised to find the lock had been removed. Nor did he mind much. He was too old to be modest. If the Inspector wanted to make a lightning check, let him. For the sake of authenticity he undid his trousers and sat.

The seat was warm.

There was only the bath and the shower cubicle. He arose, pulled up his pants and moved silently across to the cubicle.

The sliding panel was open a fraction. He put his eye to the crack and peered in.

Squatting uncomfortably up against the soap rack was a policeman.

Matlock's first impulse was to roar with rage, then go screaming to the Inspector. This lasted only a moment. His second was to roar with laughter at the ludicrous excess of zeal in this superficially so suave and world-weary Inspector. But he checked the noise in his throat.

The policeman was staring straight up at what to him must have been a mere sliver of eye, and was pressing his forefinger to his pursed lips.

Matlock moved the panel further open. It squeaked slightly. The policeman shook his head and produced a piece of soap from behind his back. Then he bent forward and rubbed it gently along the panel's running track. Finally he was satisfied and when he nodded permission to Matlock, the panel slid fully open in complete silence.

Next the man reached into his tunic pocket and produced a notebook. From it he took a loose sheet and handed it over. He was smiling broadly and familiarly. Matlock felt he ought to know him.

He read the piece of paper.

'About time. I will give you a handgun. When you go back, pretend you are going into the kitchen. As you pass the card table, start shooting.'

Matlock found himself mouthing questions like a goldfish, but quickly restrained himself. The man's familiarity still scratched at some small window in his mind. He took the proffered gun, nodded twice, turned and made his way towards the door. He was only a yard from it when a sudden noise burst out behind him.

Startled, he turned violently.

The policeman had pulled the plug.

He stood there shaking his head gently as if reprimanding a small boy's misdemeanour. Then he held up his right hand and gently waved the gun he was holding.

185

Matlock stood puzzled for a second before realizing he was clutching his own gun with no effort at concealment. Sheepishly he slipped it into his pocket. The man nodded with approval, then motioned to the door.

As he did so, Matlock recognized him. The nose was unmistakable, but something was missing.

The beard!

It was a clean-shaven Brother Francis.

But there was no time to display his knowledge further than a raising of the eyebrows, as Francis was waving him more urgently to the door. He realized why as he moved back into the living-room. The Inspector was out of his chair and moving towards the bathroom door. Brother Francis obviously had keen ears.

"You weren't going to peep, were you, Inspector?" he asked lightly, keeping his hand out of his pocket only by an effort of will.

"Perhaps. But only in the way of duty, Mr. Matlock."

"The things men do for duty. Now, gentlemen, I am moving across to the

186

kitchen where I shall make myself some coffee."

The Inspector made a negative gesture.

"Oh, no, Mr. Matlock. That would not be right. You must take some advantage of us. Sit down and we'll take coffee together. Andrews!"

One of the card-players half rose from his seat. There was no time to work out the possible advantages of this new arrangement of personae, and in any case Matlock had keyed himself up to deal with the old.

"No. I prefer to make my own."

He spoke more brusquely than he had intended, but in the event this had the desired effect. The Inspector shrugged and waved him by with a repeat of his former ironic little bow. Andrews sat down and picked up his cards.

Matlock started to move across the room.

The three policemen watched him steadily as he moved. Andrews, he noticed, still had both his hands occupied with his cards. The other two had their right hands under the table. The eldest had put his cards down, but the other still held them in his left hand.

The Inspector also, he sensed, was standing behind him watching every step. This was good, he tried to reassure himself. They could not watch him and the bathroom door at the same time. But those eight eyes coldly drilling into him left him very little room for reassurance.

He was nearly at the kitchen door. He thought of going in and postponing attack till the return trip, and though he recognized this for the procrastination it was, he had almost made up his mind.

Then he sneezed.

It was a real, natural, unrehearsed sneeze.

And just as naturally his hand moved into his pocket in search of his handkerchief.

It came out with the gun.

He shot the oldest first. The other man fired from under the table, but Matlock had not stopped moving, and accurate aim from such an angle was impossible.

Matlock shot him in the chest. It was easier than the head. He fell forward over the table and his cards slipped out of his hand.

He had two pairs, Aces, nines, with a Jack.

Andrews hadn't moved. Matlock blew a hole through his head then realized this made two.

Turning round he looked across the broken body of the Inspector to where Brother Francis stood in the open bathroom door. He found himself grinning foolishly like a schoolboy expecting congratulation, but Francis had no time for that. In two leaps he was across the room and flat against the wall behind the main door which burst open to let in the two outside guards. Matlock loosed one vague shot at them and fell sideways through the kitchen door as they ran across the room towards him, firing as they came. He scrabbled over the tiled floor, trying to squeeze himself behind the fridge but even as he regained his feet and turned, the door flew open behind him and a uniformed figure, gun smoking in his hand, stood looking down at him.

He brought his own gun up, but the other just shook his head and said, "Come along, Mr. Matlock."

"Francis."

He stood up straight.

"I feel like a cup of coffee now."

"No time for bravado. Let's be on our way."

His living-room was not the shambles he expected; only the bodies were untidy. And even they didn't stop the comfortable familiarity of the room pulling him more strongly than the sinister rectangle of space revealed by the open door.

"I don't suppose I'll be coming back here."

It wasn't a question, but Francis paused momentarily as he hustled him to the door.

"If there's something you want, get it quick."

Matlock looked around. He had had this flat for over twenty years. He had lived in it longer than any other place except his parents' house. Perhaps longer than that. He'd have to work it out. Everything he owned was here, somewhere.

"Nothing," he said. "I want nothing."

If he thought this gesture of finality would impress Francis, he was quickly disenchanted.

"Right. Out you go."

He was thrust into the corridor before he had time for a sentimental last glance.

Francis pulled the door shut behind them.

"I don't know what kind of reporting system they've got, but you can be certain it'll be pretty regular."

"Every half hour," answered Matlock. He wasn't sure where he'd picked up the information, or whether by eavesdropping or observation, but it was there.

Francis glanced at him approvingly, and said, "For Godsake put that bloody thing away."

Surprised, Matlock realized he was waving his handgun around like the hero of an old gangster film. He slipped it into his pocket.

"What about yours?"

"Once we're out of here, you're an age-offender I've just picked up. I'm taking you in. You're not happy."

"I'm not happy."

They emerged into the sunlit street without meeting anyone. Matlock was full of questions, but he knew his slender chance of escape lay in Francis' hands and he had no intention of disturbing the monk's concentration.

Once out in the open, Francis abandoned the care and caution with which he had moved in the building and strode along with all the ebullient confidence of his assumed kind. Matlock found himself being pushed and prodded almost into a trot to keep just ahead. Once he stumbled and nearly fell and turned instinctively to expostulate. But before he could speak, Francis' pistol-barrel rapped him lightly but painfully along his jawbone.

"Move," he said.

Matlock moved, though he felt for a moment that Francis was overdoing it.

Only for a moment.

Out of the mouth of a shop doorway right in front of them stepped two more policemen.

Francis jerked Matlock to a halt. The two policemen studied them carefully, unemotionally.

"Trouble?" said one of them finally.

Francis laughed.

"Not much. Grandpa here doesn't want his clock rewound. That's all."

"I see. He's got another day, you know."

Matlock looked at the man in surprise. But a glance into the expressionless face and hard black eyes assured him that this was no unexpected humanitarian, but merely a believer in the rule-book.

"In another day, this one would be over the hills and far away. Only he's got relations who don't fancy a sudden drop in their E.O.L. if the old devil made it."

Francis laughed again. Again there was no response from the other two, but the one doing the talking seemed to relax slightly and his next words were more reassuring.

"The old trouble. But it helps us. Be careful how you go. There's a smell of trouble in the air. And this is an especially controlled area for some reason."

"Right, thanks. We'll be on our way."

As they talked, Matlock from under lowering brows had been watching the other, the silent one. He had taken a step to the side, as if to let Francis past. But his eyes had been moving systematically over every square inch of

Francis' uniform since the start of the encounter.

The monk prodded Matlock forward again. Matlock stumbled and collapsed to one knee. As he rose, he turned with his gun in his hand and shot the silent man whose own weapon was half out of its holster. Then he kept on turning, the gun-barrel moved past Francis' bulk, and he sent his second shot an inch past the monk's belly into the black-eyed policeman who had had time for nothing other than to register amazement.

"What the devil did you do that for?" cried Francis kicking aside the body which had collapsed over his feet.

"You should be more careful where you get your uniforms made," said Matlock. "Your shoulder number is the same as his."

He pointed at the silent one, silent now forever. Francis nodded appreciatively.

"Thanks. Now we must really move."

There was no one else in sight, but there must have been witnesses. Matlock peered into the shop outside which they stood and was sure he saw a movement in its dark depths.

194

Then they were running, down the street. Shoulder to shoulder, partly because Matlock didn't know where they were going and partly because he had no desire to run ahead and be shot down as a fugitive by some disinterested passer-by. Partly also, of course, because after a couple of hundred yards his legs felt as strong as pipe-cleaners and only Francis' steadying hand between his shoulders kept him going.

He thought with mocking irony of his own prideful posturing in front of the mirror with Lizzie the morning before. He was as good as you could expect at nearly seventy, but that didn't qualify him for the Olympic Games, even if they hadn't stopped the Olympic Games fifteen years earlier.

"For Godsake, Francis," he gasped, "slow down!"

"Not far now," grunted the other, increasing his pressure on Matlock's back.

But Matlock was too experienced to put much faith in such vague encouragement.

He stopped dead and held Francis

back by main force while he sucked in
two great breaths. Slightly recovered, he
leaned against the wall of the anonymous
sky-scraper block they were passing and
said, "Look, Francis, do you know where
we're going?"

There was only a second's hesitation,
but it was enough for Matlock.

"So we don't know?"

"Well, yes and no. I know where I
want to be, but as things have turned
out, I don't think we'll have time to get
there."

"You mean because the alarm will have
been raised by now?"

"Yes."

Matlock thought a moment.

"Is there a deadline?"

"Midday."

It was just after eleven.

"Distance."

"About a mile and a half. Fifteen
minutes walking."

"Listen," said Matlock.

In the distance they heard a bell slowly
ring out. Then another, closer. Then
another. Till the sonorous peel rang from
nearly every building.

"Curfew. Fifteen minutes walking will get us at the bottom of a Curfew Wagon. We've got to get inside."

There was no way of telling whether the Curfew bell was being tolled because of his escape or because of the shooting which had just taken place. But it didn't matter. Once that bell sounded, everyone got off the streets. Anyone who didn't was fair game for the Curfew Police.

The next step was a building-to-building search. Every building had its own Supervisor who would do his own preliminary Curfew check, but the real trouble started when the Search squad proper arrived.

It was a good efficient system.

"Come on then," said Francis, trying to move Matlock into the nearest door.

"Wait a minute, Brother. I may not be able to beat you on the long-distance running, but there's an old head on these old shoulders. Let's see what we have here."

The building was an office block, about fifty storeys high. Matlock moved his eyes rapidly up the outside list of firms who used the building, but he had only covered about two thirds of them when Francis seized his arm again.

"Look."

Round a corner about two hundred yards away came the huge square bulk of a Curfew Wagon. Its bullet-proof steel casing gleamed dully in the sunlight. The four periscopes on top turned and turned in an angular square-dance. There were no armaments to be seen. The terror lay inside. And archaically, but most sinister of all, from the arch of metal above the great flat top of the vehicle hung the slowly tolling bell whose clang warned of its approach.

One leap took them through the doorway into the building.

"I hope to God they didn't see us," panted Francis.

"Why? They'd hardly have time to recognize us."

"But you don't usually see policemen hiding from the Curfew Wagon."

"Is there anything I can do, officer?"

The new voice startled them and made them suddenly aware of their surroundings. They were in the vestibule area of the building. There was an

198

elevator in the wall facing them, and beside it a staircase.

With a real shock Matlock discovered he was contemplating whether he should shoot this man or not.

"How easily the habit grows," he said aloud.

"I beg your pardon?" said the porter, obviously still trying to work out what degree of deference Matlock deserved.

Brother Francis took over.

"We're going upstairs. This gentleman has made a complaint against one of your firms. Come along, sir. Let's look into this."

They strode purposefully across into the elevator. As soon as the doors closed, Matlock reached forward and punched the twelfth-floor button. The lift accelerated up rapidly, forcing their feet hard against the floor.

"Why the twelfth?" asked Francis.

"Because it is two past the tenth."

The lift stopped.

Cautiously he peered out. The corridor was empty, but there were sounds of activity from the offices which lined it.

Francis looked around uncertainly. He

obviously felt that in some way the initiative had been wrested from his grasp and he was not sure what to do about it.

"Why here?"

"Not here. The tenth."

Matlock led the way swiftly to the staircase and started to descend.

"The porter will have watched which floor we got off at. I only hope he doesn't check by 'phone."

He checked that the eleventh floor corridor was empty before they swung rapidly over the landing and down the next flight of stairs.

At the bottom Matlock paused and held up his hand for silence. He had been cautious before, but now every move was as stealthy and silent as he could make it.

Again the corridor was empty, nor was there any sound of life coming through any of the closed doors.

The plaque on the wall credited all this inactivity to the Technical Education Recruitment Board. Brother Francis looked at this then turned to Matlock, his battered boxer's face (which suited his present uniform much more than his monk's robes) twisted into puzzled enquiry. Matlock pressed close to him and made a funnel of his hands at his ear. Down this he whispered, "The slightest move from anyone in there, start shooting. *Anyone.* Understand?"

Francis shrugged, then nodded. Matlock turned and led the way along the corridor to the door marked 'Enquiries'. Here he pressed himself up against the wall and motioned Francis to knock.

Nothing happened for a full thirty seconds after the knock, but Francis had lived on his intuition long enough to know that he was being scrutinized. Finally a woman's voice said, "Come in please".

He opened the door and walked in. Seated at a table opposite the door was a middle-aged woman with a bright smile on her face.

"Good-day, officer. Can I help you?"

Then her face changed and he realized Matlock had appeared beside him. Ignoring the woman, Matlock moved rapidly across the room towards the further door. The woman leaned to one side. Francis remembered Matlock's injunction but hesitated till her left hand came up with a gun in it. Then he fired. He had to shoot her twice.

Matlock meanwhile had crashed the inner door open and gone through, doubled low. Francis saw the doorway light up with the rapid brilliances of force-gun shots for a couple of seconds. Then all went dark.

A second later Matlock appeared at the door rubbing his left shoulder.

"Are you hurt?"

"Just bruised. I'm not accustomed to the acrobatics of evasion. What about you?"

Matlock looked quickly round the outer office and noted the two shot-marks on the woman. "Chivalry makes you inaccurate," he observed.

But Francis didn't hear. He was busy looking round the inner room. There had been three men in there. There still were, but all dead. All three had their guns out. Matlock must have moved fast and shot accurately.

"It would have been easier if you'd

stopped the girl from ringing the alarm buzzer. But it's my fault. I should have realized it might be a girl in there and that would slow you up."

"Matlock," asked Francis in bewilderment, "what is this place?"

"You mean you want to know who you've killed? A delicate piece of machinery is the human conscience. Well, let it rest, Brother Francis. Many years ago when I had some slight authority in this country, I made it my business to get to know as much about our various Security Services as I could. Even if I'd stayed long enough, I doubt if I'd have got to know the lot. But a myriad of little front organizations were known to me and I've kept a fatherly eye on them since. Many have disappeared in that time, of course, and I presume others have sprung up in their place. But this name I recognized outside. Either it was now legitimate and the inmates would be only too pleased to help a policeman or too scared to resist a gunman. Or it was working as before. They were a bit quick on the draw for technical education, don't you think? And this though it looks technical, is probably not very educational. Except perhaps to you."

He indicated the banks of machinery which lined the room.

"But what did they do here?" asked Francis.

"Faked things mainly, I think. Any well-run state needs all kinds of things if its security is to run smoothly. Passports, visas, paper money. And a well-run police state needs even more. Signatures, thumbprints, affidavits, wills, marriage and birth certificates."

He pulled out a drawer and emptied it, then another and another. Francis looked at the piles of legal documents, the letterheads, the blank passports.

"And the machinery?"

"Oh, that's an automatic press. That's probably some kind of ager. Developer. Enlarger. All mod-cons. And that's a radio telephone."

"Why the hell did we come here, Matlock?"

"Perhaps you'd rather be outside with the Wagon? Listen, Brother, don't have a conscience about this lot. I know they don't go around torturing and terrorizing people. But they know what they're doing. You'd have to be pretty stupid not to understand that you're forging the evidence which is going to kill someone. Or cheat someone. Or discredit someone. No one's that stupid. Anyway, more important to us is that my spotting this place gives us a chance to get out."

"How?" asked Francis eagerly.

Matlock grinned.

"I see your priorities are surfacing again. Now, during a Curfew only two kinds of vehicle move around the streets, the Wagons and Official Reds. Unfortunately Official Reds are not easy to come by for the common man. But in a place like this, your Official Red is the *only* form of transport. These chaps wouldn't be seen dead in anything else. Let's see if we can find out how to summon one."

But before Matlock could start looking, a green light above the 'phone began to flash on and off. Matlock studied the battery of dials and switches in front of him carefully. Finally he picked up the 'phone.

The noise which came out of it was

near-gibberish. Matlock flicked a switch.

"Harper? Hello Harper."

Matlock grunted inarticulately.

"Harper, you took your time. Listen. Is that Scottish job ready? The security boys are screaming for it."

"Just finished."

"Good oh. I'll have a Red round for it in a couple of jiffs. Out."

Matlock sat back with a smile.

"That's saved us a lot of bother, hasn't it?"

Francis peered down at the dials and switches.

"How did you know which was the descrambler?"

"I didn't. I merely flicked the one which looked most used."

"What do we do now?"

"Sit and wait. Perhaps you'd like to tell me now how you came to be in my shower this morning."

Francis gingerly edged one of the dead forgers out of a chair and sat down.

"We heard about four this morning what was going on."

"Heard? How?"

"Well, we rather inferred it. We got

word from the Abbey about a sudden flurry of police activity up there — not at the Abbey itself, but in connected organizations."

"My organizations, I suppose?"

"You could put it like that. Anyway, arrests were being made right, left and centre. Not just the mob, but key people. The Abbot saw at once what it must mean."

"A clever man."

"At any rate, he saw that you must be threatened. There was nothing much we could organize at such notice and as things were so vague. We had made all the agreed arrangements to get you and your friends out of London but we couldn't bring the timing forward at all. To cut a long story short, I climbed out of my beard and into this uniform."

"Which you just happened to have handy."

"Which I just happened to have handy. And off I went round to your flat at a rate of knots. There I came across a dozen or so assorted policemen making a very silent entry. I merely tagged on the back and put myself in a dark corner. Later when the bathroom was cleared and the lock had been removed, I transferred in there."

Matlock sat with furrowed brows for a while, then slowly nodded.

"I see. Tell me, Francis, how important am I?"

"I don't understand."

"This sudden activity on Browning's part. Was this his plan all along, and his approach to me just a bluff? Or was this a snap plan caused by my decision to go to ground. In which case . . . "

"In which case, how did he know about it, you mean?"

"That's right."

"Well, I knew about it. And the Abbot knew. I think I can vouch for us. That leaves you. And yours."

"Yes. You're a real comfort."

Somewhere a sharp-edged buzzer cut through the air. They both started to their feet. Then Matlock laughed.

"It's the internal 'phone."

They went back into the outer office and Matlock picked up the telephone.

"Yes?" he said.

"Hall-porter here, sir. There's a car

from the Ministry of Education here. Says he's come to collect something."

"Thank you. Oh I wonder, could you step up here a moment and give us a hand, do you think?"

"Of course, sir."

The 'phone went dead.

"Why did you say that?"

"It's better to deal with him up here than in the vestibule when he realizes we've nothing to do with this office. The Ministry of Education! I love that!"

"What do you think this job was, anyway? What did he call it? The Scottish job."

"Who knows. We haven't got time to look for it now," said Matlock, tucking more securely into his pocket the small packet he had lifted from Harper's desk within seconds of shooting the man. "That sounds like our man."

A minute later they were on their way downstairs, leaving behind them, securely bound to a chair, the unfortunate porter.

In the vestibule waiting for them in the scarlet uniform of the Official Messenger Service were two men. They looked with some surprise when Matlock, instead of

209

handing over the file he was carrying, headed for the door.

"We were told to collect. There was nothing said about you coming with us."

Matlock shook his head as if in the presence of incredible stupidity. He held up the file.

"This is no use without me."

"And him?" with a nod at Francis.

"There could be an attempt to remove this from me. I've had him looking after me for a couple of days now."

"I might as well see the job through," said Francis.

"All right. Come on."

They marched outside to where the bright-red bullet-shaped messenger car was waiting. Matlock and Francis clambered in the back, the messengers in the front.

The driver spoke briefly into his radio link.

"Twenty-three. Returning to the House."

Then they accelerated smoothly away through the deserted streets. Within a couple of blocks, they passed a Curfew

Wagon, but this was the only moving thing they saw.

Neither of the messengers showed any inclination to talk. Matlock sat busy with his own thoughts, while Francis kept a close eye on the route. Suddenly a pressure from his knee told Matlock that this was where they had to get off.

"Stop the car," he said in a peremptory tone.

The driver looked surprised but the car didn't slow down at all.

"Official Reds never stop en route," he explained kindly. "What's the trouble?"

With a sigh, Matlock reached into the file he was holding on his knee and took out his gun. (He realized he was actually thinking of it as 'his' gun.)

"This," he said.

"The trouble is," said the driver unperturbed, "that you can't take over an Official Red. Even if you shoot me, the thing keeps on going till it hits something. Then we all die."

"A cool customer," said Matlock. "Excuse me."

He reversed his gun and struck the other messenger sharply behind the ear.

He slumped forward without a sound.

"That's better," said Matlock. "Now I can lean forward and get a decent shot. I'm going to count three and then press the trigger. My force-gun is pointing, you will observe, more or less between your legs. The turtle's nest. Frying tonight, as they used to say. One . . . two . . . "

"All right," said the driver. He pulled the car into the kerb. "If you want to stop that badly, then here I stop. Now what?"

Matlock hit him in the same place. Then he and Francis got out and began dragging the two messengers from the front.

"Think you can drive this thing?" asked Francis.

"I was relying on you."

"One of us better had. Listen!"

The clang of the Curfew Wagon bell came drifting to them from a nearby street.

They let the limp bodies of the messengers drop on the road and got quickly into the car, Francis in the driving seat.

"Right, let's go."

"How?" said Francis searching furiously round. "Tell me how and off I'll go."

The control panel was simplicity itself. A speedometer, a fuel gauge. Two switches.

Matlock leaned over and pressed one.

Nothing happened.

"What's that do?"

"Say again, please, and identify yourself," crackled a loud but somehow distant voice in Francis' ear.

He shifted the switch to its former position.

"Try the other."

Matlock twisted urgently round in his seat. They were parked almost opposite an intersection. Suddenly trundling into view along the road running parallel to theirs and about fifty yards away came a Curfew Wagon. Matlock held his breath and prayed. He prayed that in the twenty yards or so in which they were in sight of each other, the Wagon would not notice them. Or that if it did, it would not consider a stationary Red worth investigating.

Francis pressed the other switch.

Rhythmic as hysteria, a great pulsating

shriek tore the air apart and sent frightening waves of sound in all directions.

It only lasted a couple of seconds till Francis threw the switch back.

"Siren," he said unnecessarily.

The Curfew Wagon which had almost moved out of sight now came to a halt, then reversed into the centre of the crossroads. The periscopes twinkled round till all four were peering down the street, towards them. They remained in that position, four blank but all seeing eyes, while the great bulk beneath them shifted round and began to move directly towards the little Red.

"Key," said Matlock, and plunged out of the car and round to the driver. He was just recovering consciousness and had half risen on his elbow. Matlock pulled his arm away from under him so that he collapsed on the road again. Then he began to prise the man's clenched fist open. It was locked like a clamp. The dreadful bell sounded nearer and nearer. He lifted the fist to his mouth and dug his teeth into the ball of the thumb.

There was an anguished screech. The fist became a hand. On the palm lay a small cylinder of metal.

The Wagon was nearly upon them. As he leapt back into the car, he saw the hatches at the front begin to slide open. He leaned over to the control panel and looked desperately for somewhere to put the key. There wasn't an aperture to be seen. He ran his fingers along under the dashboard. Suddenly he felt a slight unevenness. A hollow. He took the cylinder and thrust it in.

Nothing.

He pressed harder. There was a click.

At first he thought there was still nothing. Then he noticed the slight trembling of the fuel pressure gauge.

"We're running. Let's go."

Francis slammed his foot down on the accelerator.

The other messenger suddenly rose to his feet and staggered in front of them trying to draw his gun. The Red surged forward with such force that he was flung over the bonnet into the road behind.

"Christ!" spat Francis between pale lips.

Matlock peered through the back window. The driver was up as well now, waving his arms. A black tube like the lash of a bull-whip snaked out of the now fully open aperture of the Curfew Wagon, coiled round him and dragged him screaming into the darkness.

"I think you might have done that fellow a favour," said Matlock.

"You think so?"

They spun round a corner and the Wagon went out of view.

"Why didn't they fire at us?"

"Who knows? They like their quarry alive, they say. And a parked Red might just have been a parked Red after all. But never fear. There'll be plenty of stuff out to intercept us now."

"Let it," said Francis.

"What's the time?"

"Nearly noon."

"Just in time."

He swung the wheel hard over and the Red raced crazily up the ramp of a fifteen-storey garage. Round and round the spiral ramp they circled at the same terrifying speed till suddenly they ran out on the level plateau of the top parking lot.

There was only one other vehicle there,

a large out-of-date transporter.

The Red halted dead and Matlock used the impetus to take him out of the door.

"That?" he said incredulously to Francis.

"That."

As they ran up to the transporter, the rear board slowly unfolded. Francis had leapt on before it reached the ground. Turning, he pulled Matlock up behind him.

"Welcome aboard."

Inside the transporter, looking absurdly small, was a helicopter. At the controls in long flowing robes was a monk.

"Greetings, Brothers. Climb up, do. Will there be any others?"

"No. Get going," snapped Francis.

Others. Where are the others? wondered Matlock as he crouched in his seat.

"Something's coming up the ramp! Go!" screamed Francis.

The pilot pressed a button. Above them, the roof of the transporter split open letting in the deep blue of the sky. The helicopter's vanes began to whirl, her ground jets blasted and slowly, carefully they rose from the chrysallis of the great truck, then climbed more rapidly as a small car pulled off the ramp on to the roof. Out of it jumped a solitary figure who began to run towards the transporter, waving.

"Wait," shouted Matlock. "It's Colin! It's Colin!"

"Too late," said Francis, pointing.

Two other cars, large and official, had run off the ramp. Half a dozen uniformed figures jumped out of each and ran towards the waving man. They were antlike now, and so indistinguishable when together that to Matlock it looked as if Colin had been swallowed up.

He strained his eyes to see what was happening down there, but soon he couldn't even make out the building clearly.

Then he sat back and closed his eyes.

And wondered how it was all going to end.

7

"YOU must be tired, Mr. Matlock," said the Abbot.

"Not too tired to talk, Abbot," said Matlock, determined to take an early initiative. But in fact great waves of exhaustion were swelling over his eyes and nothing seemed more attractive than sleep.

The old wrinkled face looked at him kindly and there were the beginnings of a smile round the mouth.

"Yes, I think to talk. There is much to talk about, Mr. Matlock, and I would not have you feel that you were at any disadvantage. A few hours' sleep first. You have had a trying time."

"Perhaps you're right," yawned Matlock.

"I hope you will be comfortable. We pay more attention to comfort here in the Strangers' House than in our own cells, but our store is not great, and the demands on it are many."

Matlock looked round the simply

furnished room. A narrow bed, a chair, a cupboard.

"This is fine," he said, sitting on the bed.

"I will see you later then, Mr. Matlock."

"Of course."

Matlock drew his legs up on to the bed then allowed his head to sink back on the pillow.

"Till later then," said the Abbot as he closed the door.

Matlock was already asleep.

He awoke from a dream of Lizzie so real that he was physically excited and put out his hand to seek her beside him. Then he sat up and looked around the darkened room, taking a second or two to realize where he was.

His excitement quickly faded and he lay back, staring sightlessly at the changing dapples of light on the ceiling. Outside, the river which threw the light bubbled and hissed over the stones. It must be running low. It had been a hot summer. Mingled with it were other noises, separable only after many minutes' quiet listening. A fragment of birdsong. The long hoot of an owl (not very merry in spite of Shakespeare). Occasional water noises which were more than just the flow of the stream. Small things plunging.

If there weren't so many of us, more of us could hope to hear this, he thought. Then he smiled at the old familiar paradox of the words.

What is the answer then? Compulsory birth control? Surely it's better to control death than love? But we would not control love only the begetting of children. Then you have an old man's world, a world in which a man cannot hope to achieve anything worthwhile till he's seventy or eighty.

The Long Adolescence.

One of my phrases that. Good of its kind.

Was I right?

No matter, thought Matlock as he turned on his side and stared at the old-fashioned curtained window. No matter. What I have seen these past years is nothing of my begetting. It is not what I started.

It is not what I intended.

"It is no matter!" cried Matlock, sitting upright on the narrow, hard bed.

The window drank up his words, diluted them with the river, and washed them away as though unspoken.

He realized that a new sound had joined the noises of pure nature which filled the room. Yet in its way it too was river-like, flowing, swelling, ebbing, sinking.

It was the monks chanting at their evening service in the Abbey.

Now he rose from his bed and went to the window. He was facing the river and therefore quite unable to see the Abbey, but the chant came to him quite clearly now. On an impulse he opened the small window wide and stepped through it — with some difficulty — on to the river-bank.

The night was warm but fresh. He knelt by the water and bathed his hands and his face till he felt fully awakened. Then he moved off along the edge of the Strangers' House till he cleared the corner and was able to see across to the main group of buildings of the Abbey itself.

When he had arrived at the Abbey earlier in the day, this had been his first view of it for over fifty years. The sight which had met him was one he would never forget. He knew that reconstruction had taken place, he knew the Meek had begun to build again. But still in his mind had been that curious mixture of artifice and nature which is called a ruin, mighty pillars growing from grass; great arched windows framing trees and hills and sky; chambers with floors of turf, and paving-stones with roofs of cloud; birds nesting in clerestories and flowers growing out of capitals.

Instead as they levelled off their flight, then began to drop more sedately towards the grass before the West Doorway, he saw beneath him a complete building, arches unbroken, roofs unpierced, windows glazed, gutters leaded. The sight had struck him so powerfully that he paid little notice to the group of welcomers gathered outside the doorway, until the helicopter landed.

The Abbot had come forward smiling and greeted Francis with a chaste embrace and a kiss on the cheek. Matlock had been treated to a mere handshake, but his attention was still more involved with the building behind than the people in front of it.

"You will see it later, Mr. Matlock. All we have shall be shown to you. But first let us attend to your bodily needs."

And he had been led politely but firmly away from the Abbey itself across the grass to where, by the river, stood the Guesthouse for Strangers. Then had come the tiredness and the Abbot's insistence that he should sleep before they talked. Now he had slept. It was time to talk.

It was an eerie experience to move through the soft darkness of the night towards the source of that old music. The west window was only dimly lit and he realized that the main activity of the service would be taking place at the east end. When he reached the door he hesitated momentarily; he had been properly brought up and knew that you never interrupted a man at prayer or sex. If entry had meant opening the double outer doors he would probably have waited, but there was a smaller door built into one side of the large one and it swung noiselessly open at the touch of his hand. He stepped into an ill-lit porch and a couple of steps more took him to an inner door under which shone a faint crack of light from the nave beyond. There was no small door for inconspicuous entry this time and he had gripped the great iron ring of the door handle and was about to turn it when a thin but very bright beam of light flickered across his eyes, then went out.

"Allow me, Brother," said a gentle educated voice with a touch of Norfolk in it.

Out of the darkness came a robed figure. Matlock was still too dazzled to see him as anything but a silhouette, his grey robes just visible against the general blackness. But when the man opened the door for him and the thin light from the church spilled out he saw that he was a slight, grey-haired man with a smile whose benevolence fitted the robes of his Order.

"Brother Phillip," said the monk by way of self introduction. "We thought you might care to join us, Mr. Matlock. It is my humble duty this evening to sit at the threshold and welcome any wayfarers

225

who may chance this way in search of rest. Pray enter."

"Thank you," said Matlock and passed into the Abbey.

"I will see you later I hope, Brother," said Brother Phillip, and closed the door gently behind him, leaving Matlock pondering what kind of rest chance wayfarers might expect from the Mark 2 Force Rifle he had glimpsed propped up against the wall before Brother Phillip had closed the door.

But the interior of the Abbey swept such profane thoughts out of his mind. The nave stretched before him for a distance he reckoned at about a hundred yards, and the arch of the roof seemed almost a similar height above, though this he recognized as an illusion caused by the mingling of the dim night light filtering through the clerestory windows with the brighter but even more deceptive shiftings of fume and shadow cast by the torches below. For at first glance the only illumination, at this end of the nave at least, seemed to be these cornet shaped brands stuck in brackets attached to every third or fourth pillar. But the eye was drawn irresistibly down the nave, across the transept, through the choir (the terms came unbidden to his mind) to where brilliantly illumined against what seemed the sombre background of a great East Window, the High Altar stood.

He also realized he had viewed this scene before. On the television set at his first meeting with the Abbot.

He turned swiftly and peered up at the dark wall behind. There seemed to be some kind of cavity almost at the very top and he strained his eyes to penetrate the mirk when a rustle of noise behind him made him swing round just in time to see the floor of the nave rise up and burst into a thousand tongues of flame. The truth he realized almost simultaneously, but that *almost* left enough time to step back a pace and taste superstitious fear deep in the throat.

What had happened was that several hundred monks, dark-robed, cowled, lying prostrate on the floor and shielding close in their hands the small flame of a candle, had stood up.

Now the chant which had caught his attention as he made his way over to the

Abbey and which had so blended with the background that he had ceased to notice it, was taken up by the entire congregation and the sound rose with the multiple blaze of the candles and filled the arch of the roof. The light brought the ceiling closer but did not make it any the less impressive. Now the only part of the building in darkness was the corridor of the clerestory where the shadows of the massy pillars, whose double column ran before him down the nave, became even blacker in the new light. Again as Matlock looked up he had a sense of movement, of darker shadows in the shadow but he could not be certain.

Suddenly the chant rose to a climax then stopped. The silence was as complete and eerie as if the birds had stopped singing in an orchard on a summer's day. The light dimmed as the monks cupped their candles in their hands once more, this time to act as a windbreak as they moved slowly forward. At the end of the nave they were turning to the right (into the south transept, Matlock cumbersomely worked out) and thence, he supposed, out of the church into the working and living quarters of the Abbey. He followed them as far as the cross-aisle of the transepts. As the last monk went through the tall double door, it rolled quietly to behind him and Matlock, alone, felt the dimensions of the building, vast enough already, rush dizzily away from him till he was a pinprick of human warmth in a huge cross of space and time and cold darkness.

He turned to follow the monks, eager for human contact.

"Will you not stay a little longer, Mr. Matlock? You may find what you want here."

He recognized the voice, but could not place its source for a moment.

"Where are you?" he asked in a voice pitched slightly higher than he intended.

The Abbot chuckled.

"Here I am," he said, emerging from the shadows of the choir. "Where else should I be?"

Right, thought Matlock, if he's going to play the man of God, I'll play the man of action.

"I'm glad to meet you like this, Abbot,"

he said briskly. "There's a lot needs straightening out between us. Where can we talk?"

"Why, here," said the Abbot, unperturbed. "But do not be too keen to rush into practicalities, Mr. Matlock. We must make plans, it is true, but not, I hope, as a means of escape."

"Escape from what?"

"Why, from this."

The small gesture of the ruby-ringed finger sent Matlock's gaze and, against his will, thoughts spinning back round the shaped darkness above him.

"It's a strange thing, a church, Mr. Matlock. I mean the building, not the organization, though the two are inextricably linked. All buildings express their purpose. Obviously a house is not a shop and vice versa. And a church, whose purpose is far more complex than either of these, must express this purpose in the most complex of ways.

"At its simplest, a church is a cross. A cross on which our Lord is still crucified. In a church you are close to the body and passion of Christ at the same time as you are in his outstretched arms."

"That's a little grisly, don't you think?" said Matlock, but the Abbot went on as though uninterrupted.

"But a church is also an eye. A great eye facing East, always searching for the Light to rise which shall re-illumine the world. A telescope if you like. No wonder Galileo's claims for his little glazed tube met with the scorn of those other watchers of the sky. And it is an arrow, leaping skywards in a thousand different ways, in pinnacles, arches, steeples, buttresses. Upwards, upwards, always upwards. Lightness, airiness, that's what they were after, those great builders."

He laughed and slapped a massive pillar as they passed.

"Are you trying to convert me?" asked Matlock reasonably.

"Oh, no. No. At the moment that is the last thing I should want. Though in fact, I might be going to tempt you. I shall act the Devil for once and take you to a high place and tempt you."

The switch from religious fervour to urbane badinage did not seem at all out of place in the Abbot. They had stopped now and Matlock looked up, realizing they must be beneath the off-centre tower which dominated the external mass of the church.

"Let us ascend," said the Abbot, moving purposefully to a small door in the furthest column. "We still have a spiral staircase if you like, but I prefer this."

He opened the door, motioned Matlock ahead of him, and together they stepped back into the twenty-first century.

It was an elevator.

The Abbot pressed a button and the floor pressed forcibly against Matlock's feet. The journey only took a couple of seconds, but he noticed that there were according to the buttons another two floors they could have stopped at, though their speed had been too great for him to see anything of them in passing.

"Top floor, Mr. Matlock. Won't you step out?"

The room they entered was windowless and might have been the control room of a very tiny airport. It was in semi-darkness and two monks sat incongruously watching two radar screens while a third flicked idly from one picture to another on the television monitor before him.

"You look for God in curious ways, Abbot," said Matlock.

"Oh no. God has long been here. It is the Devil in various forms that we try to keep out. Though I am not sure I have not invited him here myself."

He raised his eyebrows quizzically at Matlock.

"But you are disappointed, I can see. You expected a fine view. Well, of course, you can view any part of the grounds you like from here. Any undue movement on the screens and a picture can be conjured up immediately."

One of the monks spoke. The brother in charge of the tele leaned forward and altered his picture. Trees, undergrowth, came into sharp focus. Through them something moved. The picture zoomed in on it.

"I doubt if you've ever seen that before, Mr. Matlock. A badger."

Matlock looked curiously at the animal which moved cautiously through tall bracken, unsuspecting that it was so closely observed.

"There are not many left now. Blunt, tough beasts who live their lives in such obscurity that when they do appear, everyone fights for a good look. They would give a great deal for such a creature in London, Mr. Matlock, archaic and superseded though it is."

Matlock shook his head sadly.

"The trouble with religion is that if you're not careful you start confusing allegory with reality, the image with the thing itself. Some people even start believing in human immortality in human terms."

"I see that nothing less than a real sight of real things will please you. It will please me also. Come."

He went to a corner of the room and pulled a lever. From the roof there swung down a set of aluminium steps. The Abbot ran lightly up them and pushed open a small trap in the ceiling. Through the hole Matlock saw a square of the night sky. The Abbot's head was black against a haze of stars.

"Come up. Do."

He climbed out on to the top of the tower and stood quite still for a moment to accustom himself to the new light.

It was a fine clear night though there was no moon. Silhouetted above the castellated parapet was the now familiar cowled head of a monk who moved away at a soft-spoken instruction from the Abbot and swiftly descended the steps, pulling the trap-door shut behind him.

"You see we do keep a more traditional type of watch, Mr. Matlock. I am glad to see these hints of a love of tradition in you. This is part of your appeal to your followers. The English have always been a nostalgic race, but nostalgia has never been a real political force. During our own youth there were always plenty of people willing to talk longingly of the twenties, the thirties, even the forties and fifties. But no one ever really wanted to get back to them, or at least only an insubstantial minority. But things have changed. For the first time ever in our history there is a real desire to go back, to reverse the tide. And you are our Canute."

"And just as helpless I suppose."

"Oh no. If Canute had really wanted to impress the people, which he didn't, he would merely have worked out where the next high tide line would be, and stood there. That's what you can do. Nothing is really changed by man. It's just that some men happen to be about when the changes take place. But you are full of questions, Mr. Matlock. Why not ask them?"

"Right. Question. What has happened to my friends?"

The Abbot shrugged eloquently.

"The first time we met, I gave you what I believe was true information about your friends. That is, that at least two of them, the woman Armstrong, and the man, Colquitt, were in Browning's service. I fear that you disregarded this information and continued to take them into your full confidence. Ask yourself what seemed to be known by the authorities and what did not. And compare this with what you told your friends."

"I have done so a hundred times, Abbot. Nothing conclusive appears. Are you suggesting that Browning's latest moves are the result of this alleged betrayal?"

"Not directly. The timing, I think; yes,

that might be. But this was carefully planned, not hastily put together overnight. In any case, he had information which was not yours to give. Names, places, times."

"Just what has happened? I only know what the tele-news told me."

The Abbot leaned against the old stone of the parapet and stared out down the valley through which the scarcely audible river ran.

"Our organization was not a tightly-bound thing, you understand, with levels of control and authority clearly marked. In no sense a pyramid. No, it was a loose union of diverse interests — and individuals linked together by a common aim. Revolution. The overthrow of Browning. The repeal of the Age Laws. Such diversity required a focal point. That's where you came in, Matlock. The Apostate. The man who had the blinding vision which converted him and could convert the world."

"Who was in this organization?"

"Oh, many thousands you would not know. Could not. But there were four or five main groups scattered over the North.

The North West was controlled by an old friend of yours. The Chief Constable of Manchester. Don't be surprised. He played his part well whenever he met you. He was a pillar of strength to us."

"Was?"

"He was shot during last night's purge. Resisting arrest they say. My informants tell me he was shot in bed before he opened his eyes."

Matlock was silent, remembering the man. And his own puzzlement when he had appeared personally to escort them from the hall where Percy was killed. He really was protecting us, he thought bitterly. He really was.

The Abbot was speaking again.

"The other main rallying points for our cause were the Head of the North East Development Corporation, who has disappeared without trace, and the Doncaster Poetry Appreciation Society and the Women's Guild of Nottingham, neither of whose ridiculous guises proved strong enough to fool Browning. The President of the Doncaster Society was hanged after a summary trial and his entire committee arrested; while the ladies of Nottingham have either gone to earth or been put to earth. Nothing has been heard of them since yesterday. There have been many arrests in the rank and file, but Browning's too clever to overdo it. Prisoners are a nuisance, and become martyrs. Freedom with fear is much more useful. His men have let so many of ours know that they *are* known that even those still unsuspected go in fear of constant observation."

Matlock shivered in a light breeze which momentarily touched the tower.

"Tell me," he said, "why in all this activity have the Meek remained untouched?"

"You must ask Browning that," laughed the Abbot. "It seems to me that here at Fountains we have one advantage not shared by our colleagues. We are a united group. All together. All in one place. To destroy us would need a major operation. As I've said, Browning doesn't want this. He wants to cut the beast's hamstrings, not butcher the body. He knows we are warned. He knows that alone we are impotent. And though our strength lies in our unity, so does our weakness. For

239

we are easy to watch, both from inside and outside."

"So," said Matlock, clutching the parapet tightly, "it is over. You have shown me the Promised Land, then turned me back to the wilderness."

"Why, the atmosphere of the place is affecting you after all, Mr. Matlock."

"I want no jokes. What happens now?"

"Now? I think bed, Mr. Matlock. Bed I think."

He moved back towards the trap, but Matlock stepped smartly in front of him and grasped his robe.

"What about the future, Abbot? Is there any hope?"

The Abbot disengaged himself gently.

"There is always hope, Mr. Matlock. We shall see. Let us wait in patience."

"I can't wait too long. I have a birthday. Remember?"

"Oh don't let *that* concern you one little bit. We have our own adjusting machine. We'll give you another fifty years in a jiffy."

The rush of relief through his whole body made Matlock ashamed. He found himself talking to try to stem the selfish joy which the news had brought him.

"And Lizzie? Ernst and Colin? You'll try to find out about them?"

"Of course I will. Though I suspect that the first two are either reaping the rewards of their success or paying the penalty of their failure. It just depends how Browning looks at it. But let's go down now. It is rather chilly up here. I have duties to perform. Only my duties are important here. All else can wait till tomorrow."

Four days later Matlock was still waiting for this tomorrow. He had woken up the following morning, breakfasted simply but well, and then he had set out across the grass towards the main buildings determined to get some outstanding matters settled. But as he approached the Abbey a smiling figure he recognized as Brother Phillip, the guardian of the porch, had come to meet him.

The Abbot, he explained, had a great deal of work, both administrative and pastoral, to catch up on just at the moment and he had asked if he, Brother Phillip, would look after

Mr. Matlock's needs until an interview could be arranged.

Brother Phillip smiled sympathetically as he said this and Matlock felt his anger evaporating under the charm of the man.

"I see why you were picked for the job."

"I hope that's a compliment, Mr. Matlock. Would you like to see round the Abbey?"

"Why not?"

So had begun a conducted tour of the buildings. Phillip had proved to be such a good guide — informative, intelligent, humorous — that Matlock had found himself enjoying the day despite his sense of time fleeing past; time important in any plan to overthrow Browning, and time even more important to himself.

His birthday was now less than a week away. But he had determined to make as good use of this waiting period as possible. The set-up at the Abbey was obviously a great deal more complex than the Abbot had implied and he felt pretty certain there must be other reasons for its immunity from Browning's purge than those he had been offered. So he questioned Phillip closely about everything he saw, but had to admit that the monk seemed to answer freely with no attempt at concealment. Yet Matlock at the end of four days felt himself no nearer the solution of any of his problems.

The very beauty of the place only made him feel more cut off from reality. It was many years since he had felt himself so secluded from the great cities which now covered so much of the countryside. There was not a sign of their existence visible from most of the grounds which had been exquisitely laid out in the eighteenth century with a series of ornamental lakes, lily-ponds and classical statues. It was not until you reached their easternmost end where the Skell poured smoothly down a small but impressive drop that the distant edge of the multicity which comprised Ripon, Boroughbridge and Harrogate, could be seen.

There was a set of stepping stones or rather slabs over the river just above the fall, and a rather curious incident took place here on the fourth day.

Matlock was sitting in the grass looking out towards the cityscape and wondering what was going on in the world of men and action he seemed to have left behind. Suddenly impatient for activity he jumped to his feet and without a word to Phillip set off across the stones. As he trod on the first one a hooded monk started across from the other side. When he saw Matlock he stopped sharply and stared right at him. The sun was striking athwart his hood and only the barest hint of features could be made out in the dark shadows beneath.

Then he stepped back to the bank. At first Matlock took this to be merely an act of courtesy but as he continued over the stones, he saw the monk, pulling his cowl still further over his head, set off briskly along the path beside the river.

Matlock stood in the middle of the river and watched him go. He heard Phillip come up behind him.

"He didn't want to meet one of us," Matlock said.

"Surely not. A change of plan. Something remembered which took him back that way. That was all."

"If you say so."

But Matlock was beset by a strange sense of familiarity as he watched the now distant figure.

"Tell me, Phillip," he said, "are there two types of monk here? Or degrees or ranks? The Abbot said something about this when we first met, and I've noticed that many of the Brothers always wear their cowls up indoors and outdoors."

Phillip paused a while before answering.

"That's two questions really," he said. "Yes there are degrees of course, under the Abbot. Degrees of responsibility in the running of the Abbey and degrees of religious initiation. But the wearing of hoods is only indirectly related to this. Some of our brethren prefer this ultimate in withdrawal, this final abasement of self, the concealment of the face, or most of it anyway. It's a logical spiritual step, if that's not a contradiction."

"It must make things rather difficult. Surely you want to be able to recognize people at some time."

"Why? We are interchangeable, equal before God. Even our names are borrowed.

245

We have them chosen for us on arrival."

"Do you shed your old identities completely?"

Phillip laughed.

"That would be very difficult. We are still under the Law here. We must report ourselves according to the dictates of the Law."

"And your heart clocks?"

Phillip looked at him quizzically.

"When our time is up, we must be accounted for like anyone else."

"But I thought the Meek would inherit the earth?"

"A metaphor, Mr. Matlock. A metaphor."

Matlock grunted, trying not to sound too disbelieving. His mind was once again sharpening for action and he didn't want to show the full depth of his dissatisfaction. There was much here in need of investigation and he was not altogether certain whether Phillip was merely his guide or also his guard.

That evening Matlock made a great play of borrowing a history of the Abbey, saying he was going to get some real insight into the traditions and aims of the place. He almost overdid it for Phillip became very keen to stay with him in the Strangers' House and guide him through the labyrinthine chapters of the massive tome, but Matlock finally persuaded him to leave the discussion till the morning and join the others in the usual pre-midnight service.

"They'll drum you out if you don't start paying more attention to your religion and less to me," he said lightly.

"Same thing," said Phillip, "you're the lost sheep."

Blacksheep, thought Matlock as he watched Phillip move across the grass to the church. Then he turned swiftly and went back to his room. He had chosen this particular time for two reasons. The first was that in a few minutes nearly all the monks, including the Abbot, would be participating in the service. The second was that the watchers in the tower would be more easy to fool if they happened to be scanning the area between the Strangers' House and the main buildings. At least he hoped so, as he pulled from his bed the tattered remnants of the blanket he had spent the previous night hacking to pieces. Now he draped it over his shoulders and carefully set another piece on his head.

He only had a small shaving mirror and from what he could see of himself in that, he didn't look much like a monk. But he hoped that on the television screen, if he was unfortunate enough to appear there, his shadowy image would pass muster.

He moved to the door of the Strangers' House and peered out into the darkness. He saw a couple of figures move swiftly across an open space, then they disappeared into the shadows. Taking a deep breath as though he was about to dive into water, he stepped out into the night.

When he reached the protecting wall of the main building, he felt a sense of relief but recognized it instantly as premature. He had no way of telling if he had been observed or, if observed, whether he had been detected in his disguise. But there was nothing else to do now but continue with his plan.

Plan was perhaps rather too organized a word for what he had in mind, he thought as he slipped through the low arched door into the Cellarium, the Abbey's main store-house. His destination was the Abbot's private rooms and his purpose — he shrugged, and the blanket nearly slipped off his shoulders. To look around. To test a few suspicions. To do something instead of waiting for something to be done to him.

It was eerie down here in the Cellarium. Almost as long as the church, but much lower roofed, the building was totally unlit, and he stood for a while till his eyes grew used to the darkness.

Gradually the long row of central pillars began to form themselves out of the darkness like an exercise in perspective; then the arches of the vaults which sprang out of them. And finally, prosaically, the shadowy shapes and forms of the crates, boxes and cans of provisions which packed the vaults.

Distantly he heard the now familiar line of chanting which told him the service was under way. As quietly as possible, he made his way across the Cellarium and through the door that led into the cloister court. Compared with the darkness he left behind him, thin starlight glinting on the faintly damp grass was very bright indeed. He kept to the right, as far as possible moving always in shadow. He had no anticipation of meeting anyone, but the instinct of self-preservation seemed to have strengthened in him during the past few days.

I have the cloak, he thought hugging his blanket closer. Now I only need the dagger.

Surprisingly, he suddenly felt in need of a weapon. The gun he had had with him when he first came to the Abbey had disappeared during his first sleep. He hadn't thought it worth mentioning to Phillip. Either he would know, in which case he would be an accessory to the theft. Or he wouldn't know. In which case he wouldn't know.

In any case it had been Francis' gun.

Francis. He hadn't had even a glimpse of him since the first day. Matlock surprised a sentimental fondness for the man in himself. They had been through trouble together. Such things had an illogical binding power.

But Francis was very firmly the Abbot's man. Never forget that.

The thought of the Abbot suddenly snapped his mind back to the present. He had been moving forward with a stealth which was purely physical. His mind had been only half concerned with his progress. And his return to full alertness almost came too late.

He was just at the corner of the court nearest the arch which led through into the Chapter House. Inside he heard the shuffle of sandalled feet.

Silently he moved sideways till he came up against the wall.

Out of the Chapter House came a cowled figure who walked slowly, as though in deep thought, over the square of bright grass.

Matlock recognized instantly the figure which had turned away from him at the stepping stones that morning. But some deeper, older nag of near-recognition was scratching at his mind.

He shifted his position slightly to try to get a better view of the man. Under his shoed foot a stone clinked.

The monk stopped and turned. He seemed to be peering doubtfully towards the shadows where Matlock stood, but the shadows on his own face were still impenetrable.

"Is that you, Brother James?" enquired a querulous, high-pitched voice.

A remembered voice.

An old man's voice.

"My God," said Matlock.

"Who is that?" asked the old man. Then with a sudden strength which echoed ancient authority.

"Who is that, I ask? Come out and show yourself."

My God, breathed Matlock, now certain, but still desperately uncertain. Believing and incredulous at the same time.

He took three steps forward out of the shadows, then stood and shifted his hood back.

The monk stood like a weather-worn statue for a few moments then imitated the gesture revealing a thin ascetic face topped by a wiry tangle of white hair. It was a face which should have been long decayed in the earth. But the eyes were too full of a lively intelligence to belong to a ghost.

"Hello, Matt," he said.

"Carswell?" said Matlock. "Carswell!"

8

THE old man suddenly looked furtively around, pulling his hood back over his head.

"Come," he said, beckoning like a figure from a Gothic novel, and he moved swiftly back into the Chapter House.

Matlock followed more slowly, still trying to catch his thoughts. His suspicions about the Abbey had been along these lines, but this dramatic and personal confirmation of them had caught him entirely unprepared.

Carswell, his one-time father-in-law had led the Party for over forty years, finally retiring well over the E.O.L. to enjoy the year of grace permitted to anyone retiring from a post which had held exemption privileges.

He should have been dead for seventeen years.

Now he sat like Death itself on the white marble which showed the last resting place of John de Cancia, the thirteenth-century abbot who had been responsible for many important developments at Fountains.

"Well, Matt," he said, "I didn't think we would ever meet again. Not after the last time."

Matlock thought back to that last occasion they had come face to face.

A wet day. October. Gusty. Umbrellas full of air interfering with dignity. Substituting irritation for grief.

Edna's funeral.

They had stood facing each other across the grave, the priest between.

Nothing had been said. Nothing dramatic was done much to the disappointment of the reporters and photographers with closely focused zooms resting on the cemetery wall.

"You should have let me know," he said. "I'd have sent you a telegram on your hundredth birthday."

Surprisingly, the old man laughed at the gibe.

"You remember that? The King used to do it. To mark a rarity. Even rarer now, isn't it, but no telegrams.

Wouldn't do at all."

"No, I suppose not. Well, Carsie. What's the set-up? Are you going to tell me, or just leave me to make intelligent guesses?"

"You'd be good at that. But not Carsie, by the way. Adeste."

"Adeste?"

"Brother Adeste Fideles. That's me. We choose our own religious names. It seemed fitting."

"O come all ye faithful."

"That's right. Wouldn't do for you, Matt, would it? You shopped us all."

A shadow passed over Matlock's face then his mouth puckered with distaste.

"And you, Brother Adeste Fideles, have betrayed yourself."

The old man grinned, his teeth gleaming white in the cavern of his cowl.

He's in good nick, thought Matlock. Over a hundred. We could all be like that.

As if catching his thought, Carswell nodded vigorously.

"Here we are on the same side again, Matt. After all these years. That might

256

be good. It might be bad. I don't know. I'm too old for memories. Memories are the debris of life. When you get to my age, you start again. Dump the junk. But I do remember that you're a dangerous man. That's the first thing I thought when I first met you and talked with you. Here's a dangerous man, I thought. Like Cassius. Or rather, like Brutus, the really dangerous one because it didn't show too much to most people. But to me it showed. And you made my party. And you made my daughter. I suppose in a way, you made me. Leader of an insignificant minority group to Prime Minister of the most powerful government this country has ever known. Do you remember that day we met, the first cabinet, at my house? In the orchard? Every tree seemed packed full of the fruit of the tree of life. It was there for the picking. There for the picking."

Matlock found himself trembling, with what emotion he did not know. The old man hadn't finished.

"And I picked it, Matt. That's what I've done. Me and a hundred others. All these Brothers going round with their cowls up. We're the new immortals, whip back those hoods and you'd find a few faces you thought long gone. But you'd guessed all this?"

"In general terms. I was suspicious."

"And that's what you're doing now? Having a prowl around to see what you can pick up? I bet you were headed for the Abbot's rooms?"

He seemed to relapse into thought for a while, then he leapt to his feet.

"That's not such a bad idea still, Matt. There are one or two bits of the jigsaw I've lost sight of lately. I'll join the expedition if I may. In fact, as I know the layout of this place better than you, I'll lead it. It won't be the first time will it, Matt? Me leading, you in charge?"

There was nothing bitter in his voice but Matlock felt constrained to say something. He caught the old man by his arm as he brushed lightly past.

"Carsie," he said. "I was sorry about Edna. Truly sorry."

"Memories are debris, Matt. I told you that. You'd better be ready to ditch them if you're joining the club. It's the only rule."

They set off together, the old man slightly ahead and seeming to find no need for stealth. They turned left out of the Chapter House, then left again down a passage which led into a smaller covered court, and then into another corridor, the Cloister Passage which Matlock knew led to the Infirmary with a branch off to the Chapel of Nine Altars and the body of the Church. He also knew from what Phillip had said and what he had seen in the Abbey plans in the history book that the Abbot's rooms were above the court they had just left and that his own private corridor to the Church ran parallel to and above the Cloister passage. But how to get into the rooms other than by entering the Church (impossible while the service was on) and working back he did not know.

They now reached the right-angled offshoot to the main passage and without hesitation, Carswell turned up it. As they progressed along it, the sounds of the service in progress ahead grew louder and louder. Matlock became afraid that the old man intended to march full into the sanctuary and announce his presence.

He reached forward a restraining hand.

"Not to worry, Matt," said Carswell reassuringly. "Nearly there."

"Nearly where?" hissed Matlock.

For answer the old man stopped and began feeling the wall.

Momentarily there was utter silence in the Church and Matlock was too intimidated by it even to whisper.

"Uh-huh," said Carswell. "There we are."

A section of the wall, to the eye solid stone, slid back smoothly and Carswell stepped into the space revealed, pulling Matlock after him.

The stone slid behind.

The floor rose beneath their feet so unexpectedly that Matlock's knees buckled slightly and he stumbled against his companion who gripped his elbow.

"Careful now. You've got to watch things at your age," said Carswell with open irony. "It's just a lift. Likes his creature comforts, does our dear Abbot. Here we are."

The door slid open and they stepped out into another corridor. It might have been another world. There was no ancient stone here, dimly lit by smoky flambeaux but a smooth metal wall, with a plastic coated floor, all lit by concealed fluorescent lights.

The old man moved from one foot to another, almost dancing in his glee at the revelation.

"Like it? Nice eh? You've got to be special to get up here, you see. Not one of the religious boys."

Matlock kept his face impassive as he looked around.

"Yes. Very nice, Brother Adeste. You mean there really are genuinely religious monks here?"

"Oh yes. But of course. We all are, really. But some of us have rather more esoteric Gods. But the most are your gen-u-ine Bible-punchers. Come and see."

Matlock followed the old man to the nearest end of the corridor. Carswell reached up to the wall and slid aside a small section revealing a peep-hole.

"Look."

Matlock peered through. He found he was looking down into the Abbey at right angles to the High Altar, at which stood

261

the Abbot, his head bent in prayer. Then he was shoved aside and Carswell peeped down.

"Come on," he said. "They're skipping through it tonight. We haven't got long."

As they moved back, Matlock noticed a door in the wall to his right.

"What's behind that?" he asked.

"That leads into the clerestory gallery. You can get right round it into the tower. But not tonight. It's full of people who'd ask questions. This way, if you don't mind."

They pressed on back down the corridor, turning once through a right angle which confirmed Matlock's estimate that they were following the exact line of the passage below.

"Here we are then," said Carswell, coming to a halt before another door. "In we go."

Matlock expected another great performance with concealed locks and catches, but Carswell merely thrust the palm of his hand forward and the door swung open. They passed through.

Once again there was a change of period, not so violent as the transformation from medieval to modern, but merely the gentle step back of about a hundred years. Or more or less, depending on how you dated it. It was a style which men of wealth and culture had affected for their private studies for many many decades and Matlock didn't know whether its origin was Edwardian, Victorian, Regency or whether indeed it was any kind of historical style at all. Oak panelling, solid comfortable furniture, silver candelabra, a wall full of leather-bound books, a huge fireplace with what looked like a potentially serviceable arrangement of logs in the hearth, old prints on the wall and what looked like an ancestral portrait over the mantel-shelf. The figure depicted there wore eighteenth-century dress. His face was familiar, but the dress confused Matlock sufficiently to delay his recognition by a few seconds.

It was the Abbot, or someone closely related to him.

"Oh it's him all right," said Carswell at his elbow. "He's got one of himself in an Elizabethan ruffle, but we all laughed so much when he brought that one out that he's hidden it away."

Matlock shrugged the picture's fascination off him and turned to the rest of the room. There was an elegant writing bureau in the far corner and he moved purposefully over to it, ready to use violence. But it was unlocked and for the next couple of minutes he rifled quickly through all the papers it contained while Carswell stood and watched him. There was nothing there but the kind of paper one would expect to come across in the administrative centre of a place like the Abbey. Bills, accounts, work rosters, what looked like sermon notes.

Frustrated, he dumped the lot back where he'd found them and began casting round the rest of the room.

"What are you looking for, Matt?" asked Carswell politely.

Matlock stopped and faced the old man. "I'm not sure, Carsie. But now I come to think of it, you showed me up here, so there must be something you hoped I'd find. You tell me what that is, and perhaps I'll be able to tell you what I'm looking for. In fact, I think we should have a long talk now. You might be able to tell me so much that I needn't look for anything at all."

The old man shrugged.

"What do you want to know, Matt? But wait a minute. Let's know where we are, eh? Or rather where he is."

He reached into a recess beside the bookcase. A television monitor slid silently forward. He flicked a switch. The screen glowed, then the High Altar appeared on it with the Abbot in clear view.

"That's nice. Now Matt."

He stood there with a kind of naive expectancy on his face. His cowl was down again and Matlock found it strangely hard to look into those still bright blue eyes.

This was a man he had once respected as much as anyone in the world.

But to the world it had seemed that he had used him then betrayed him.

Finally, controlling his voice with his will, he said, "How many of you are there here? Over the top, I mean."

"One hundred and sixty-three over. Twenty-two waiting."

"Who are these men?"

Carswell grinned.

"Oh, all sorts and conditions. Lots of old friends. Thurlow, my Chancellor — you'll remember him; Jenkins; Whitmarsh from the Treasury; Field Marshall Curwen — he's a great help — Sir Augustus Terce, the old King's physician; Herb Slattery of Force Physics Inc.; oh you could write a Who's Who from our ranks, or rather a Who Was Who, eh?"

"Tell me about this place, Carsie."

The old man settled into one of the voluminous armchairs drawn up by the hearth, lighting a cigar from a box on one of the many stone ledges of the fireplace. As an after-thought he pressed a switch near the floor and instantly the logs burst into flame.

"You fool," said Matlock. "He'll know."

Carswell smiled and moved the switch again. The flames died. The logs were unchanged.

"It's like hell. All-consuming flames which never consume. Here we go again."

The flames licked their way up the chimney once more.

Seating himself opposite the old man, Matlock found that the scene — the dark panelled room, the great fire, the white-haired benevolent looking old monk, his features now sharp now shadowed in the shifting light of the fire — was having a strangely soporific effect upon him. It was like moving into the archaic world of a picture on a Christmas card. He had to wrest his mind round to full attention to the old man's words. He had dropped the flip, casual style of speech he had effected since their meeting, and reverted to the old lectorial style Matlock remembered very clearly.

"The main difficulty of beating the Age Laws has always been one of organization. Any fool with enough money can go for Op, skip the country and lead whatever precarious semi-legal life his wealth can buy him in whatever other country will let him in. Switzerland's the only real answer in Europe and they're so full of Age-Law refugees of all nationalities that they work an unofficial quota system — and only the very *very* rich even get on the waiting list.

"Scotland's the only other European

country without Age Laws and at best all an Englishman can expect there is confiscation of his assets and a labour camp. Utopian rumours of certain South American states reach us from time to time. But what trust can you put in rumour? and we're all so isolated now.

"And in any case, escapes of this nature immediately lay all one's family open to the rigours of the Age-Law Evasion Act. Of course, that bothers some people less than others. I must confess that were the penalties applicable to relations by marriage, I might have made my evasion public just for the satisfaction of doing you down."

The old man rocked forward and back, letting an occasional whimper of his amusement escape. Matlock cursed him for being so long winded and glanced at the monitor but the Abbot still seemed to be fully occupied.

"Hurry it up," he said.

Carswell gave him a reproachful look and sucked at his cigar.

"As I say, what was needed was a comfortable life with no comeback on the nearest and dearest. Indeed, an opportunity for them to join you when their time was up. Like the 'In Memoriam' poems.

'*He waits for us behind the door,*
Not dead, but merely gone before.'

"So one or two old friends got together and had one or two chats. And gradually the idea evolved of this place. Not an evasion of the law, but an extension of it. The kind of extension which you as a pragmatic politician, Matt, must have regarded as logical, but unfortunately like many ideas reasonable in themselves it was quite impossible democratically. The public accepted, albeit reluctantly, the notion of limited exemption for active members of the Government. But further than that they would not go, though I need hardly list for you the arguments for not terminating the existence of certain peculiarly important men in the key walks of life. So our organization had to be clandestine. You take my point?"

"Oh yes," said Matlock. "I take it. Was this started before or after I left the Party?"

"Oh before. Just before. We thought of approaching you, but it didn't seem worth taking the risk at the time. You were so sincere. And so young. It seemed best to let a bit of age and experience fix your ideas rather more firmly. And you see, we were right."

Matlock felt something like admiration as he looked at that smiling old face.

You cunning bastard! he thought. And I believed I was using you too much. And the whole world thought you were my puppet on my string! Dear God! Is there a time in my life when someone somewhere hasn't been using me?

"So you formed the Meek?" he asked.

"Oh no. Certainly not. The Meek formed themselves. We just joined them. Never create your own cover if someone else will create it for you. One of the first principles of Security.

"But then, you never really had much to do with Security during your term of office, did you Matt? That's the P.M.'s prerogative. Even if he is just a figurehead.

"But to continue. The Meek existed, a vague religious group whose reaction to the Age Laws was the kind of pure unreasoning emotionalism which men dignify by words such as spiritual or mystic. They would have died away in a twelvemonth if we hadn't injected them with a bit of firm positive purpose. I mean, of course, our dear Abbot."

They both turned and looked at the figure on the screen for a moment. He was now facing the congregation, his arms outstretched, a look of exultation on his face. Matlock felt vaguely uneasy. Carswell shook his head.

"Sometimes I feel that he really did join them. Then he does something so amorally Machiavellian that all doubts end. At least all *those* doubts. We poured a bit of money in. There was no shortage. And this place came into being. So there you have it. A retreat where the best and most important minds of our age may be preserved instead of prematurely destroyed. What can be wrong with that?"

Matlock did not speak for a while. He sat with half-hooded eyes considering the defensive note on which the old man had ended. The broad outline of the scheme he grasped easily and this was enough, he felt, for his purposes. But the details still niggled away in his mind.

"What actually happens when your E.O.L. is up?" he asked finally.

The old man waved his hands airily.

"Oh, death is reported, all the necessary records completed. You know the drill. You helped to work it out, after all."

Smiling, he began to rise. But Matlock reached forward and pressed him back into his chair.

"Yes. I helped work it out. And we made it foolproof. Or as near as possible. Carsie, there's got to be a body. The Public Registrar or his representative has got to see it before the funeral. Carsie, you had a state burial. I saw it on the tele. Who was buried, old man? Who was buried?"

With surprising agility, Carswell leapt up and made for the door, but Matlock had him in a couple of strides. Slowly he bent the old man's head back till his eyes began to stand out like balls of marble and an inhuman rattling came from his throat.

"Let's have it, Carsie. The truth. Or

else I'll do the job your heart clock should have done years ago."

He slackened the pressure on the old man's neck, but didn't let go. Carswell coughed and spluttered for several minutes, his face changing from streaky purple to a mottled grey.

"Now talk."

"All right. You always were a physical man, Matlock. Not enough mind. All right. Not again. I haven't survived this long to let myself be strangled by a failure. So there has to be a body. So we help ourselves to a body — one of the faithful, the true believers. So far as the rest are concerned he's just joined the Hooded Chapter, to fill the vacancy which will be caused by the imminent death of one of these specially devout brethren. Does that make you happy now you know? Are you glad you asked?"

Stunned, Matlock slackened his grip and the old man pulled free and stood almost spitting at him, his head pushed forward, his long bony neck bruised by Matlock's fingers, his eyes full of venom.

"That's the way it goes Matt. You

started it. You should have learned by now that all democracy does is to ensure the survival of the very fittest."

"Fit for what?" said Matlock dully. "I had come to think that I'd caused many evils. But this is the worst of them all."

Still coughing, the old man turned to go. Matlock made no move to stop him. But as he reached the door, he spoke.

"Carswell."

"Yes."

"One last thing. There must be more. You might be able to fool local Registrars and Enforcement Officers by substituting bodies. But everything goes back to the Ministry. Identi-Cards. Thumb-prints. Cardio-X-rays. It's foolproof. You can fool the rest. You can't fool the Minister."

He didn't recognize at first the cracked sound which came almost visibly from the old man's throat. It was laughter.

"Don't you know? Why, Matt, you're even more naive than you used to be? But you must know! They're all on the waiting-list. All the top people come here. It's one of the perks of public service. Didn't Browning tell you?"

"Browning?" said Matlock, feeling himself gawping, but unable to do anything about it. "Browning is in on this?"

"How could we survive otherwise?"

The old man laughed again, then the cracked notes died away.

"If you don't know about Browning, then why are you here, Matt? You don't know, do you? Then bringing you here's even more dangerous than I thought."

He glanced anxiously at the monitor screen. The Abbot was still addressing the congregation. Reassured, he turned again to the door.

"I must bid you good-night, Matt. I've got to talk to one or two people. Things are worse than I thought. I wouldn't hang around here too long if I were you."

He opened the door and stopped in his tracks for a moment, then took two or three uncertain steps backwards.

"Good-evening, Brother Adeste. Those were wise words. Probably your wisest tonight. Good-evening, Mr. Matlock."

Into the room stepped the Abbot.

Matlock glanced from him to the monitor.

"I thought his gestures were a little too flamboyant," he said as coolly as possible.

"Sharp of you. Shall we sit down."

He moved lightly across to the large old fashioned desk which stood in the corner diagonally opposite to the bureau. Behind him came Francis, his beard beginning to grow again. Through the door Matlock could see another two or three monks. Francis turned and said something to them. They nodded, he closed the door and stood with his back to it.

"Now," said the Abbot. "Let us talk."

9

"YOU see," said the Abbot, "there is and always has been a basic contradiction in the make-up of our organization. This stems from a contradiction in your Age Laws, Mr. Matlock. When you first propounded the idea, an Expectation of Life of ninety years or thereabouts seemed not unreasonable. But two things have happened. Firstly because of gross mishandling of the nation's economy after your departure, first by Brother Adeste here . . ."

The old man stirred in protest but Francis took a step forward and he relapsed into a vicious silence. The Abbot continued unperturbed. " . . . and then by his successor, Browning, the E.O.L. has dropped steadily year by year for many years until, as we all know, it has at last reached the Bible Barrier. At the same time medical science has not been standing still. There are drugs, techniques, which delay the ageing process considerably. But it seems rather pointless putting these at the disposal of those who are never going to be able to benefit from them."

"To those that have shall be given. From those who have not . . . " Matlock trailed away dully.

"Well done, Mr. Matlock. I see the Abbey is having a positive effect on you after all. Turn that monitor down, will you, Francis? I must have a word with Brother Duplex about those arm movements. You're right, Mr. Matlock. He's developing a style of his own. Well, to continue. The contradiction present in our set-up has always been that the old guard was being preserved with the connivance of the new, who looked forward to similar preservation when their time came. And there has through history never been any love lost between the old guard and the new.

"But this state of things would have continued quite happily, were places such as this merely hermitages where the worthy old could live out their last few years in peace."

"Places?" interjected Matlock. "Plural?"

"Oh yes. That's one of the results of the contradiction you see. We had to expand. But more of that in a moment. No, the real trouble was that because the E.O.L. in law got less and less while the E.O.L. in medical terms got more and more, our customers started arriving here with upwards of quarter of a century of life still before them. Look at Brother Adeste here. He should by the estimates of twenty or thirty years ago be at best a bed-ridden dotard, more likely a worm-eaten corpse. But he's still hale and hearty, apart from some interesting contusions round the throat. The outcome of these changes in circumstance was twofold. Firstly over-crowding. We started getting too many because the oldest weren't dying. And our customers began to grow discontented. These are men not used to anonymity, to sitting back without influence while others wield the reins of government."

He paused and pursed his lips as though in private amusement.

"And?" prompted Matlock, eager to

hear the rest now. Whatever the future held, he had decided, he must play his part, big or small, in full possession of all the facts.

"We solved the first problem by developing other centres on similar though less magnificent lines. Lindisfarne on Holy Island, Lanercost in Cumberland. Our neighbour Bolton. Of course this made the problem of keeping the secret more acute. Not that we feared anything from the *ultimate* if anything got out, but *local* authorities and newspapers might have been able to do a great deal of damage before the muzzle was applied. As it is we have come under a certain amount of suspicion, but never any direct accusation. Or at least none that was published.

"So far so good. But I had noticed in my dealing with the Prime Minister in recent years a growing uneasiness with the situation. While the thought of another thirty years of life appealed greatly to him, the prospect of passing it certainly in obscurity, probably in constant danger of discovery, and most unbearable of all, in the company of men who had been his unrespected superiors for most of his working life, did not appeal at all.

"Meanwhile back at the Abbey Brother Adeste and others began to fret at the bit. They have attempted to assume some kind of vicarious power with me as their plenipotentiary to the P.M., but Browning was having none of that. So more positive methods were sought. Power is a drug of strange potency, Mr. Matlock, as I am sure, you know."

"I have lost the taste for it Abbot," said Matlock.

"Nonsense. You are drinking in every word I say in the hope that you might be able to use it against me. Or someone. And so you may.

"Well now, at this point in time some two and a half years ago, just when I was beginning to feel the horns of my own personal dilemma pricking very hard — I mean how best to preserve myself in the developing clash between the Hooded Brethren and Browning — a strange and fortuitous event occurred. I was approached, subtly and indirectly, by a member of the Anti-Age-Law movement, your group if you remember, Mr. Matlock. It was the President of the Doncaster Poetry Appreciation Society as a matter of fact, up here allegedly to have a word with Brother Michelangelo, one of our genuinely religious brethren with some claims to being a minor Minor Poet. This man paid a courtesy call on me. I soon realized he was looking for an opportunity to sound me out on certain topics. I encouraged him, gave the kind of answer I saw he wanted, and soon I was being invited to join your conspiracy. A very naive kind of man really. I cannot but feel he deserved his fate, whatever it was.

"At first I was merely amused by the irony of the situation. But soon I began to see in it a kind of insurance against any possible move Browning might make against us. I told Browning I had been approached, of course. He probably knew already. Indeed he might have arranged it. Anyway, he advised me, as I hoped, to join."

Mixed with his revulsion, Matlock felt a strong sense of relief. This seemed to let Lizzie and Ernst off the hook.

"So it was you who betrayed us," he half whispered.

"Oh no. Not always. I had to give him a lot of information, of course. But I was only one of a thousand sources. As far as you're concerned, Mr. Matlock, I have been very tight-lipped. Any information about your activities came from other sources, probably those I have suggested to you already.

"No, I was very interested in making the Anti-A's a going concern. I found a considerable amount of enthusiasm, often positively militant, among the Unhooded Brothers. People like Brother Phillip for instance. He's a great fan of yours. Of course they don't know about Brother Adeste, and the others; I don't quite know how they'd take that. But they're tremendously useful as guards and patrols. And of course I have my own picked band of Brothers led by Francis here whose loyalty is to me and me alone. Mercenaries you might call them. But not ungodly men for all that, eh Francis?"

Francis smiled, his eyes still fixed on Carswell who sat still, but taut as a spring, in the great armchair.

"The Hooded Chapter, of course, were kept abreast of events. At least, as much as I thought it good for them to know."

Carswell moved then, squirming with hate.

"I never trusted you, Abbot."

"Indeed? Then I'm pleased I never voted for you or your party in my life.

"Well, recently things began to come to a head. I was influential in the movement, you understand, but not its leader. The Scots had been approached, not through me. I was much against it. I have reason to believe they are not very fond of me either."

"They're not," said Matlock, remembering.

"Curious folk, the Celts. You see, what I wanted was not a revolution, but the threat of one. I wanted a gun to point at Browning should he look troublesome. But the gun was now cocked and it had a hair trigger. Matters were out of my hands, the climax was fast approaching. So I looked at my cards, then volunteered to be the one to contact the charismatic Matthew Matlock. You'll be interested to know, Mr. Matlock, that not even the leaders of this motley gang of revolutionaries knew just how much or little you yourself knew. But you were our unifying factor, our rallying point. Under you, the Anti-A's could move as one in a way they couldn't under any other single individual.

"So I wanted you with me. I still couldn't see which way was best to go. But with you, I had a double chance."

"You mean, to use me as a figurehead, or to trade me in to Browning?"

"Exactly. But Browning moved too quickly for me. My intelligence service was limited. He squashed the plot and got you. Your value to me was less now, but still worth a risk — your risk — to get hold of. So Francis brought you out and here you are."

Matlock closed his eyes and was surprised to find he could almost have slept.

Oh Lizzie, Lizzie, he thought, I long for your arms to shelter me from these men who turn me, and turn me, and turn me again, till I face the way they want, but never know which way that is.

285

"Are you all right?" asked an anxious voice.

He opened his eyes. The Abbot now stood beside him, his face all benevolent anxiety. The oak panels glowed gently in the shifting light of the flames. All seemed well. Even the flickering whiteness of the monitor screen seemed safe, domestic. He shook his head.

"What now, Abbot?" he asked. "Why do you tell us all this? What has happened?"

"Yes, Abbot," came Carswell's voice. "I guess you've been with Browning these last few days. What have you been up to?"

The Abbot smiled and rested his fingertips together to form a Norman arch.

"True, Brother. I have been negotiating with him. And very amenable I have found him. He doesn't want trouble at this point in time. His position is precarious enough as it is, though he has made a great deal of political capital out of the uprising that never was. Of course he has not mentioned that its main purpose was to overthrow the Age Laws.

No, he has subtly insinuated that its main purpose was to steal the property of, and rape the wives and daughters of, every good citizen. Fortunately, Mr. Matlock, he still regards you as a person of some importance. In the hands of the Scots, say, you could still guarantee sufficient support in the North to make an invasion feasible. So I have promised to keep you safe and sound.

"I did have to make a couple of concessions, Brother Adeste. One of them involves you, I fear. He fears for your health up here in this bleak place. A man of your age needs what comforts the South and the metropolis can offer him. He has sent a special escort of men with a long history of medical training to accompany you on your journey."

Carswell stood up, slowly, as if his years had suddenly grown heavy on his shoulders.

"I will not go."

"You must."

"I will not. I will not. You bastard. You traitor!"

He turned and ran desperately to the door. Francis' waiting arms wrapped round him and he kicked for a moment, then hung like a rag doll.

"Are they here, Francis?"

"Outside, Abbot."

"Good. Give him to them."

Francis turned and opened the door, Carswell didn't struggle but turned his head as he was carried through and raised a limp arm towards Matlock.

"Matt," he said, and again, "Matt."

Matlock didn't move. In the lighted square of the door over Carswell's pathetic white hairs he saw two men, not robed but in suits, their dark-blue ties split down the middle by a thin silver line. One looked him straight in the face for a second, then the door closed behind Francis and they were gone.

"Abbot," he said.

"I'm sorry about that, Matt — I may call you Matt now, I think — but . . ."

"Abbot," he interrupted. "Those men. Browning's men. They saw me."

A shadow crossed the Abbot's face for a moment, but he then gave a smile.

"I take your point. They know you're

288

here. But not for long eh? We'll move you along in a very short while. It's all laid on. But first, and very important, we mustn't forget your imminent birthday."

"Abbot," said Matlock, "you don't know Browning as I do. You should do, but you don't. You can't. It won't be hours. It might be minutes. You must stop those men. You must . . . "

His protests died as the wall panel at which the Abbot had been fumbling moved away and out of the gap revealed there slid a shining silver machine.

It was a Heart Clock Adjuster.

"Just step over here please, Matt, and we'll put you on a few years. We have to keep you alive now, don't we?"

All Matlock's fears came rushing back.

"It can wait a few moments, Abbot, but those men can't. Get hold of them, for God's sake."

The Abbot hesitated.

"I fear you are exaggerating the dangers, Matt. Of course we don't want Browning to know your exact whereabouts. But by the time those men make a report, he'll know you could be anywhere. In any case they will not be allowed to leave without clearance from me."

"You bloody fool," screamed Matlock, his own fears suddenly, horribly, hardening to certainty. "Haven't you seen a wrist-radio? Don't you think Browning wouldn't be happy to take this place apart if he thought he could get everyone here at one fell swoop?"

"He wouldn't dare. We know too much. He wouldn't dare."

But the Abbot's voice was full of uncertainty and suddenly he moved purposefully across to his desk-phone. But before he could touch it, it gave off a high-pitched urgent scream which only stopped when he picked it up.

"Yes," he snapped, jabbing a button. The picture on the monitor leapt from the Church, where the acting-Abbot was saying the benediction, to the control room in the tower. A worried looking monk peered out towards them.

"Abbot," he said, "something's happening out by the gatehouse. We're trying to get in close-up . . ."

He dissolved before their eyes and the screen went blank. A split second later the floor rocked beneath their feet and a huge explosion blasted their ears.

"Dear God," said the Abbot, white-faced. "Dear God!"

The door burst open and Francis rushed in.

"The tower. They've blasted the tower."

"How, for God's sake?"

"How should I know? Rockets, I think."

He was shouldered aside by another monk.

"Abbot," he cried. "They're coming in. Helicopters full of men."

Suddenly he and Francis stiffened together like some ghastly double act, then toppled forward into the room. The Abbot stood stock still, but Matlock moved forward so quickly that he caught Francis' gun before the dead monk hit the ground and revealed the smoking hole between his shoulders.

Matlock threw himself out into the corridor his finger pressed hard on the trigger. The speed of the attack surprised the two men who stood outside. One of them went down to the first burst of shots, the other dropped flat and took aim, but there was no time for aim.

Matlock heard the Abbot come out beside him.

"They came back," he said. "Conscientious perhaps. Or glory-seekers. They came back to do it themselves."

"We'd better move," said the Abbot. "This is a bit of a dead end up here."

He made to move off down the corridor but Matlock's gun jammed in his belly.

"Don't forget that," he said. "I need it."

The Abbot went back into his study and picked up the Adjuster.

"You're right. Even if you didn't need it, it's worth a million of anything you name. Shall we go now?"

The lift door was open, the lift occupied. It was Carswell.

For a moment Matlock thought the old man was alive but the blank unseeing eyes told him the truth even before the frail corpse slid down the wall against which it had been propped and sprawled across the floor.

"They must have killed him in the lift, radioed their news to Browning's men, then come straight back up for us."

292

The Abbot did not reply but started to drag the body out into the corridor. The Adjuster impeded him and he could only use one hand.

"In the interests of speed, Brother," he said, "could you help me here?"

Overcoming his distaste, Matlock seized the old man by the shoulders and heaved him out. When he straightened up his hands were tacky with blood.

"No time for obsequies, I'm afraid," said the Abbot. "Down we go. Do keep that gun ready."

But there was no need for it below in the cold passageway, dim and shadowy by contrast with the brightness they had left. As yet it was deserted, though the sounds of war were all about — the crackle of guns, the shouting of men, now and then the loud explosion of something more than a hand-gun.

"Where are we heading?" asked Matlock.

The Abbot stood uncertain for a moment, then seemed to make up his mind.

"This way," he said and they set off at a jog down the passage which led to the Cloister Court.

The Abbot talked breathlessly as he ran.

"Browning won't stop till he's razed the Abbey. Now he's committed himself, he can't just go halfway. But he'll want proof we're dead first. Not just a pile of rubble we might or might not be under."

He stopped talking to gasp in great lungfuls of air.

Matlock shouted back, "How does that help us?"

The Abbot stopped and leaned up against the wall.

"It doesn't much. But at least it means they'll want everybody. There are one or two others he'll want to be sure are not wandering round the countryside."

"But his men will recognize people they know should have been dead years ago."

"So what? That's exactly his justification for this attack. The Age-Law evaders revealed. A plot against the country. There is one law for all, rich and poor. Can't you hear him? This will make him."

They were almost at the end of

the passage where it came out beside the Chapter House. The Abbot peered carefully out into the Cloister Square, now no longer dark but fitfully lit by flashes of light from the fighting which seemed to be centred in the adjacent Church. Overhead swung helicopters and their searchlight beams swept across the Square and up and down the whole complex of Abbey buildings. Even as they watched, the dazzling light poured down on to the close-mown grass and transfixed there three monks. They turned to run, one tripped over his robes and, falling, clutched at another. A gun chattered above them and they both lay still. The third disappeared into the protecting shadow of the cloister walk.

The light moved away.

"Come," said the Abbot.

They slid round out of the passage and into the Chapter House. Unhesitating, the Abbot moved among the marble pillars till he came to the tomb of John de Cancia. Matlock stood and watched, still trying to accustom his eyes to the new darkness.

"Help me," hissed the Abbot. He was

fiddling at one corner of the marble slab, and now he began to pull.

Matlock knelt beside him and added his weight, still ignorant of what they were doing. Slowly at first, then smoothly and easily; the marble moved, and Matlock found himself peering into a dark uninviting hole.

"Ah," said the Abbot with satisfaction. "There we are. These places were often fitted with tunnels for various purposes. This one is very old and runs to How Hill, a mile to the south. I merely had it extended to open up here. Who wants to enter the tomb, after all?"

"Ingenious," said Matlock. "Shall we go?"

There was a sound behind him. He spun round, gun at the ready, but hesitated when he saw the figure who had so stealthily approached was a monk.

"Thank God I've found you, Abbot," gasped the man. He moved forward so that his face was visible. It was the Abbot.

"Ah, Brother Duplex," murmured the real Abbot. "How clever of you to know about this. You made more use of our rehearsals than I thought. What's happening out there?"

"They're massacring us. We're out-numbered both in men and firepower. Brother Phillip's organized what defence he can, but it can't last long. We must hurry."

"Indeed we must," said the Abbot. "Brother, I see you are well armed. I have nothing, let me have a gun."

He reached out his hand. Matlock saw that he was right. Duplex must have paused long enough at some arms cache to grab a couple of hand-guns and a belt of grenades. The monk now thrust one of the guns into the Abbot's hand and turned to the tomb.

The Abbot spoke.

"When doppel-gängers meet, one must die," he said, and shot Duplex twice in the back.

"Now Brother Matt," he said turning, "look not so disapproving. It suits me very well to have my body found by Browning's soldiers. And two's company they say. Come."

He stooped to pick up the Adjuster. Over his bent back, Matlock saw Duplex half turn on his left elbow, his right hand plucking at his grenade belt. Matlock brought his gun up, but the Abbot rose at that moment blocking his aim. He thrust him aside and fired, but the lost second had been crucial. From Duplex's nerveless fingers rolled a primed grenade. A whole pack of wild thoughts ran madly through Matlock's mind. Lizzie, Colin, Ernst, Edna, Carswell, his parents, all rose before him and reached to him and tried to talk to him. But like Ulysses in the underworld, he knew these phantoms needed blood before they could speak. And in his mind he stood and wept silently, futilely before their dreadful pleas.

But his body moved independently. Two strides forward, the grenade scooped up, arm thrown back and the metal egg hurled into the one place which offered them any escape from its blast.

The tomb.

He lay on the ground till the ground stayed still and the stones stopped falling about him. Then he rose.

"Abbot," he whispered, his eyes still dazzled by the flash, "are you all right?"

But the Abbot was up already and peering down into the tunnel.

"You bloody fool! It's blocked. We can't get through. You stupid . . ."

His voice trailed away as he saw Matlock's face.

"Yes of course. There was nothing else to do. Of course. Well, lead on. It's up to you now. Your quick thinking saved our lives. Let's see if your quick thinking can save us from the results of your quick thinking."

"What about the river?"

"The river? Yes, the river perhaps. Perhaps."

Matlock hit the Abbot in the face with the flat of his hand.

"Wake up, Abbot. Despair is the sin against the Holy Ghost, isn't it? How do we get to the river without going outside?"

The Abbot stood in silence for a while. Whether in thought or in shock, Matlock didn't know. But finally he said, "The Cellarium. That is built over the river. We can get at it through the Cellarium."

Outside in the Court they could still

hear the sound of the battle raging in the Church. But they crossed without incident and cautiously entered the long, cool vaults of the Cellarium. In there it was absolutely quiet and even the sounds of fighting outside seemed distant and disconnected.

Matlock was now leading, the Abbot close behind. He had discarded his gun and was clutching the Adjuster with both hands, whether for reassurance or because his strength was failing, Matlock didn't know. But he knew he was worried about the Abbot whose will seemed to have suddenly bent, if not broken, under the strain. Matlock wondered again how old he was, who he was, or rather, had been to be given this job.

Perhaps it was these thoughts which distracted him. Certainly he thought later, he should have been aware a couple of steps earlier that they were not alone in the cellar. Even then, he was so keyed up to action that as the two darker patches detached themselves from the wall ahead he was moving sideways.

The beam of light caught his face, he shot at it and heard a hoarse cry. Then

300

something struck the wall about three inches from his head, a sliver of fine stone raced across his brow and he fell.

It felt like hours, but his unconsciousness must have lasted only a couple of seconds. When his eyes opened again, it was to see a strange nightmarish tableau. In the middle of the great stone floor, bathed in torch light, knelt the Abbot. Approaching him with gun in one hand and torch in the other was a young soldier, a boy of about twenty. Matlock could see the pallor of his face in the light reflected back from the silvery metal face of the Adjuster which the Abbot still clutched to his chest.

The Abbot's face was working as though something lived under the skin. His lips moved, but no words came. Matlock began to feel around carefully for his fallen gun. The boy was standing right over the Abbot now, his face taut with fear — or disgust.

Suddenly the Abbot thrust the Adjuster up at him.

"Take it! Take it!" he screamed. "You can live for ever. For ever. Take it!"

Whether the boy thought the machine

301

was a weapon, or whether he knew what it was and acted in hysterical disgust, Matlock didn't know. But he jerked back a step, then began to pump bullets through the machine into the Abbot's body.

The Abbot remained kneeling for a long time. He hissed through his pale lips. "Life, life," a couple of times, the Adjuster fell apart in his hands, then he collapsed forward.

Matlock rolled over and tried to push himself up. His hand touched the still hot barrel of his gun. Clumsily, noisily, he shifted his grip to the butt. He needn't have worried — the boy stood stock still over the Abbot's body and heard nothing. He didn't even move when Matlock, his head still dizzy with pain, missed with his first shot.

His second tore the boy's chest open, and the third removed the terrified face.

Staggering to his feet, Matlock made his way over to the Abbot and turned his body over. Amazingly he was not yet dead. Words bubbled redly from his lips.

" . . . too young to bribe with age,

Matt . . . too young."

Then he was dead.

Matlock spared a few moments to look at the shattered Adjuster. It was obviously beyond repair. It was five days to his birthday.

He ran his hand over his forehead in perplexity and found it thick with blood. He must have looked very dead.

Bending over the soldier he went swiftly through his small pack till he came across the field dressing he was looking for. He had no time for refinement but drew a smear of antiseptic cream across his brow and wrapped a bandage round twice.

All the while his mind raced on.

Was it worth it? Even if he escaped it meant only a few days of uncomfortable, frightened, waiting freedom. Wouldn't it be better to go out now with a gun and die fighting the enemy.

What would that do? Kill a few boys like this?

He looked at the faceless youth at his feet.

Better surely to look for someone worthy of death. Perhaps in four days

303

he could find Browning. Perhaps in five days . . .

Perhaps I'd just rather die in five days than five minutes, he told himself and the admission made him feel almost light-hearted.

He turned and headed back up the Cellarium. The river was still his best bet, he felt, but without the Abbot's guidance, he decided it would be easier to get out of the Abbey buildings altogether and take his chance in the open.

His first thought was to make his way out of the door through which he had entered the Abbey buildings earlier that night. The thought went through his mind that if he had stopped quietly in bed, Browning's men could not have been certain he was in the Abbey that night and the attack might not have taken place.

But he found that a small profitable side-effect of his sense of being a pawn in someone else's game was a dilution of self-reproach, and the thought was pushed completely from his mind when he reached the outer door and peered through.

The Strangers' House was a roaring inferno around which the black outlines of men scuttled like insects on a burning log. The greensward between the House and the Abbey was as bright as day, if daylight could properly be likened to this red and white fury.

Exit from this door was impossible. Matlock felt the beginnings of despair and suddenly four days seemed a lifetime to lose. He began to make his way back, looking for refuge in the dark shadows of the great building. But now a new and stranger horror began to pursue him. For the darkness around him suddenly brightened, began to redden, to tremble, to dissolve as though it was being burnt away.

He spun round. The great wall behind him seemed to be full of a terrible flame and his mind began to spiral to some safe insanity of terror as he watched. Brighter and brighter it grew. Then as he turned to run, the truth flashed on him, still stimulus to terror but not to madness.

A glance back confirmed his guess. The flame was the glow of the raging bonfire which had been the Strangers'

305

House. He was seeing it through the wall, more clearly each second.

The wall was made of poro-glass and someone had operated the transparency control. And even as he ran, the implications of what he had seen leapt eagerly into his mind.

The whole reconstruction of the Abbey must have been done in poro-glass, a type so refined that it was possible to create the exact colour of old stone in it. He was trying to escape like a rat running through a glass maze.

As he ran, the walls about and behind him misted greyly then cleared to perfect transparency. Searchlights, flames, even the thin sliver of moon which had edged into the crowded sky, all shone through the clearing roof and walls as though aiming their beams at him. He tried desperately to recollect from those childhood memories of the Abbey ruins which walls had been intact, which walls he could hide behind without fearing that they would turn into a sheet of glass.

For the moment he seemed to have outdistanced the transformation process. He thanked heaven it was based on a slow chain reaction and was therefore gradual not instantaneous. He had lost his bearings in his panic and now he stopped to find out where he was. A little thought told him he was back in the Cloister Passage. Up ahead must be the Infirmary, but that he was certain was part of the reconstruction and must be avoided. He leaned back against the wall and tried to calm his turbulent thoughts.

Without warning he was bathed in hard white light. Turning he saw that the wall on which he was leaning had become transparent, but the other side must have been in utter darkness and he had no warning. Now there was a little group of soldiers there with two or three high-radiancy torches. They stood and stared at him through the wall for a moment, then one of them came so close that his nose touched the glass and for a second he looked like a small boy with his face pressed against a sweetshop window.

Matlock saw a look of excitement cross his face, then he turned to the others and his mouth opened and shut in silent agitation. The others all came forward then and peered closely at him.

Matlock knew he had been recognized. It was eerie to stand there and see these men within a yard of him, silently plotting his death. One of them brought his gun up and pointed it at the wall, but another said something sharply and the gun was lowered.

Matlock smiled. With hand weapons they were more likely to damage themselves than him by firing pointblank at a three foot-thick poro-glass wall.

He began to walk slowly, almost casually along the corridor in the direction of the Infirmary. The soldiers kept pace with him, one of them speaking excitedly into a wrist-radio.

The wall to his right was still a wall. Real or poro-glass he did not know, but at the moment it was beautifully opaque.

He prayed silently that there would be a door in it. At the end of the passage would be the Infirmary which must by now be as bright as day.

When the door appeared, he almost believed in God. Then he entered and found himself in a small windowless store-room with no other exit, and his new-formed faith crumbled.

He glanced around looking hopelessly for something that might help him. The room seemed to be some kind of medical store-room and it was full of crates and bottles. Leaning against the far wall was a row of gas cylinders. There seemed to be two types. Matlock was not expert enough to decipher the markings on them but one of them he was certain must be oxygen. And the other . . .

Swiftly he moved along the row, turning each tap full on. Then he bent and picked up a bottle he had noticed by the door. Phosphorus. Memories of chemistry lessons in the old smelly laboratory at school more than half a century before came back to him.

He eased the stopper half out and turned the bottle on its side. The liquid in it began to ebb out. Carefully he propped it up against the wall so that its mouth pointed to the floor at an angle of forty-five degrees.

Then he stepped back into the corridor and pulled the door shut behind him.

Looks of relief appeared on the faces of the men opposite. They too must have been praying that there was no other exit.

"A simple example of the democratic nature of prayer," said Matlock to the unhearing men, and moved slowly away along the passage. After fifteen paces he stopped. This ought to be safe enough. He sat down and made himself as small as possible. Back in the store-room he imagined the gas hissing out of the cylinders and the insulating liquid dripping out of the phosphorus bottle. And he wondered how long it would be before the other soldiers got round to him. He was surprised that they had taken so long. He could only surmise that Brother Phillip was keeping them occupied with a hard rearguard action.

Distantly he heard the sound of trotting feet. Booted feet.

He didn't bother to get up but glanced back the way he'd come. Within seconds he saw them, four soldiers and an officer moving towards him at the double, guns ready. He wondered dismally whether they had been told to capture him or kill him on sight.

Then as they passed the store-room door, there was a small bang, followed immediately by a vast explosion. The door was hurled from its hinges squashing two of the soldiers flat against the poroglass. A great tongue of flame licked out into the corridor bearing with it chunks of store-room wall. Protected though they were, the men opposite flung their arms before their faces in horror and fear.

Matlock rose slowly and without looking at them moved carefully back through the smoke to what had been the storeroom. One of the soldiers was still moving. He shot him as an act of mercy and taking a deep breath, he plunged into the smoke and reek of the room, stepped through a wall of flame, thought for one horrified moment that the wall had not been breached, then felt the cool night air on his face.

A minute later he was being carried by the river underneath the Infirmary and out into the inviting darkness beyond.

Looking back later, he realized what risks he took then. But somehow the river had been identified with safety and escape, and once in it, a trance-like confidence came over him. He made no effort at concealment when he clambered out, but strode openly across the grass, even pausing to look back at the red glow which was all he could see now of the Abbey. He supposed that similar scenes must have taken place at the other centres mentioned by the Abbot.

Browning's dissolution of the monasteries, he thought almost jauntily as he struck across country.

An hour later he was wandering through the outer streets of Ripon. It seemed as if his luck was going to hold.

Then minutes later he was sucked into the cavernous depths of a Curfew Wagon.

10

THE first torture wasn't too bad. Indeed as he swam back to the surface of consciousness, he realized that it was his own refinement of fear, plus the physical debility resulting from the night's activities, which had caused him to faint rather than any real intensity of pain. The pain had been administered quickly, almost casually. It was obviously routine. You got it no matter what your story was. They hadn't even asked to see his papers to check the incoherent, jerkily-told tale he had offered them to explain his presence on the streets. A sick daughter — a telephone call — action without thought. It sounded weak enough to start with, and he hadn't been able to project much sincerity into his voice.

But the curious thing was that they were ready to believe him. He could feel it as the young sergeant leaned down over him and slipped those terrible

metal bands from around his wrists.
Their nights, he realized, must be full
of people like him, curfew-breakers with
good reason, or at least real reason,
sad reason, even tragic reason. And
they would all stammer and tremble
when caught, all sound guilty of every
treasonable crime in the law books.

"Right, Dad," said the Sergeant. "Just
give us the story again."

He gave it again, as best he could
remember it.

"Right," nodded the policeman.
"Papers."

He held out a confident hand. Matlock,
feeling very hammy, started to go through
his pockets.

"I'm sorry," he stammered, "I was in
a hurry. I've put on the wrong jacket."

"Not even your cardio-card?"

"No, I'm afraid not. I'm sorry."

Even now the Sergeant was still happy
to believe him. At least that's how he
interpreted the mock severity of the
man's gaze.

"You oldies are all the same. What's
the matter with you, getting age-happy?"

Age-happiness. The state of being too

near your final birthday to care what you did, who you offended. Matlock stared up at the young man's face. Square-jawed. Broad nosed. Archaic military moustache. Not much imagination there. Might make another rank, but certainly no further.

He tried to look like a frightened, fuzzy-witted old man near his death.

It wasn't difficult.

Shaking his head, the Sergeant lifted a 'phone from the wall.

"Inspector," he said. "There's an old guy down here. On his way to see a sick daughter. Forgot his papers."

Then a period of listening.

"Yes. I reckon he's OK. Address? Hang on."

He hissed down at Matlock. "The address?"

"Address?" said Matlock, puzzled.

"You daughter's. Where are you going? Come on!"

Matlock's mind did a leap.

"The Hospital. Ripon General."

He hoped such a place existed. He prayed it did. After another period of listening, the 'phone went down.

"You're lucky," said the Sergeant, "the Inspector feels kind. We pass the Hospital this sweep. We'll drop you off. Smoke?"

Matlock didn't. Never had. But now he felt the urgent need for something to calm his nerves. He took a cigarette. Within seconds the nerve-caressing smoke had damped down his fears and he began to look around.

A mobile dungeon. That's what these things were. There was no hope of escape if you needed to escape, and just being there meant you needed to escape. Unless you were very lucky.

Superstitiously he diverted his mind from his own lucky break. Leaning back against the bulkhead, he felt a slight tremor which told him the wagon's powerhouse lay behind him. Not that that told him anything much. He knew that the engines lay dead in the centre of these machines, insulated from assault by compartments such as the one he sat in now. Not that anyone had ever tried to assault a Curfew Wagon.

The Sergeant was seated at a small metal table bracketed to the wall. He was filling in some kind of form with

316

practised ease. On the wall to his right hung the 'phone. To his left was the only other object which relieved the uncompromizing metallic squareness of the compartment. This was the simple control panel for the electric manacles which now dangled casually above his head.

There were, of course, stories of the interiors of wagons which made medieval torture chambers seem very dull unimaginative places and which peopled them with psychopathic manipulators of human flesh.

The truth was even more frightening, Matlock decided. Conscientious men, unaware of any need to examine what they were doing, and with the power to apply the exact level of pain desired to any part of the body.

The Sergeant caught his eye and smiled.

"Won't be long, Dad," he said.

The 'phone buzzed. He picked it up, listened, said, "Right," then replaced the receiver.

"Come on," he said to Matlock, "we're nearly there."

"This is very kind of you," said Matlock with incongruous but real gratitude.

The Sergeant looked gratified.

"Think nothing of it. We're here to help, one way or another. Up you go."

He helped Matlock up the little aluminium ladder he had pulled down from the roof and which led to what seemed the only exit from the room.

"Hurry it up," shouted the Sergeant below, prodding him unceremoniously in the behind.

"Which way?" asked Matlock when they were both upright in the corridor.

"Along there," pointed the Sergeant.

Matlock, his heart beating fast in the anticipation of getting out of the wagon, moved smartly along. The end of the corridor seemed blank, but the Sergeant reached over his shoulder and by some sleight of hand conjured up a door into a well-lit room.

There were four men in the room which was obviously the eyes and ears of the machine. Two of the men were watching a bank of television monitors which gave 180 degrees visibility round the wagon. A third was obviously in charge of the radio equipment which was fixed to the wall in front of him.

The fourth, standing with his hands behind his back which was towards Matlock, had an air of authority even from behind which told Matlock as clearly as his lack of uniform that he was in charge.

This was immediately confirmed by the Sergeant.

"I've brought the old fellow, the one for the hospital, Inspector."

"Right," said the Inspector without turning.

A door slid open in the wall opposite Matlock. This led into a protective bulkhead. Beyond, another door opened and Matlock found himself looking out into the night. A draught of cool air rustled in, refreshing, invigorating.

"Go on," prompted the Sergeant.

It was only half a dozen paces across the room. Another two would have taken him outside, but some built-in, deeply conditioned politeness made him pause a second, turn and say to the room in general, "Thank you. Good-night."

The Inspector glanced round. Casually.

Then with growing disbelief.

He took a step towards Matlock, his face still full of doubt. But even before the doubt disappeared, his hand was full of gun.

"It can't be. No. I don't believe it. But it is! It is, isn't it? Matlock. Matthew Matlock. Step back inside do! You may not remember me, though I haven't changed as much as you!"

Matlock remembered now too well. Manchester. This was the man who had been in control the night Percy died.

At his back he still felt the cool night air, but even as his memories of the man flooded back, he heard the doors slide shut behind. Over the Inspector's shoulder he could see the Sergeant's face, bewildered, worried, angry.

"Sergeant," said the Inspector.

"Sir!" snapped the Sergeant.

"This poor old man you're so eager to help is none other than Matthew Matlock, one time politician, cabinet minister, Deputy Prime Minister, now rebel, terrorist, wanted on any number of charges. Don't you recognize him?"

"I do now, sir," said the Sergeant

with nervous reasonableness. "But you must admit he doesn't look much like his pictures, sir. He looks . . . older. Doesn't he, sir?"

"Older? Perhaps. But we'll talk more about your lapse later. I suggest meanwhile you take Mr. Matlock back below."

The Sergeant, his face a blank of subordination, moved smartly across to Matlock who looked with some unease on the savage eyes which burnt through the mask. His arm was seized violently and he found himself being dragged bodily across the room. In some far corner of his mind he heard the Inspector instructing the radio operator to contact his Headquarters and give them the news. Then he was out in the corridor, being bounced from wall to metal wall. The Sergeant never uttered a word but used the rock-hard edge of his hand with controlled viciousness. When they reached the trap which led back down into the 'dungeon', Matlock attempted to drop cleanly through it, realizing his particular vulnerability here, but one boot came down on his hand and crushed it against the floor while the other swung at his unprotected face. He ducked as best he could but felt a gaping wound flower on his forehead as the boot crashed home. Then the pressure on his hand was released and he fell backwards.

He didn't become unconscious, but was only distantly aware for the next few minutes of what was going on. There was a hubbub of voices, he was lifted up and sat down, and when he finally managed to re-focus his eyes and his mind, he found that the Inspector was leaning over him bandaging his head, which was nice.

Then he tried to move his hands and discovered that he was once again wearing the electric manacles. Which wasn't nice at all.

The Sergeant was standing stiffly, resentfully, to attention. It was a small comfort to realize he was being reprimanded.

"It is our business to act within the law," the Inspector was saying severely, "and though there may be times when sheer brute force is the only kind of force available or suitable, this can never be the case in an establishment like this.

322

We have absolute electronic control over the amount of persuasion we administer. It is measured and recorded. Should accusations of maltreatment and abuse of power be brought against you, those measurements and recordings are your defence. You know the precise limits of your authority. But who can measure a kick in the face? You might have killed him. Just weigh the consequences to yourself of *that* for a moment."

It was nice to know that there were precise limits to the amount of pain these men could administer, but Matlock reckoned they would be far beyond his tolerance if his earlier experience was anything to go by. He kept his eyes nearly closed in an effort to postpone the interrogation he knew must follow, but he soon became aware with sinking feeling that the Inspector, the bandaging now finished, was carrying on with his preparations quickly and efficiently. He realized now that the Sergeant's brief application of shock earlier had indeed been casual, routine. Then he had only worn the manacles. Now there was a variety of wires and tubes being attached to his body. At first he thought they were merely refinements of the actual pain-inflicting apparatus, but as his mind cleared, he realized that their function was less directly unpleasant but at the same time more sinister. This was recording apparatus. The Inspector would be able to keep a close check on his pulse, breathing, temperature, degree of consciousness, etc. while questioning him. Through the fringe of his nearly closed eyes he saw the man move back to the control panel and throw a switch.

"Well now," said the Inspector, "I see that you are, or at least ought to be, fully awake."

Matlock didn't move. The Inspector did, and a split second of fearful pain coursed round his body.

"There you are. Try not to drop off again. Right, Sergeant. I think we can begin."

The Sergeant produced a small radio-microphone which he attached to the wall apparently magnetically. He switched it on.

The Inspector spoke.

"Zero one-thirty hours. Thursday 13th

September. Interrogation of Matthew Matlock by 0576621 Inspector Ross P.K."

The Sergeant spoke.

"Witnessed and recorded by 3789552 Sergeant Hamer P."

"Now Mr. Matlock," said the Inspector. "Let me sketch out to you briefly the information I wish to obtain from you before we reach Headquarters. Firstly, with regard to your escape tonight from Fountains Abbey, it seems unlikely that you could have done this unassisted. I want to know first of all which members of the attacking force aided you. Secondly, I want to know where you were going when we picked you up."

Matlock opened his mouth, but the Inspector raised his hand.

"No, don't speak yet. We'll take your first answer as spoken. People always lie the first time. Let's just say we don't believe you."

He moved his hand.

The pain this time lasted several seconds and left Matlock feeling as though his nerve-ends had been rubbed raw.

"Now I'll ask you again. Who helped

325

you to escape? Where were you going?"

Matlock opened his mouth again, but before he could speak, the pain returned, longer lasting, more violent, and the words turned into a high, drawn-out shriek.

"That was just in case you were thinking of lying again. Now the truth, please."

"No one. Nowhere," rasped Matlock from a dry, rough throat.

"Really? That is helpful. You should perhaps realize Mr. Matlock that I can take you to the edge of unconsciousness and keep you there for some minutes without actually pushing you over. That's the beauty of these things."

He caressed the control panel affectionately.

"Why not truth drugs?" muttered Matlock.

"Those will come, never fear. But in laboratory conditions. For all I know, you are pumped full of one of the many neutralizing drugs which have been developed. For rapid accurate results, nothing can beat this. Now I don't like your answer, I'm afraid."

Again pain, taking him to the brink of a deep dark pit into which he tried desperately to fall, but always he was pulled back, always he swayed on the edge.

"No one. Nowhere. Truth," he muttered again.

Then he was back by the pit, screaming to be plunged into the oblivion which swirled vaporously below.

His mind now wanted to say something, anything, which would satisfy the Inspector, but he could think of nothing, he was incapable of imagining, of inventing. Some very remote, still controlled part of his mind noted the effectiveness of the torture, but it was light-years away. Then like a headlight in the fog it came slowly, imperceptibly closer and closer till suddenly it rushed on him with unstoppable impetuosity and he opened his eyes to a world beautifully free from pain, but still hideous with its memory and its threat.

The respite had been caused by an interruption. Clambering down through the trap was a constable. In his hand was a message form.

327

He saluted.

"Radio from H.Q. Sir."

"Read it," said the Inspector.

"It's coded, Sir."

The Inspector motioned to the Sergeant who took the paper. The constable saluted again and climbed out.

The Sergeant stood hesitating for a moment.

"Do you want me to . . ." he began.

"You're studying for your promotion exams, aren't you?" said the Inspector with the slightest hint of a sneer.

Without replying or saluting the Sergeant left.

The Inspector spoke into the mike.

"Interrogation pause. Zero One-Forty-Seven Hours." He switched off and said conversationally to Matlock.

"We've got to have a witness."

Seventeen minutes, thought Matlock. At this rate the few days that remain to me can seem longer than the previous seventy years.

The Inspector was quietly smoking a cigarette and making a note of some figures on the control panel.

"You're a pretty fit fellow, Mr. Matlock.

I can understand how you feel about the Age Limit. But you couldn't really hope to do anything about it, could you, now?"

He sounded almost reproachful.

The trapdoor opened and the Sergeant's well-set figure filled the square. He came slowly down and stood at attention. Matlock even through his weakness felt he detected a kind of triumph in the way the man stood, though his face was the old subordinate blank.

"Message decoded, sir," he intoned expressionlessly.

"Not bad, Sergeant," smiled the Inspector. "Read it please."

The Sergeant held the paper up before him, but Matlock got the impression he did not need it. His eyes seemed to be focused on the Inspector.

"From Commissioner One," he began. The Inspector became absolutely still. This was not the message-source he had expected, Matlock guessed. Commissioner One was the man responsible directly to the Prime Minister for the police force of the country.

The Sergeant went on in the monotonous

voice usually reserved for the giving of evidence in court.

"Your message acknowledged. Bring prisoner quickest repeat quickest to local H.Q. Do not stop for any reason whatever repeat do not stop for any reason whatever. Pick up no one repeat pick up no one. Do not commence interrogation of prisoner. Ensure that all further messages concerning prisoner are encoded repeat encoded. Message ends."

There was a silence.

"Sergeant," said the Inspector softly, "didn't the operator encode my first message."

"No, sir."

"Despite my instructions?"

This was an invitation, Matlock decided, an invitation to cover up. But he saw the Sergeant was in no mood to conspire.

"You gave no instructions, sir. I checked. There were three constables present. Shall I file the interrogation tape, sir?"

The Inspector pulled himself together and managed an ironic smile.

"Yes, you better had, Sergeant. At the

same time ensure the time of receipt of this message is clearly recorded, send off an acknowledgement, and pass the instructions about not stopping or arresting to the control room. No, on second thoughts I can do that more quickly from here. You might be delayed."

There was an unmistakable stress on the 'you', but the Sergeant showed no reaction and busied himself removing the radio-microphone, while the Inspector moved over to the telephone.

Matlock's relief at realising he was temporarily free from the threat of further torture brought him new strength. His mind began to regain its old agility and he had watched the Inspector closely, realizing that despite his effort at unconcern here was a sadly worried man. More interesting to Matlock than the Inspector's personal worries, however, was the background to the message.

Obviously the news of his arrest had been channelled right up to the top, to Browning himself most likely. Hence the reply from Commissioner One. He felt mildly flattered, but more interesting still was Browning's desire to save interrogation till he personally could deal with it. Matlock smiled. There were things about the setting up of the Abbey which the Prime Minister would not want blurted out by a tortured and obviously truth-telling man.

But most interesting of all was the reprimand for not encoding the message about his capture. The implication was that they were worried about possible interception of messages. But by whom? And to what effect? Rescue must be out of the question. Even if there was anybody desirous of rescuing him and capable of arranging action in the twenty minutes or so since the message was sent, he was now imprisoned in the strongest most impregnable vehicle ever known to man, on his way to what he suspected was going to be even closer confinement.

He surfaced from his discomforting thoughts to hear the Inspector speaking rapidly and authoritatively into the 'phone. He was giving instructions for the utmost speed.

"Also," he added, "stop for nothing.

If you can't go through it, go round it. And no further arrests, not even on the move. Understood?"

Even as he spoke, a small panel in the wall above his head flashed red and white.

"I said no arrests!" he screamed angrily.

Matlock surmised that someone had been spotted and swept up automatically (as he had been) just as the order was being given. The Inspector's next words seemed to confirm this.

"All right. No. We might as well keep him now we've got him. Put him down. But no more! Understood? Right."

He replaced the 'phone and turned to Matlock.

"A little respite for you, Mr. Matlock. I'm glad in a way. I was beginning to believe that you had nothing to tell me and nothing isn't really an end to justify these means. How are your friends?"

"Friends?"

"The ones I met in Manchester. The night the old man was killed. You were wrong about that, by the way. Nothing to do with us. Our orders came from

333

the Chief Constable and he was hardly likely to arrange to murder one of his fellow-conspirators, was he?"

"No. I don't know. I forget about . . . him. My friends? I don't know. I don't know where they are. I don't know. I don't."

Amazed at himself, Matlock felt a couple of large tears swell at his eyes and begin to course down his cheeks. He tried to brush them away, but his hands were held by the manacles.

"Could I . . . ?" he asked, looking down.

"Of course," said the Inspector and moved over and unfastened them, at the same time removing the wires taped to Matlock's body.

But he hadn't finished this when there was an interruption. The trap opened and a pair of legs appeared, not uniformed legs, but short massive limbs straining to the limits the worn yellow trousers which clothed them.

"What the hell's this?" snapped the Inspector.

A constable's face peered through what little remained of the gap and he said

334

anxiously, "It's the prisoner, sir. You said to put him down."

"Not down here, for God's sake!" said the Inspector violently. But it was too late. The man let go of the ladder and dropped to the floor, landing with a heavy crash but not even bending his knees.

Even without the curfew he looked villainous enough to be arrested on sight. Above the yellow trousers was a voluminous and evil looking green donkey-jacket. Above this, a vast head, its features squashed between a narrow deeply corrugated brow and a blue triple-cleft chin. The figure only stood about five feet high, but in terms of sheer volume, it was the largest in the room. The accompanying constable had dropped down after him and stood with gun drawn. But the arrested man was by far the most menacing figure present.

Matlock recognized him at once as Ossian.

"Get rid of this thing, Sergeant," cried the Inspector. "Lock him up somewhere. We'll interrogate later. God, this used to be an efficient unit."

335

The Sergeant moved forward to Ossian who had been slowly looking round the room. His gaze had rested lightly on Matlock for a second, then moved on. The Sergeant put his hand on his shoulder and said, "Right. You, up!"

Ossian nodded and slowly began to climb the exit ladder. The constable came close behind. As he reached the trap, Ossian jerked back one of his legs and backheeled the man beneath the chin. His neck snapped audibly and he was thrown back into the dungeon with great force. Then Ossian shook a small metal object from one of his voluminous sleeves, dropped it into the room, pulled himself up and closed the trap.

The constable lay where he had fallen, his head strangely askew, the Sergeant leapt up the ladder, the Inspector rushed across to the 'phone. Matlock saw them both stiffen almost simultaneously, the Sergeant's hand stopped almost a foot from the rung he was grasping at, the Inspector's three times that distance from the 'phone. Then both dropped, and Matlock almost had time to think, "nerve gas!" before he fell forward, oblivious to the pain as the tape holding the remaining wires ripped away from his skin.

But his subconscious raced on filling his sleeping head with visions of Ossian like some monstrous troll running across the world, himself over his shoulder, and all men falling dead before them.

When he awoke he thought it must have been true for he was looking down at the surface of the earth from a great height. It seemed to be revolving very quickly beneath him and he could not understand why he was not falling. Then it seemed that he was and he closed his eyes in terror waiting for the impact.

When he opened them again, he knew instantly that he was lying on the floor of a helicopter with his face pressed to the observation panel. Looking up he saw Ossian, his ugly face expressionless if you discounted what seemed its perpetual look of brutal malignancy, a pink plastic respirator thrust up over his beetle-brow like a pixie's hat.

Beside him at the 'copter's controls was another vaguely familiar figure. Attracted by Matlock's movement he glanced down and the moonlight which was so clearly etching out the landscape below picked out his features in patches of shadow and brightness.

It was the man with the hole in his head.

Matlock felt he ought to say something. Perhaps ask how he got there. It could have been no mean feat for one man, even armed with nerve-gas grenades, to take over a Curfew Wagon, rescue an unconscious man and get him into a helicopter.

But he didn't really feel interested, and only slightly grateful. He was more amused that Ossian who could have no personal love for him, indeed must bear a strong grudge against him, should have had to take such risks on his behalf.

He did wonder, however, why they were flying so low. The ground now did not look more than about fifty feet below. And they were crossing pretty hilly terrain. He shivered as he looked out of a side port and saw they were flying lower than the peaks of some of the hills.

Ossian touched the pilot's arm and pointed; Matlock automatically followed his finger, looking straight into the moon which was halfway down the sky. He saw nothing at first, then thought he picked out a sudden gleam, then unmistakably saw a dark shape flash across the gleaming saucer.

"Are they looking for us?" he asked.

Ossian ignored him but the man with the hole in his head answered in his precise Scots tones.

"That's right. If they find us, we've had it. But don't worry. Down here there's little enough chance of that. They're too fast, too high."

"Then we're safe?" said Matlock seeking the repetition of reassurance.

"Oh, no," said the man. "They've got helicopters too. And they'll be waiting at the Wall."

"The Wall?" enquired Matlock stupidly.

"Don't say you've forgotten the Wall, Mr. Matlock? It was restored at your instructions. After standing for centuries as a monument to the ruthless persecution and the unquenchable spirit of a great race, you resurrected it from history and gave it its old role again. Aye, Hadrian's wall. Pushed a bit further north in places, but the same thing. Matlock's wall some of the lowlanders still call it."

"What about it?"

"Well, we have to cross it. They'll have been alerted, the guardians I mean, and it's well fortified as you may know. We'll have to go up to get over it safely, and up there there's lots of the Few waiting to blow us out of the sky. If we keep too low, they'll drop us from the Wall, or get us with their 'copters."

"Thanks," said Matlock.

"You're welcome."

In fact the Wall was easy. The great metal-plastic structure, sixty feet high throughout its length, prefabricated in a month and dropped into place section by section in less than a week, looked sinister enough as it snaked away to east and west following the roll and turn of the hills, but only one gun started up as they leap-frogged over at a height of several hundred feet, and that was well out of range and soon stilled.

Matlock relaxed, but soon tensed up again when he saw no signs of similar relaxation in his two companions.

"What's the matter," he asked finally.

"The Wall's past. We must be in Scottish air space now. What's the trouble?"

"You don't imagine the sovereignty of Scotland bothers the English Air Force, do you?" sneered the pilot.

"The reverse is certainly true," rejoined Matlock.

"And lucky for you it is, Mr. Matlock. No, the Wall itself was little enough obstacle as long as a chancy shot doesn't take you. But if I was in charge of this operation, I'd send my 'copters fifty miles or so over the Wall into Scotland, wait till my observers on the Wall had spotted us, then give the ambushers our crossing point, speed, direction, etc."

"Dear God," said Matlock, his mind racing now. "Then why don't we land as soon as possible and proceed by road?"

"What a good idea," said the pilot ironically.

He pointed ahead. At first Matlock could see nothing, then suddenly out of the darkness he picked a point of red light, then another, then two more.

"Now if we can just get down without being spotted, they can trespass up above as much as they like."

Slowly they dropped towards the square of safety. A kilted figure appeared and began to wave them down. Others stood further back, guns at the ready. The lights were extinguished even before they touched.

"Out," said Ossian.

Matlock realized as he tumbled out on to the long wet grass that this was the first word he had heard Ossian speak.

A small reception party approached, headed by a tall uniformed figure who saluted the man with the hole in his head, then held out his hand.

"Mr. Boswell, I'm Colonel Mackay. Glad to see you safely here, sir."

"Thank you. Is there a car for us?"

"Aye, it's all laid on. We'll have you in Edinburgh within the hour."

Boswell stiffened slightly and Matlock had an impression of a new alertness, but his voice was as soft and even as ever when he spoke.

"It was Glasgow we were to go to."

"I know sir. A change of orders. Those are my instructions."

"I see. Well, let's be off."

He half turned then said with a small

gesture, "This is Mr. Matlock," before walking briskly towards a group of vehicles just visible as dark outlines in the slight mist rising from the sodden field.

"I thought it would be," said Mackay. "Matlock, eh? Well now."

His tone was quite neutral, but Matlock felt glad when Ossian propelled him after Boswell with what might have been meant as a gentle push.

Rubbing his arm, he hurried away and clambered into the back seat of the awaiting car which jerked forward before Ossian, squeezing in behind him, had time to close the door. They moved slowly at first over what seemed a very rough track, if that, then began to pick up speed as the surface improved. Glancing back he was surprised to see distantly the red guidelights flicker to life again.

Boswell followed his gaze and answered his unspoken question.

"Now we're safely out of the way, these soldiers can have their rough fun. They're lying in the heather with their guns all ready, hoping that some of our trespassers will spot the lights and fly low to investigate."

He laughed at Matlock's slight flicker of distaste.

"Don't worry too much, Mr. Matlock. Your countrymen have grown rather more cautious than they used to be about taking such bait. Our soldiers will probably just get cold and wet for nothing. But it'll sharpen their appetites; oh yes, it will do that."

The lights were now completely out of sight. Matlock settled back with a sigh. Then he managed a half-smile as he remembered Colonel Mackay's insignia.

"It's probably too far back for you to recall, Mr. Boswell, but when I was a young lad in the late sixties, I can remember seeing posters and stickers on car windows which said, 'Save The Argylls'. I suppose in a way I did."

There was no reply and the rest of the journey went by in silence.

Dawn was breaking as they ran smoothly through the silent suburbs of Edinburgh. As they turned into the long steep street that led up to the dark bulk of the castle, Boswell let the window down and on the sharp-edged breeze that blew in Matlock smelt the sea.

11

IF he had expected quick answers to the hundreds of questions crowding his mind, he was soon disappointed.

He had heard the ancient cannon, which still boomed out the hour at one o'clock each day, twice startle the birds roosting on the ramparts. And still there was no indication of what their purpose with him might be.

He was surprised to find he had the beginnings of a cold. It was a quarter of a century since he had had a cold and he had thought his resistance had been permanently built up. But evidently the course of injections he had undergone did not cater for men of nearly seventy wading along rivers and not changing out of their damp clothes for several hours thereafter.

He was inclined, however, to blame his present quarters as much as his ducking. The apartment they had given him was sumptuously furnished and bright and

345

airy. Too airy. He had forgotten that rooms as draughty as this could exist for people to live in. It was bad as the ancient halls his meetings had only half filled. And the sumptuousness of the furniture was appreciable aesthetically rather than ergonomically. It was all several hundred years old and the whole room reminded him of the 'public' apartments of the old stately homes, open for a season and an admission fee to the gawping mob. In fact, the room had exactly the same faintly dank smell as these places, the same aura of unlived-in-ness. He would not have been too surprised to wake up and find himself being observed from behind a rope of red velvet by a group of bored sightseers.

This sense of archaism did not end outside his room. He found that he was able to stroll quite freely around the battlements of the castle, though he was always aware of being overlooked. The city which lay spread out beneath him seemed incredibly old fashioned. He could look out across the New Town (New!) to the distant pale scar which was the Forth, and see almost the same view as the French prisoners held in the castle during the Napoleonic wars.

Even the shops of Princes Street, seemed still to belong firmly to the twentieth rather than the twenty-first century, while the gardens below looked as well-tended and attractive as ever.

"I see they never finished this side of the street," he said to a soldier who had come up beside him (to stop me jumping over? he wondered). He knew this was an old Glasgow jibe at the pretensions of Edinburgh to be the nation's capital, but was surprised to see the hostility which flared briefly in the man's eyes.

"Just a joke," he said, and returned to his staring.

That evening after finishing his lonely meal in his room he spoke to the orderly who came to clear it away.

"Please tell whoever is in charge here that I must speak to him."

The man did not reply and after he had left, Matlock settled down to his reading of the only book he had been able to unearth in the room, the *Complete Poems of Robert Burns*. He had not read very far when there was a gentle knock at the door.

"Come in please," he said.

The door opened to reveal Colonel Mackay.

"You wished to speak to me."

Again the neutrality which frightened more than hate.

"To you, Colonel, or to anyone who can convey a message for me."

"I am no errand boy, Mr. Matlock."

"As you will, Colonel. But here's the message all the same. I would like Mr. Boswell to be reminded that it is my seventieth birthday the day after tomorrow. Tell him I hope he will be coming to the party."

The Colonel left without a word. Matlock wondered whether he would make any effort to deliver the message, then shrugged and returned to his book, surprised and half pleased by his own feeling of complete indifference. But his sleep that night was troubled and uneasy.

He awoke with a start and sat up. For a moment he thought that his idle imaginings had come true and a party of tourists was being shown around the room. Standing round the bed were half a dozen men all peering down at him.

The only one he recognized was Boswell.

"Thank you for your message, but you need not have bothered. You were not forgotten. Indeed quite the contrary. You have been in the very forefront of our minds day and night. Please come now."

He started to dress but Boswell prevented him.

"It is not necessary. Just put on your dressing gown."

Slightly uneasy, Matlock slipped his robe over his shoulders and allowed himself to be escorted from the room. They moved swiftly along bare stone corridors. No one spoke, but Boswell noticed Matlock shiver as they turned a corner and walked into a keen-edged draught, and he increased the pace still further. Matlock was reminded of his wanderings through the echoing passages of Fountains and shivered again at the strangeness of it all.

"In here, please."

The door was held open for him and

he politely muttered his thanks as he passed through. No one came after him. He heard the door close. He was in an operating theatre.

Four white-clothed, gauze-masked figures stood round the operation table, forming a tableau of terrifying hygiene.

"Take off your clothes please, Mr. Matlock, and step over here, won't you?"

It was a pleasant, reassuring voice and Matlock began to undress without hesitation, unaffected by the dispassionate professional eyes that watched him. But as he moved over to the table he sensed that at least one pair of eyes was anything but dispassionate and professional. The amount of emotion which can be registered by the two inch strip of face below the hairline and above the nose is obviously limited. It was equally unidentifiable, but Matlock felt there was something familiar about those eyes. Their owner stood behind the other three as though she were an onlooker rather than a participant in whatever was going to happen.

"Just a wee operation," said the reassuring voice, "and then you can

350

enjoy your birthday."

"You mean, you're going to take it out?" asked Matlock.

"Of course we are. Lie down here please."

Matlock climbed on to the table.

"Turn your head slightly."

He turned his head and looked up into the brown eyes which he was so near now to recognizing. A name came scrambling up to the top of his mind as one of the others leaned down and pressed an anaesthetizing disc to the side of his neck. He blinked once and spoke.

"Lizzie."

She leaned down over him, unmasked now, her long black hair freed from the unbecoming restrictions of a surgical cap.

"Hello, Matt. How are you feeling?"

"Why, fine. Fine."

He looked around. He was back in his bed and there was a dressing taped to his chest.

"Is it done?" he asked incredulously, then he laughed. "That's a stupid bloody question, isn't it?"

"Yes it's done," she said, her face

strangely solemn.

"But you, Lizzie, here! This is marvellous!" Matlock said, pushing himself upright on the bed.

"Today I should be dying, but I'll live. And with my life I get you!"

For a moment the sheer joy of the moment so pressed in on him that his head began to swim and the room seemed to stir slightly on its foundations. Lizzie reached out to him anxiously but his head cleared almost instantly and he pulled her down beside him and pressed his lips deep into her hair.

"Oh Matt, Matt!" she whispered.

"Lizzie!" he whispered in reply. "My darling."

His right arm tightened over her shoulders and his left hand moved down from her face, along the slimness of her neck and came to rest on her breast. For a second she thrust herself against him, then gently pushed him away.

"Later, Matt, later. But now, before they come, we have to talk."

"Before *who* comes? Anyway I don't give a damn who comes. *You* come here!" He reached out for her laughing

352

and caught her hand. "Some of the early doctors seriously suggested that the warmth of a naked girl was the best palliative for the illnesses of age. I think they may have been right."

But Lizzie leaned back so that the whole of her weight pulled on his arm and he could not move her.

"No, Matt. Please listen. They'll be here soon. They want your help, Matt. They need you. You must help, Matt."

He let go of her hand and dropped his arm, but the tension between them did not fade with the relaxing of tendon and muscle.

"Why must I help?"

"Because you are here, helpless. You can look at it that way if you like. But also because it's right that you should help, Matt. It's the only way to achieve what you've been aiming at."

There was a note of passionate sincerity in her voice which filled him with foreboding. She was standing over him now her face flushed with emotion, her body within easy reach, but he made no move to touch her.

"Why are you saying this to me, Lizzie?

353

What are you doing here anyway? How did you escape?"

"What does it matter, Matt? I *am* here, that's all that matters, and you are too, and there's an opportunity to do what's seemed so important to us both for so long. Overthrow Browning."

Matlock fixed his eyes steadily on her face.

"The Abbot tried to tell me you were one of Browning's spies, but I wouldn't believe him. I told you, remember? Did you laugh as I told you?"

"No, Matt. No!"

"Did the Abbot just get the employer wrong? Was that all?"

"No, no. Please try to understand."

But he only understood what was now obvious. Lizzie was in the pay of the Scots and had been since the beginning nearly twenty years before.

He turned his head away and stared blindly at the wall.

"Yes, try to understand, Mr. Matlock."

When he looked round again, Boswell had appeared from somewhere and stood at the foot of the bed.

"Do not be hard on Miss Armstrong.

She has served you at least as well as us over the years. She could have been moved from the assignment any time she wished after it became apparent that your real political value had disappeared completely. It's only in the last four or five years that you began to become important again. For the rest of the time there was nothing in it for her as an agent. And at no time was there ever any real clash of interests."

"How convenient for her," said Matt dully.

"Oh, Matt," cried Lizzie in a voice husky with strain, "Matt, I love you. I've loved you for years. All I wanted was to marry you, it didn't matter for how short a time. And I believed in you and all you were trying to do. I couldn't foresee all this, Matt, not this. I thought all this was over for you years ago."

"But it wasn't," interjected Boswell swiftly. "Now, Matlock, the position is this. At the expense of much time and energy, we have got you safely away from the wrath of your countrymen. But back in England, Browning is still firmly in control, men who have worked with you,

355

for you, even if you did not know it, are now in danger, are now being arrested. Imprisoned. Murdered. We in Scotland are preparing to intervene in support of the forces of democracy before it is too late."

"Intervene then. What do you want with me?"

"We need you to show our goodwill. There are many hundreds of thousands of your countrymen ready to take up arms against the dictator, but they will be reluctant to support what Browning will surely designate as an invading army. If we're not careful, our intervention could make him stronger, not weaker. But with you at our head, there would be no room for doubting our motives."

Matlock laughed.

"Motives? And what are your motives?"

"Can't you *see*, Matt?" Lizzie came forward again, her hands raised as though she would force conviction down on him. "We want to help. Both our countries are failing because they each lack what the other has. The North of England at least belongs with us geographically, economically. We can create a new and greater nation than ever before."

"A second act of Union!" sneered Matlock. "Tell me, Boswell, why didn't you come over the Border a week ago when Browning started his purge? Then we needed help. Then we would have welcomed you. Could it be that you were happy to see all the top men chopped down? Could it be that you didn't want an underground movement as well organized as ours to be in existence when you made your own bid for control?"

"Oh, Matt, why won't you understand?"

"Why won't you understand, Lizzie?" asked Matlock gently. "I suspect that there's even more than meets the eye at stake here. Who's in charge at the moment, Boswell? Glasgow? Hardly. Inverness? Or is it really Edinburgh? Is that what's been going on these past few days while I've been lying here listening to my life tick away? You've been sitting round the table waving your tartan banners and rattling your claymores at each other, trying to reach a compromise. And you've come out on top. A bit precariously perhaps, but still on top. Perhaps because you convinced the rest that I'm a king-pin in the invasion plans. And I belong to you. But only if I'll play."

Boswell fingered the hollow in his head and smiled slightly.

"You paint us blacker than we are. And more primitive. But there is not time enough to reason your co-operation out of you. I am sure we could, even if it was only by appealing to your sense of history. You can't afford to wait another thirty years for your chance, Matlock. You have some power now. But only by using it can you preserve it."

"I am sorry you can't be bothered to reason with me," said Matlock. "I should have been interested to hear your plans."

Boswell was unperturbed by the gibe. "I can do better than that. You shall see them in action. We mobilize in forty-eight hours."

"I will not help without reason," said Matlock, "and I have heard no hint of reason yet. Only promises. Vague claims."

Boswell came round the side of the

bed now and stood over him, a menacing figure, but his voice was still calm.

"Here are two reasons then. The first is, we are attacking through Carlisle. Your birthplace I believe. We will try to talk our way in. If not, we will smash our way in. You are a well-known talker."

He relaxed and turned as if to go.

"And the second reason?" asked Matlock.

Boswell leaned forward and tapped the dressing on his chest, then nodded at Lizzie.

"She'll tell you," he said as he left. "I'll be back later. You'll want to talk with your military advisers."

Matlock pressed his hand against the dressing and seemed to feel his heart beating dangerously near the surface.

"What did he mean, Lizzie?" he asked tightly. "What is it? Didn't they take the clock out?"

Lizzie turned her back to him so he could not see her face. Her shoulders were rounded and he knew without needing to see that she was crying.

"Yes Matt. They took it out. But

they put in one of their own making. It will have to be reset daily. Without Boswell, you can never have more than twenty-four hours to live."

There was no weakening of the flesh. His vision did not blur, his head did not swim. His mind felt as alert as he had ever known it and his muscles seemed stronger than at any time since his arrival in Edinburgh.

But he felt something die in him at that moment and he smiled to himself without humour.

"For the past many days I have been an ally worthy of everyone's wooing," he murmured. "Now at last I think my enemies have made of me an enemy worthy of their hating."

"What do you say, Matt?" asked Lizzie anxiously.

He smiled up at her.

"Nothing, my dear. Fetch Boswell back, would you? We have things to discuss."

Tears of joy welled up in her eyes.

"Oh Matt!" she cried. "Matt! It is the right thing, the only thing! For you, for the country. For us. When it's done, when it's finished, then we can begin to live!"

Begin to live? he wondered as she left the room, almost running in her haste to find Boswell. Poor faithful Lizzie! Loyal to too many things. Able to reconcile all she loved.

A year ago, a month ago, I would have tried to persuade her, used words, arguments. A liberating army whose own country has already developed its own heart-clock technology! She would have seen the paradox, understood the dangers. She might still — if there were time. But now there is never more than twenty-four hours. Never more than another sunrise. Whatever I can do I must do in a day!

Boswell's plan was simple. His forces were massed in readiness for the invasion which was timed for seven o'clock in the evening two days hence. At six-thirty on that same evening, it was his intention to over-ride all the usual English television transmissions with a broadcast of his own. They had the signal power to be able to do this with a hundred per cent success in the Border Counties and this was where success was most important.

361

The main feature of the broadcast was to be a speech by Matlock.

"Live?" he asked hopefully.

Boswell shook his head with a cynical smile.

"Taped," he said. "We wouldn't like to lead you into temptation."

The script was much what Matlock expected. It contained much that he had been saying in draughty twentieth-century slum halls for years. But it was more forceful, more violent, more emotional. It could go down very well, for he had to admit it was beautifully written. He felt something almost like pleasure at the thought of the vastness of the audience being offered to him. Then he thought of William Joyce, of poor Ezra Pound, of others who had broadcast for and given help to the enemy in long past wars.

He had to make the speech four times before Boswell was satisfied with the video-tape.

"How much help do you think this will be?" he asked the Scot. "I'm not universally loved in England, you know."

"More than you think," replied Boswell.

362

"This will get us well into Cumberland without more than token resistance. Your home town has a reputation in history for opening its gates to the Scots whenever they decided to march south! And once in, with the help of follow-up broadcasts, we'll have a popular uprising to support us right down to the Midlands. Your supporters have been keyed up for this for a long time, Matt. We've got our own intelligence network widely spread."

"I know," said Matlock glancing at Lizzie who, along with Ossian, was now his constant companion.

Boswell looked at his watch.

"I must go now," he said. "Only twelve hours till the start. You're lucky, Matlock. I'll be lucky to sleep again in two or three days. You can go back to bed now for the rest of the day."

He looked mockingly at Lizzie.

"You forget," said Matlock. "At ten o'clock every morning I have an appointment to keep."

He tapped his chest.

Boswell nodded.

"Of course. Don't forget it, will you? And don't forget to watch this evening.

363

We'll fetch you down as soon as we need you again. Look after our guest, Ossian."

With a casual wave, Boswell left. How sure of himself he looks, thought Matlock. His plans are all perfectly prepared. And mine?

He poured himself another cup of coffee and settled down to wait.

There were two key times in his day. The first was ten o'clock when he was re-wound-up, as he was beginning to think of it, for another twenty-four hours.

The second was four-thirty p.m.

This was the time that the full technical staff would come on duty at the television transmission station which he could see from the castle ramparts spread out over that other rocky eminence once known as Arthur's Seat. These stations were automated to the point where they could almost run themselves. But for tonight's transmission, Boswell was taking no chances, and a full staff would be on duty. But not till half past four.

The hours moved by slowly. Matlock tried to act normally, but normality in such conditions was hard to define.

Lizzie, chameleon-like, took her own cue from Matlock's mood and there was little conversation between them.

Ossian sat in the corner, squat, toadlike, watchful.

He'd love an excuse to set about me, reflected Matlock.

And outside in the courtyard of the castle, at all exits, were guards whose orders too were to keep him inside.

He turned his mind away from them and thought of all he had tried to do with his life.

The one o'clock gun boomed, making him start. It would take a lot of getting used to.

It would soon be time.

At three o'clock he knew he could wait no longer. He stood up.

This was the most hateful bit of the plan.

He went across to Lizzie and leaned over her ostensibly to look at the book she was reading. He let his hand brush against her breast, gently at first then with greater urgency.

Surprised, she looked up at him. He grinned down at her and motioned with

365

his eyes towards the bedroom door. For a moment he thought it had gone wrong. He saw doubt, suspicion, in her face. Then it vanished. She smiled widely, moistened her lips and stood up.

Ossian watched without revealing any thought, any emotion on his great flat face.

They walked together to the bedroom door and went in, Lizzie first.

She stopped just inside the bedroom, her back still to him as he locked the door.

"Matt," she said in a low voice. "I love you. I know you don't want to make love to me now. Whatever it is you want to do, do it quickly."

He struck her sharply with the edge of his hand along the side of her neck and caught her as she fell. Quickly he gagged and bound her with the strips of sheet he had torn up earlier in the day and rolled her under the bed. Then he took from inside his pillow the one object he had borne with him through all his vicissitudes since that now so distant mad escape through the streets of London.

It was the small package he had taken from the Technical Education Board, Browning's forgery centre.

Now he opened it, as he had done once before at the Abbey. It contained a single flat oblong of a material which seemed half metal, half plastic. At first sight he had suspected what it was. Since arriving in Edinburgh he had had his theory confirmed by seeing them in use.

It was a top-level security pass. If the electronic code printed on the reverse side were the one currently in use, there would be a repeated two-tone whistle from the check-machine into which it was pressed by the thumb of its owner — if the thumbprint electronically printed on the other side matched the presser's thumb.

There were a lot of 'ifs'. Too many, thought Matlock. He could only hope that Browning's security men were up-to-date in their knowledge of the Scottish coding. And that the thumb space had been activated but blank till he pressed his own thumb into it.

But before he could find out this

he had to deal with Ossian. Ossian would not contravene his orders even at the direct command of God Almighty, let alone for a mere security pass. He possessed the unbluffability of the single-minded.

It would take the full persuasion of the small gun Matlock had removed from Lizzie's side.

He undid his tie, and ruffled his hair. It was only three-ten. Ossian might be suspicious of such a rapid performance, but he could wait no longer.

He opened the door and stepped out yawning.

Ossian watched him unblinkingly, then suddenly some animal instinct made him grab for his gun.

Matlock shot him carefully between the eyes.

Lizzie was coming round as he pushed Ossian's body under the bed beside her.

"I'm sorry," he said, but that was all he could find to say, so he went quickly, leaving her with her grisly companion.

The first check was the worst. The guard was surprised to see him, but instantly accepted the potential authority of the pass, fitting it into his check-machine and offering it to Matlock to press.

He said a prayer and his knees went weak as he heard in reply a clear two-tone whistle.

After that it was easy and he was only challenged twice after leaving the castle, the second time being both challenge and opening signal at the door of the television station.

As he had hoped there were only two technicians there. Even their presence was obviously superfluous; they were sitting playing cards. They stopped as he entered, obviously surprised to be interrupted at all, let alone by him.

The older of them looked even more surprised and went very pale when Matlock beat his companion unconscious which took two blows from his gun.

"You can work this equipment?" he demanded.

"Aye, sure," said the old man placatingly.

"Then let's make a film," said Matlock. "It's quite simple. I'm going to speak for a bit. I want it put on video-tape. Now if you misbehave yourself when setting up the equipment I'll shoot you. When I'm actually speaking, I'll be holding my gun to the head of your friend here who'll be lying on the floor. If you misbehave then, *he* gets it. Understand?"

"Aye," said the technician, glancing surreptitiously at the wall clock.

"And also," continued Matlock, "if I see any indication that you're trying to delay matters till four-thirty, then I'll kill you both. Now move!"

The man didn't speak another word, but went about his business with quiet efficiency. For all that it was nearly four o'clock when Matlock finished his short speech.

"Now play it back," he said. He didn't want a critical viewing — there was no time for a retake — but he had to make sure that the man hadn't fooled him in any way, that the speech was actually on the tape.

It was. He nodded in satisfaction.

"Good," he said. "Now, one last job. You were here yesterday when they recorded my other speech, weren't you?"

The man nodded.

"Well, I want that bit of tape removed from tonight's broadcast and this put in."

The man didn't move.

Now he knows what it's all about, thought Matlock. I hope to God he's not the martyr type.

"What're we waiting for?" he demanded.

"I can't do it, Mr. Matlock," the man said with a dignity made all the more impressive by his obvious terror. "It'd mean they'd know about the attack. It'd mean the death of hundreds of our boys."

Matlock sighed. This man's very virtue was going to be his weakness. He should know. He was himself a bit of an expert on weakness.

"Perhaps so," he said. "If you don't, though, it'll mean the certain death of this boy here."

He prodded the unconscious man with his toe and pointed his gun down.

"I'll count three," he said. "The first one will be in his stomach."

He didn't even have to start counting. Quietly the man went to work.

371

It was four-ten.

Matlock watched him closely. Video-tape equipment on a small scale was sufficiently common in households now for him to have some idea of what the man was doing. He might even have been able to manage it himself but it would have taken him much longer. Too long.

As it was, it was after four-twenty when the job was finished. But he still had to check. He picked up the stretch of tape which had been removed.

"Now play this," he said.

It was the right piece. He pressed the accelerator switch and it whizzed across the screen at a great rate.

It was nearly four-thirty.

"Where are the unused tapes?" he asked. "The other three versions of this?"

The man took him to a store cupboard and silently pointed out three cylinders. Matlock saw his name on them. Quickly he removed the tape from each and replaced the cans on the shelf.

Distantly he heard the two-tone bell. Someone had arrived.

"Pick him up," he said, pointing to the unconscious youth. "Now let's go."

372

They made their way out of the studio, down a long corridor and up a flight of stairs.

Behind them doors were opening and shutting.

"Angus!" cried a voice. "Are you there? Where are you man?"

Matlock pressed his gun to the unconscious man's throat.

"Answer him," he said.

"I'm up here, Jimmy," called the man.

"Tell him you'll be off home in a minute. Tell him to enjoy himself. Be natural!"

"I'm just off, Jimmy," the man called again. "See you later. Enjoy yourself."

"I will," came the reply. "When I sign off, I will!"

Silence fell. Matlock listened long enough to make sure no one was after them.

"On we go," he said.

They stopped finally in a small office which did not look as if it received very frequent use. Matlock still did not know what to do with these men. Perhaps it was his very concern with this problem which helped him solve it. The older man, Angus, had laid his friend on a desk. As he turned he must have noticed the break in Matlock's concentration. Or perhaps he had just reached the point of desperation. Whatever the cause, he leapt forward. He might have succeeded if he'd been faster, come in lower, used his feet. Instead he came swinging a punch at Matlock's head like an old-fashioned pugilist.

Matlock shot him twice before the blow could land, and fired a third time as he fell. This shot burned a hole in the side of the young man's head.

An accident. Matlock mouthed the words silently as though they could help. But he knew how little of an accident it was.

There was a key on the inside of the door. He took it out and locked the room behind him as he left.

All he had to do now was keep out of the way till the broadcast was over. It would probably have been as safe as anything for him to have remained in the transmission building, but something drove him out into the fresh air. He paused only to drop the rolls of tape he was carrying into a refuse shaft. Then he abandoned caution for a while as he strode down into the town again, feeling the fresh east wind clutching at his cheekbones. But once the buildings began to grow up around him again, he realized just how foolhardy this was and turned away from the broad thoroughfare he was approaching into darker, meaner streets that would have been a Curfew Area in England.

Here, he thought, there will be less chance of recognition, more chance of finding somewhere to hide. But as he turned out of the narrow streets to go down an even narrower, darker passageway between two ancient buildings, he cannoned into a long, stooping figure who cursed him violently in good, broad Scots at first, then stopped, peered closely at him and said in perfect English, "Dear God. Matlock!"

"Oh, no," said Matlock. "Not you too."

"I'm afraid so," said the man as he thumbed his force-gun to stun and applied it to Matlock's head. "Sorry, Matt. But you're going to have to come back and answer for yourself."

Matlock made a hopeless gesture towards his own gun, the force-gun popped gently and he fell forward into darkness and the arms of his one-time friend and agent, Colin Peters.

12

THE first thing he saw as he clawed his way up out of darkness was the wall clock. It read nine-forty-five.

So it was over. Nearly three hours over. The broadcast would have been stopped of course. They must have checked. The invasion would have proceeded without it. Or perhaps they'd made copies of the tapes he'd destroyed. Perhaps they had just gone ahead according to plan. If they had, they might still want to use him. They might keep him alive a bit longer.

The thought came as no comfort to him.

He would have to face Lizzie again, he supposed. At least they would be rid of pretence. That was one thing he had done with, pretence. He had had enough of it forever. From himself. And from others. From professionals like Browning and the Abbot, you expected it. But Lizzie. And now, Colin. Colin! It just didn't make sense. Browning's police had captured him. He had *seen* them capture him, long ago, on that rooftop as he rose up in Francis' helicopter.

The door opened and Colin came in. "Feeling better?" he asked brightly.

"Better than what?" asked Matlock.

"Ah, you are feeling better. Smoke?"

"No thanks," said Matlock, swinging his legs out of bed. He saw for the first time his clothes had been changed again. He was now wearing a kind of loose fitting house-suit.

Everyone's at it, he thought. Stripping my clothes off as soon as I close my eyes.

"It's nice to see you again, Matt," said Colin.

"Yes. You showed it."

"I'm sorry about that. I didn't know."

"Know what. And where am I?"

The room was strange and at the same time faintly familiar. He shook his head in an effort to clear away either the strangeness or the familiarity, but both remained.

Colin looked at him and laughed.

"Where are you? What a question. Here!" he said and reached up to the window and pulled up the venetian blind.

For a moment Matlock thought he had fainted again. There stretched out before him was an unforgettable, unforgotten panorama.

It was the skyline of London. And from a familiar viewpoint.

He realized now where he was. He was in a room of the Prime Minister's apartments in the House of Commons.

But something else struck him as well. The light outside. It wasn't the light of late evening. It was the light of morning.

It was now nine-fifty-five in the morning.

He opened his mouth to speak, then closed it again. There wasn't time to do anything. The Scottish machine was not the same as the English. It would have to be an operation. And why should they want to do anything in any case?

And why should he want anything done either? He was weary of it all. Now was the time to go.

But perhaps a few answers first.

379

"So you were with Browning all the time?" he said.

"With Security," corrected Colin.

"And you weren't captured on the rooftop? You were in pursuit?"

"I'm afraid so, Matt. I'm sorry, but I was just doing my job. You became quite a problem, you know. Browning was very concerned about you for a long time. You should have accepted his offer. He did everything in his power to persuade you. Why. I even had to blow a hole in your window with a force-gun to give you a scare!"

"That was you?"

"Yes. But without harmful intent. I thought you'd be still in the lounge. Browning really wanted you, you know. It wasn't till I reported on your traffickings with the Abbot that he decided on the crash-budget and the security blitz. It was really all your fault in a way."

"It's all been my fault, it seems," said Matlock bitterly. "Tell me, how did we get here?"

"Well, I'd just been planted in Edinburgh — I'd only been in the place about twelve hours when we met! — to

380

find out what was going on. There'd been a bit of a purge, it seems, and lots of our men had been picked up. We thought you'd be there. We believed you'd be helping them, but we had to find out more. You can imagine how I felt when I bumped into you like that, wandering around unattended in that part of town! Anyway, I got in touch with my contact on the Wall right away, put you in the back of my car and drove out, up into the hills where a 'copter picked us up. I didn't know about the broadcast till we got back here. I'm sorry, if I'd have known, there wouldn't have been any need to knock you out. It would have made things easier for both of us. But I thought you'd really gone over!"

"Broadcast!" snapped Matlock. "You mean it went off all right? What's happened?"

"Let me tell you that, Mr. Matlock," said a voice from the door. Matlock turned and stared at the tall, grey-haired figure who stood there, recognizing the thin face, long nose and archaic steel-framed spectacles.

"Sedgwick," he said, recognizing the

381

leading Minister of Browning's cabinet, the man who had taken over his old office when he resigned all those years before. He too had been young then.

"We haven't met for a long time, have we?" said Sedgwick.

"You were saying about the Scots . . . "

"Ah yes. Well, the broadcast came on at six-thirty. I do not know how you got that piece of film in, but I take it that it was not part of the original programme. Boswell spoke briefly, saying that a Scots force was being sent at your request to assist the uprising against the Browning government. Then you came on. If you had spoken in support, I dread to think what kind of civil war might have resulted. As it was you picked your words quite magnificently. You were only on thirty seconds before they cut you, but it was more than enough."

"And the invasion?"

Sedgwick looked serious.

"I'm afraid that we are in a state of war with Scotland. They managed to breach the Wall in several places and despite the slight warning we had and fierce resistance, they have managed to occupy most of the Carlisle multicity but we are holding them at a line along the fells north of Kendal. Where they would have been if your broadcast had supported the attack it is impossible to say. We are most grateful."

Matlock began to laugh. He lay back on the bed and let the great peals of mirth come forth unhindered.

"So this is it!" he gasped between outbursts. "So the net result of all my efforts has been to save Browning! I bet he's grateful. I bet he laughed all the way to the House this morning."

Exhausted, he lay still regaining his breath.

"No, Mr. Matlock," said Sedgwick sternly. "You are wrong. The crisis facing the country as a result of the Scottish invasion has had far reaching effects. A vast number of members of this House in view of Mr. Browning's recent performance could not feel any great confidence in his ability to cope with this situation. He had assured the country only two days ago that he had had long talks with the Scottish Ambassador

383

and that the situation was well in hand. There was no chance of war, he told us. And in any case, such was the state of our Northern defence line, that the Scots would be quite incapable of breaching it. He has been proved miserably wrong on every count. This morning, acting on the advice of his Cabinet, Mr. Browning has recommended to his Majesty that you, sir, be invited to form a new government. We have transport waiting outside to take you to the Palace. I am here, sir, to say that if you accept, you will have behind you the unanimous support of the Uniradical Party and, I believe, of all the minority parties in the House."

"But . . . " said Matlock. "But . . . "

He stared wildly round, his eyes finally coming to rest on the clock.

It was ten-fifteen.

Sedgwick followed his gaze and smiled coldly.

"You were examined on your arrival, sir," he said, "and when it was realized you had a heart clock which would not respond to our own Adjusters, you were sent for Op. The clock has been removed."

Matlock's hand automatically went to his heart.

"No. Nothing has replaced it. We have an X-ray machine available if you wish to check."

"Yes," said Matlock gently, his mind beginning to surface from the whirlpool into which it had been sucked. "Yes. I will check. But later. Later. I must not keep his Majesty waiting. Are there clothes? I cannot go dressed like this."

"Through here, Prime Minister," said Sedgwick, leading the way into a neighbouring room.

Matlock paused in the doorway.

"Colin," he said. "What happened to Ernst? Was he one of . . . ?"

He left the question unfinished.

"Oh no," said Colin. "The bloody fool. He was killed resisting arrest."

"I see," said Matlock half to himself. "The fool. He was the fool. The other fool."

He went to change his clothes.

As he drove back to Westminster some time later he was only dimly aware of the cheering crowds lining the streets. Already the need for decision was pressing hard upon him. There were the immediate decisions to be made about the conduct of the war. Should he use planes to smash the enemy armies occupying the Carlisle multicity? Should low-fall-out nuclear weapons be employed against the Scottish towns? And then there was the composition of his Cabinet. Dare he omit such old enemies as Sedgwick whose support he realized was linked more with personal survival than altruistic patriotism? And then in the long run there were the questions of his policy for the future. What support could he expect for economic and age reforms once the war was over?

And the question kept on bobbing up to the surface of his mind like a playful dolphin — would he be able to afford such reforms after the expense of such a war?

And how much would it matter to him if he couldn't?

He walked quickly into the House not responding to anyone.

Where was Lizzie? Would they ever meet again? And poor Ernst? The fool. The poor loyal fool.

"The House is assembled, Prime Minister. The Members are waiting to hear you."

It was Sedgwick. Courteous, deferential. Could he be trusted? Or rather, how far should he be distrusted?

"Give me one minute please," he said, turning into the Premier's great office. As he did so, he recalled the last time he had been here, listening to Browning's offer. The miniature was back on the wall he noticed.

And tidying up the desk with care and affection was an old, bent, familiar figure.

"Hello, Mr. Matlock, Prime Minister, sir," said Jody with a welcoming smile. "It's very good to see you back again."

Matlock looked around carefully, thoughtfully. And a whole minute elapsed before he said in a low voice, as though speaking to himself:

"Yes Jody. It's good to be back."

TO FIGHT THE WILD
Rod Ansell and Rachel Percy

Lost in uncharted Australian bush, Rod Ansell survived by hunting and trapping wild animals, improvising shelter and using all the bushman's skills he knew.

COROMANDEL
Pat Barr

India in the 1830s is a hot, uncomfortable place, where the East India Company still rules. Amelia and her new husband find themselves caught up in the animosities which seethe between the old order and the new.

THE SMALL PARTY
Lillian Beckwith

A frightening journey to safety begins for Ruth and her small party as their island is caught up in the dangers of armed insurrection.

THE WILDERNESS WALK
Sheila Bishop

Stifling unpleasant memories of a misbegotten romance in Cleave with Lord Francis Aubrey, Lavinia goes on holiday there with her sister. The two women are thrust into a romantic intrigue involving none other than Lord Francis.

THE RELUCTANT GUEST
Rosalind Brett

Ann Calvert went to spend a month on a South African farm with Theo Borland and his sister. They both proved to be different from her first idea of them, and there was Storr Peterson — the most disturbing man she had ever met.

ONE ENCHANTED SUMMER
Anne Tedlock Brooks

A tale of mystery and romance and a girl who found both during one enchanted summer.

CLOUD OVER MALVERTON
Nancy Buckingham

Dulcie soon realises that something is seriously wrong at Malverton, and when violence strikes she is horrified to find herself under suspicion of murder.

AFTER THOUGHTS
Max Bygraves

The Cockney entertainer tells stories of his East End childhood, of his RAF days, and his post-war showbusiness successes and friendships with fellow comedians.

MOONLIGHT
AND MARCH ROSES
D. Y. Cameron

Lynn's search to trace a missing girl takes her to Spain, where she meets Clive Hendon. While untangling the situation, she untangles her emotions and decides on her own future.